REVIEWS OF THE PIER

"Louisville author Bill Noel, himself a seasoned photographer, has followed his debut offering, *Folly*, with another engaging Folly Beach mystery. Armed with a gift for creating ultra-quirky yet believable characters, Noel shows how a healthy dose of cynicism—even among untrained, nonprofessional types—can lead to solving a murder mystery that the police had initially decided wasn't even a homicide."

-Kentucky Monthly
September 2008

"He knows how much information to give his readers, how to make his characters realistic and interesting, and how to carry the plot along to a satisfactory conclusion. And although there is a murder at the center of his story, he has a light enough touch to add bits of humor to the dialogue and narrative."

"Spend a little time at the Lost Dog Café ("Coffee and a bite") with Landrum and his troupe of amateur sleuths, and I bet you'll be glad you made the trip."

-The Voice-Tribune
September 2008

THE PIER

THE PIER

A FOLLY BEACH MYSTERY

BILL NOEL
AUTHOR OF FOLLY

iUniverse Star

New York   Bloomington

The Pier
A Folly Beach Mystery

Copyright © 2008, 2009 by Bill Noel

This is a work of fiction. All of the characters, names, incidents, organizations, and dialogue
in this novel are either the products of the author's imagination or are used fictitiously.

iUniverse Star
an iUniverse, Inc. imprint

iUniverse books may be ordered through booksellers or by contacting:

iUniverse
1663 Liberty Drive
Bloomington, IN 47403
www.iuniverse.com
1-800-Authors (1-800-288-4677)

ISBN: 978-1-4401-2698-7 (pbk)
ISBN: 978-1-4401-2861-5 (ebk)

Library of Congress Contol Number: 2009923910

Printed in the United States of America

CHAPTER 1

"Let's have a toast to Chris Landrum, the newest resident of our beloved Folly Beach …"

A high-pitched, piercing police siren overrode the rest of the speech offered by my new and very strange friend, Charles Fowler. My house was only two blocks from the small barrier island's police station; the sudden, loud warbling sound of the emergency vehicles' warning sirens was prone to startle rather than get gradually louder. This was one more sensation I'd need to get used to as I adapted to my new home.

"Look on the bright side, Chris," Charles continued as the sirens moved away from the house and our eardrums recovered. "Last time you were here, it only took three days for you to stumble on a murder. Now, you've been here a whole week before you have the police running all over the place."

"Yeah, Chris," chimed in Amber, Charles's sort-of date for the evening, "it took the natives months to recover from your visit last year."

Time to change the subject—this was a housewarming party I'd thrown for myself, and I didn't want it ruined. I had just taken early retirement from my former life as a health-care company executive in Kentucky. Through a couple of lucky real-estate investments and a nice corporate buyout plan, I was fortunate enough to buy my retirement home two blocks from the Atlantic Ocean, fifteen minutes from historic and beautiful Charleston, South Carolina, and within easy walking distance of some of the strangest, nicest, and most caring folks I'd encountered in my fifty-seven years. Most of them had honored me with their presence tonight. I hoped they had come to see me, although I suspected the free food and libations contributed more than a little.

"Okay, folks," I announced cheerfully after the sirens faded, "turns out this wasn't the destination of Folly's finest. So, drink up and enjoy the food." Clearly without need of further cajoling, my friends refreshed their drinks, filled their plates, and checked out each corner of the weather-worn, screened-in front porch of my new beach house. Actually, it was only new to me … and not quite on the beach, either. The small, one-story, weathered clapboard house had lived through many a hurricane and storm rolling off the Atlantic, and its blue paint was chipped and faded. But it was now my home, complete with rope handrail beside the brick steps leading to my porch, tin roof showing stains from every imaginable bird and airborne pollutant, and plenty of character.

Despite my efforts to play the warm host, a festive housewarming wasn't to be. Not fifteen minutes after the sirens faded into the cool February evening, Brian's cell phone played the opening notes of the theme from the old television show *Dragnet*. Brian, who was known to most everyone on the island as Chief Newman, served as the director of public safety.

None of us were surprised by the call. In fact, I was surprised one hadn't come earlier.

CHAPTER 2

"Folks, duty calls," said the chief as he retrieved his uniform jacket from the living room. "Seems like we've got ourselves a floater at the pier behind the Holiday Inn. I'll try to get back and let you know what's happening. Don't eat all the food." He stared at Charles.

With that comment, I could tell the wind had gone out of the festivities. Amber gasped loud enough for all to hear. Bob, the stoic one, whispered, "Oh no."

"I think he really means 'Don't drink all the beer,'" offered Charles, in a moment of deep insight and in an effort to break the somber mood.

"Enough about our police chief," I said, then attempted to get everyone's attention by tapping my plastic wine glass with a plastic spoon. The sound was quite underwhelming, so I stomped my foot on the wooden porch. "I'd like to offer a toast to the best real-estate agent a guy could ask for. If it weren't for him, I wouldn't have found this aged, dilapidated, overpriced cottage. Here's to my favorite—and only—Realtor, Bob Howard."

Bob looked like Santa out of season. He had the well-endowed belly and scruffy white—actually, gray—stubble of a beard. But he sorely lacked the jolly laugh and pleasant demeanor of the Christmas icon, and Bob also hadn't aged as well as Santa; he looked his sixty-five years.

"Damn, Chris, you sure know how to pay a compliment," said Bob, his face reddening more than usual in response to twelve clapping hands. "I already got my commission check—and, of course, gave it to my lovely wife, Betty—so I don't care what you say. As long as you use me for any of your further realty needs, that is."

Bob had been one of the reasons I decided to make Folly my full-time retirement home after I had spent a month here on vacation. My original plan had been to buy a vacation home on the small island and split my time between Louisville and Folly Beach. But, in less than a month, I had accumulated more friends—although most a bit off-center, I'll admit—than I had back home. I hadn't expected my social life to take off on a scrap of land only six miles long and a mile wide; even after retirement, life could certainly be full of surprises.

"Bob," I said. "I'm honored you dressed up for tonight's party—I didn't know you had a shirt that wasn't wrinkled or said something like 'I'm with Stupid!' or 'USA—Love it or Suck Raw Eggs.'"

"You'd be amazed how few of my clients invite me to a party after they're done with me," replied the mostly rumpled agent. "I thought I'd better show how *GQ*ish I am. Besides, Betty wouldn't let me leave the house dressed like I wanted to."

Neither of these things had surprised me. Bob, who generally failed to shave, detested eating anything healthy, and had never met an insult he didn't like, must have owned an overly abridged dictionary if he could find the word "*GQ*ish" anywhere near "Bob Howard"!

"Chris, do you still plan to open a fine art photo gallery on Folly?" asked the always proper and earnest Bill Hansel, as he moved between Bob and me.

Drastically different from my other, much more irreverent friends, Bill held his own in the area of uniqueness. He was one of Folly's fourteen or so African Americans, out of two thousand plus residents. To add to his extreme minority status, he hailed from the north, was a conservative Republican, held a doctorate in travel and tourism, and taught as a tenured professor of hospitality and tourism at the College of Charleston. He was also a great guy who had been my neighbor for a while last year.

"Yes, Bill," I said as I switched my attention away from Bob—no easy task. "I don't know how I'll do it, but since I've been taking photos for more years than I can remember, I'm going to give it a shot—pun intended. Besides, I'll need to do something with my time."

I offered to get Bill another glass of the finest box wines that Piggly Wiggly had to offer. He declined.

"You can always help with my gardening," he said, in the deepest bass voice I've heard from someone as thin as Dr. Bill Hansel.

"Don't bet your hoe on that. I'll come over and occasionally watch," I replied.

Looking through my camera's viewfinder was as close as I wanted to get to gardening and flowers.

*   *   *   *

A small space heater did its best to warm the porch from its position near the side wall, but cold winds had traveled the few blocks from the ocean and were beginning to take their toll on my guests. The party was clearly winding down, and the alcohol was running out; even the stash of Pepsis for Betty was running low. Chief Newman pulled up in front of the house in his unmarked Crown Victoria just as Bill was preparing for his three-block walk home.

"Welcome back, Chief. I saved you some cheese puffs," said Charles as he waved his hand-carved oak cane in the direction of the food. "What's up?"

Brian walked toward the food table. "I don't know much, other than the body was a white male and looked to be in his fifties—but even that's hard to tell with a floater. Water does terrible things to a body," he said as he filled his paper plate with the diminishing fare. Apparently, death didn't affect his appetite. "The guy was well dressed—had on a dark suit, a red bow tie, even a matching pocket handkerchief. Amazing how it stayed in the pocket after what the corpse had been through."

"Any idea what happened?" I asked as I followed him to the Styrofoam cooler sitting on the floor.

"Not really," said Brian before he popped a cheese puff in his mouth. "There didn't appear to be any gunshot wounds. There were a few cuts on the head, but they could've been caused by the rocky sea bottom while he churned around. We'll have to wait for the coroner's report before we know much. Unfortunately, we average about one of these every couple of years; people continually ignore our riptide warnings as if we're issuing 'em just to amuse ourselves. But I'll admit this one doesn't fit the profile. Few folks go for a swim dressed like they're going to the opera."

I noticed Bill, who had been standing by the door and getting ready to leave, had suddenly turned pale—or, for him, the color of cream-infused coffee—and sat on a plastic porch chair while the chief was speaking.

"Are you okay?" I asked Bill.

"No, I must say I'm not," he said in a voice barely above a whisper. "Chief Newman, I believe I know the poor soul you just described."

I think that's what he said, but it was hard to tell. His voice cracked, still nearly inaudible. The rest of what he had to say was easily heard; the wildly speculative chatter of my guests abruptly dropped to just below the decibel level of a pin dropping.

CHAPTER 3

All eyes were turned to the professor—all eyes and the battered, black notebook Chief Newman pulled from his jacket.

"Some of you know I'm a member of Preserve the Past," said Bill, his voice strengthening. "We meet each month and talk about ways to raise money to draw attention to the plight of the slowly sinking Morris Island Lighthouse. I've been going to these meetings for four years or so. It's sad how few people are really concerned about saving the historic lighthouse ... so sad." Bill bowed his head, supporting his chin with both arms.

"Umm, Bill? You say you know the deceased?" interrupted the chief.

That jolted Bill back to the present.

"Oh, yes," said Bill. "I believe you described Julius Palmer. He's been to almost every meeting since his wife died three years ago. I think that's how he channeled some of his energy after being left alone; he didn't have children. We became friends—I think mainly because we both had lost spouses to cancer." Bill's wife had died of the dreaded disease eight years ago; he still spoke of her often. "Besides that, we really have little in common. Julius owns an antique shop in Charleston. Chief, I hope I'm wrong, but who else would wear a bow tie and pocket handkerchief here?"

Good question, I thought—no one I knew, to be sure.

One other notebook got a workout that night: the one that belonged to Tammy Rogers, crime reporter extraordinaire for the *Post and Courier*, Charleston's daily newspaper. Besides being a fine reporter, Tammy was my date, my girlfriend, my significant other, my whatever; I had no idea what the appropriate term was for a middle-aged couple in this day and age. Regardless, Tammy took a keen interest in what the chief and Bill had said.

*   *   *   *

My guests—all but Tammy, to my great pleasure—had gone their separate ways after the party-stopping revelation by Bill. Bob left in his typical grumpy manner, instructing me to call only when he could make a commission in real estate. "Or when there's more free booze," he said. Betty smiled; I suspected she did a lot of that around him. This was the first time I'd met her, so I wasn't sure.

The chief, saying he needed to get back to the pier, thanked me for the invitation. He said he was glad I was finally getting settled in his fair city and ordered me to stay out of trouble. Bill, with hardly a word, left with his chin resting on his chest—in as gloomy a mood as I'd ever seen from him. Charles and Amber were the last to leave—with the exception of Tammy, of course. Charles and I had become amazingly close after spending time together last spring. He was a few years younger than I, and we were opposites in most every respect. I had taught him photography (some, anyway); he had taught me how to kill time while not working for a living—a condition he had perfected many years ago. I had a bunch to learn. During my previous month-long stay, Amber had been my best source of gossip, cheer, and flirtatious overtures, all while serving the best food on the island at the Lost Dog Café. Charles and Amber's relationship had sparked and ignited during the last seven months. She was especially eager to get home to her ten-year-old son, Jason.

For about an hour, Tammy and I were sad to see my friends go. But then we decided to focus a little more of our attention on each other. After that, we quickly forgot the party—and most everything else, to be accurate.

CHAPTER 4

Two early assignments required Tammy's return to the city that morning. With her short, blonde hair and minimal makeup routine, she wasted little time preparing for the day. We were up and ready a little before sunrise. My two previous visits to Folly Beach had been in late spring and summer; I still wasn't used to how cold it was now in the predawn hours. Fortunately, I hadn't thrown away my coats from the less tropic Kentucky climate.

The ongoing investigation of last night's unpleasant discovery was absolutely none of my business. I hadn't even met the late Julius Palmer, if he was the drowning victim, but I couldn't get the image of Bill out of my head. I'd never seen him anything but pleasant, upbeat, and kind—and a bit erudite. But what could one expect from a college professor—especially a tenured college professor in his fifties? He was somewhat of a loner, except for his acquaintances in Preserve the Past. His look when he realized Mr. Palmer was gone made the eyes of a basset look gleeful.

$*$ $*$ $*$ $*$

Tammy called around three with the not-so-surprising news. The police had confirmed the body as being Julius Palmer, age fifty-five, of West Ashley Avenue, Folly Beach, South Carolina. Bill was right.

On Folly, nothing was far away. Palmer's house was less than six blocks from my new abode. Tammy had also learned that he was considered "wealthy," whatever that meant. He had inherited his father's antique shop on prestigious King

Street—the affluent shopping address in Charleston. His shop specialized in European antiques, and anyone lacking a well-heeled wallet needed not enter. But unlike some dealers, he was liked by everyone in Charleston.

I walked three blocks to the Holiday Inn for a cup of complimentary coffee. The nine-story hotel was the tallest building on the island and Folly's only chain hotel—only chain anything, for that matter. The corporate office of the mega-chain interpreted "complimentary" differently than I—something about the adjective only applying to beverages consumed by their guests. Fortunately, the always friendly desk staff at *my* Holiday Inn entertained a more liberal interpretation. We assumed it meant for anyone who lived on Folly Beach. Besides, I dropped in around sunrise a few days a week, so I gave them someone to talk to. Early mornings were slow at a resort-area hotel during the off-season.

"Morning, Diane," I said to the young, attractive, efficient desk clerk. As curvy as a bowling pin and as chipper as a squirrel (well, at least on days when no one had washed up dead recently), Diane was always a good conversational partner. "I hear you had some excitement here last night."

"I didn't come on duty until eleven, so I missed most of it," she said as she looked up from the computer monitor. "The police stuck around here until after one."

I leaned on the check-in counter and spoke in low tones to avoid alarming the guests. It was a wasted effort, since the lobby was void of any paying customers. The only other sounds came from water cascading from the aqua-colored ceramic water feature in the center of the lobby. "What was so interesting until that late?" I asked. "From what I hear, the police think it was a drowning."

"I'm not sure. Officer Spencer—you know, the young, cute one—told me they were confused about what the guy was wearing. He told me they were trying to find out if we had any events last night where the guests would be in suits and ties."

"Were there?" I asked. "I wouldn't think you would have many of those on the beach, especially as laid-back as most folks are here."

"You're right," she said and looked around the empty lobby. "If people want something fancy, they aren't going to have it here—that's what Charleston is for. Even if we were that sort of place, we didn't have anything special last night. This isn't much of a convention town in February."

"Did Officer Spencer say why he was here so late?" I asked. While I waited for an answer, I took a sip of coffee from the Styrofoam cup.

"Not really. He mentioned something about hanging around to see how some of our other guests were dressed when they came in," she said. "I didn't feel it was my place to tell him we were only about twenty percent full and would have been surprised if anyone was still out at one in the morning. Besides, he's so cute, it was fun talking to him."

"Just like it is with me, right?"

"Well, you are really nice," she replied, trying to hold back a giggle.

I guessed she simply forgot to say "cute." Anyway, I'd take "really nice" anytime.

Fishing for compliments had worn me out, so my coffee and I relocated to a comfortable chair overlooking the pool and the ocean. It was still early, and the temperature was in the low fifties, so my view of the ocean was uninterrupted by swimmers and sunbathers. I hadn't known Mr. Palmer, but Bill was my friend, and our brief conversation last night had clearly shown his devastation. He had mentioned he would be going to church this morning, so I decided to walk to his house around one to see if he wanted to talk. I hoped he would know by then that the body had been confirmed as his friend; I didn't want to break that news.

✳   ✳   ✳   ✳

As I approached Bill's house, I spotted him in the side yard, raking dead branches, leaves, and assorted pinecones from his garden. He spent much of his free time in the garden.

When my silhouette shaded his efforts, he looked up at me. "Oh, hi, Chris. What are you doing on the wrong side of Center Street this afternoon?"

He looked anything but professorial in tattered jeans, dust-covered tennis shoes, and a jacket that any self-respecting thrift store would reject.

I leaned on the corner of his house, only a few feet from the garden, and tried to stay out of his way.

"I was in the neighborhood and thought I'd stop by."

"You're a terrible liar," he said as he stopped raking. "There's nowhere to be around here that would qualify as a neighborhood. I don't see your ubiquitous camera, so you're not taking pictures. Why the visit?" He had already leaned the rake against the wall and was heading for the door. "Want to share some hot tea? I've done about all I can out here anyway. I need to warm up."

"You caught me," I said, then followed him to the door. "To be honest, I was a little worried about you. You seemed to take the news of Mr. Palmer's death pretty hard. And, yes to the tea. That sounds good."

Bill's house was small—normal-sized by Folly standards, in other words— neat, and comfortable looking. I gazed around after taking a seat in the living room. One wall was covered with bookcases. They held a variety of textbooks, boxes of student projects, and a few hardback books by authors ranging from Malcolm X to Dick Francis—an eclectic group, to say the least.

"I guess you're right about me taking it hard," he said and handed me the steaming tea. "Julius is—was—one of my closest friends. You know I don't have many friends. At the college, I'm sort of an outcast, and on the island I don't know many people, despite my six years here. I do have an interest in history and the Morris Island Lighthouse, but the main reason I joined Preserve the Past was to meet folks."

"Do you feel people are being aloof because of race?" I asked, gingerly approaching the topic.

"At first I did, but I finally realized I'm sort of an odd duck," he said between sips from his white College of Charleston ceramic mug. "I could have chosen to live in Charleston, where there is a much larger African American population, but I love the water. I could play the political game at work; that would keep me in much better stead. But that's not me. Even in my chosen field of study, I have little actual work experience. I don't really like the travel and tourism industry. I love to teach and saw hospitality as the easiest way to get there. It's not really how people react to me, but my choices."

Bill had a unique talent for talking circles around a difficult topic until it made sense in the end—most of the time.

"You know, Chris," he continued, "I really fit in better on this small, idiosyncratic island than I did in the north, or at work, or even around my fellow descendents of slaves."

"Did you and Julius have much in common?" I asked, matching him sip for sip.

"Grand question. We only had one thing in common: losing our wives to cancer. I was in Preserve the Past with him for two years before we had a conversation. Sure, we nodded, said hi, and smiled, but that was it. Then his wife died, and I offered a sympathy that I felt on the most personal level imaginable. That was the spark." Bill hesitated, took another sip, and continued. "Other than that one bond, about everything else about us was opposite. He was rich; I'm a college professor. His family owned slaves; mine were slaves. He loved antiques; I consider most of them just old things. He hated the water; I crave its presence. He loved his work; I tolerate mine. See what I mean?"

"Back up a second. What do you mean about him hating the water? His house is just a block off the beach."

"Chris, he inherited the house along with the shop in Charleston. The only reason he was in Preserve the Past was his love for old things, antiques, and history. It was a joke in the group that he wouldn't go within twenty feet of the ocean. The best view of the lighthouse is from the end of the old deserted Coast Guard station."

"You don't have to tell me that, Bill. I'm intimately aware of that spot."

"Oh," he replied. "I almost forgot that's where your troubles began last year. So you know what I mean about the view. Anyway, when the group met out there, Julius wouldn't go any closer than the top of the dunes—about fifty feet from the water, I would guess. Once a year, the group would charter a boat and go to the lighthouse ... our pilgrimage, we called it." He paused, ever the gentleman, to inquire whether I wanted more tea. In my efforts to become more of a gentleman myself, I politely declined. "Julius wouldn't even entertain the thought of going," he continued. "He was the butt of many a joke from the other group members. Now that I think about it, maybe that's another reason we became friends. I would never make fun of someone for being different. I'm too well acquainted with that condition."

"If he was that afraid of the water, any idea how he could have drowned?" I asked. "Why would he have been so near the water—not to mention so dressed up?"

Bill stared at me and slowly lowered the mug from his lips. I could almost see the lightbulb's glow emanating from his ears.

"I've been so distraught," he said, "I haven't given any thought to what could have happened. I just know he would never, never have gone close enough to the water to fall in. The clothes, I understand. He was an extraordinarily formal person. He believed that if he was selling expensive antique pieces, he needed to show total respect to the antiques and the discerning buyers. He did that with his polite, formal manner and his attire. He dressed like that at work. He worked most Saturdays, so he would have looked that way yesterday. Could he have gotten sick, disoriented? Could someone have done this to him? Could ... I just don't know. I don't have a clue. Chris, I just know I miss him."

Our tea cooled as our conversation waned. Bill seemed to be withdrawing into memories of his departed friend. I felt awkward and told him if he needed anything, I was there and to let me know. I said I needed to be going (not totally true) and left after we said our pleasantries. On my way out, Bill said he really appreciated my visit. I knew he meant it.

The walk home gave me time to mull our discussion—especially the part about Julius being deathly afraid of the water.

CHAPTER 5

My favorite spot for free coffee may have been the Holiday Inn (although the atmosphere was a bit too predictable—too Holiday Innish for me, which I suppose isn't surprising), but my favorite breakfast location was the Lost Dog Café, hands down.

Only six blocks from my house and just off Folly's main drag, the café had moved from its former location to bigger digs on Center Street since my visit last year, but it was still number one in my heart and stomach. The establishment's name was a misnomer; if anything, the café could stand to lose a few dogs. The rustic, unpretentious former Laundromat turned restaurant was full of dogs—more accurately, photos, paintings, and statues of dogs. I'd once heard from an obviously bored tourist that more than two hundred canines could be counted in the place. None of them—dogs, not tourists—appeared lost. With the slogan "Coffee and a Bite" and the images of canines everywhere, the owners never had to field questions about whether they were cat people or dog people.

In addition to having the best breakfast on the island, the Dog was the hangout for locals. Some would have stayed there from sunup to sundown, but were run out when the restaurant closed in midafternoon.

Before I let go of the door, I heard Amber, my favorite waitstaff person in the world, speak her well-rehearsed and wordy, yet endearing, greeting: "Good morning, Chris. I'll be doing everything I can to make your breakfast experience as positive as possible." She said it louder than usual. She had told me that I was one of the few people who actually listened. Most placed their orders without acknowledging her existence—without a doubt, their loss.

The first time I'd met Amber, she told me a significant portion of her life story. I knew she'd been on Folly for almost ten years, having arrived in her late thirties, had a son with a massive imagination, and had left a less-than-successful career as a McDonald's manager trainee. Even if she hadn't told me a thing about herself, I would know that she was funny, sexy, flirty, and prone to gossip, the magic elixir in many small towns. If I hadn't met Tammy, I'm pretty sure I would have gotten to know Amber much better than I did—and I knew her pretty well.

"Okay, Amber, you've had more than twenty-four hours to put your ears to work. What's the latest on the untimely death of Mr. Palmer?" I asked as she brought my coffee.

"You're not going to believe this," she said. "In fact, this'll hurt my reputation: I haven't heard anything. Everyone coming in here asks me for information instead of dispensing any. Only two of the regulars even knew who Julius Palmer was. One was Cameron Little, one of the agents at Bob's firm. He went to a few of the Preserve the Past meetings and spoke briefly to Palmer, but that was about it. Then Mayor Amato said he was aware of Palmer because he had been in Palmer's antique shop and recognized him from the Pig. But that's it; I've failed you."

She bowed her head, slumped her cute shoulders, and acted as if she were begging for mercy. Even the dog on the logo of her well-fitting polo shirt looked sadder.

"That's a little disappointing for someone with your skill, but there's still time," I consoled her. "It's only been a day. I have faith in you."

She smiled—pleased with the reprieve, I assumed.

"Did you see the new dog saying we added to our board?" she asked, her spirits buoyed.

I confessed I hadn't noticed anything new on the large chalkboard just right of the entrance. After a while, I had seen enough dogs.

"I found it in a magazine, and they let me put it there," she said.

"If a dog's man's best friend, the dog has trouble" was written in chalk in Amber's neat, legible script. I couldn't argue with that. I had just finished reading this Amberism when Chief Newman entered, walked directly to my table, and took a seat. This was clearly a man on a mission—rare in the Dog. There was something comforting and equally distressing in knowing that the police chief felt comfortable joining me whenever he wanted to. We had gone through some strange times together during the brief time I'd known him. Most of that time, I had been a thorn under his badge. I had wreaked havoc in his department—

unintentionally, I must add. Such misdeeds, no matter how well-meaning, were not usually an ingredient for friendship.

"Amber, could I get some coffee?" he asked, then turned to me. "Chris, I know you and Bill are friends. I think he should hear this from you, rather than from the police or the media."

Not the best way for a conversation to begin.

The chief slowly sipped the coffee Amber had unobtrusively placed in front of him. "The coroner called and said unless something extraordinary appeared in the toxicology results, she was going to rule Palmer's death suicide. The tox reports won't be back for a few weeks, but damage to the body—a few contusions on the head, arms, and back—are all consistent with churning in the surf ... hitting rocks and all. There were no significant wounds. And there was seawater in his lungs, which meant he was alive when he hit the water. She speculated he jumped from the end of the pier. The currents at the time would have taken the body to where he was found."

The Folly pier jutted more than a thousand feet over the Atlantic and was one of the most visible tourist attractions on the island. I pondered the notion of a man creeping along it while battling his intense phobia of the water surrounding him.

"Chief, I spent some time yesterday with Bill. He told me something you should know—especially now."

I shared everything Bill told me about his friend, placing emphasis on his strong fear of water. The chief listened, but I could tell he didn't want to be inconvenienced by anything that didn't fit with the prevailing theory, now that he had one.

"Suicide is a strange thing," he offered, barely looking up from his steaming coffee. "You really never know about someone. Maybe he chose to jump just to show he could face his fear and end his life that way."

"Maybe, Chief, but it sounds unlikely," I said.

I didn't want to tell him how to do his job (we weren't nearly that close), but before retiring, I'd spent several years working in the human-resources section of a multinational company and had a degree in psychology. Nothing in my experience or education was consistent with the chief's explanation. The "facing his fear" bit sounded good, but promptly following such a triumph with suicide just didn't compute. At least it wasn't my problem.

"In a minute," I continued, "I'll walk over to Bill's house. Thanks for the heads-up. It does need to come from someone he knows."

I just wished it wasn't going to be me ... but then, who?

Amber stopped by the table as soon as the chief left—one of her not-so-covert techniques for gathering intelligence. I gave her a brief synopsis of the conversation.

"I've been thinking," she said. "If he really killed himself, why would he dress up to kick the bucket? You think he wanted to look good to meet his maker?" She paused, picked up the chief's empty coffee cup, and then continued. "But then again, if that's what he thought, isn't killing yourself one of the no-nos for getting into heaven? And, if you're not going to heaven, why would you want to have a nice suit on to meet the horned guy?"

Occasionally, some of Amber's questions were of the overly philosophical variety. I thought I detected a couple of those in her barrage. At this rate, we would soon be discussing whether a waitress could still gossip in the forest if there was no one around to hear her.

I countered with an insightful, "Heck if I know."

*   *   *   *

I could have walked more slowly to Bill's house, but I wasn't sure how. I dreaded our conversation. At least I didn't have to ruin a good mood; he answered the door and faced me with a deep frown.

"And what have I done to deserve two visits in as many days?" he asked through a sad attempt at a smile.

"Could I come in, Bill? I have something to tell you; it may take a few minutes."

"Sure, of course, come in," he said. "I apologize for being so rude. I'm really having trouble getting my hands around Julius's death."

"I understand. I'm afraid this won't make it any easier."

"I figured that, or you wouldn't be here," he said. "Let's have it."

I shared what the chief told me. I didn't try to soften it; I wanted Bill to hear the facts—at least as they were known then—as clearly as possible. I felt terrible at the sight of his pained grimace.

"Chris, I don't understand. I was serious yesterday when I told you he was deathly afraid of the water. There is absolutely no way he would walk to the end of the pier. Sorry, but the police made a mistake."

"I know what you're saying," I continued. "But there's really no way to truly know what someone will do—especially if he was depressed."

To be honest, I didn't believe that myself. My commentary wasn't an attempt to cheer Bill up—more to help him get through the situation.

"Chris, I value our friendship and hope what I'm about to say won't endanger it, but you're wrong—so very, very wrong. That's all there is to it." He chopped his right arm through the air like a hatchet, cutting the conversation off.

"I told Chief Newman what you said about Julius being afraid of the water. If you want, I'll go back and let him know how strongly you feel."

"Go ahead; if you want, have him come talk to me," he said. "I don't know if I can convince him, but he needs to listen. Chris, I was up all night trying to figure out what could have happened. I couldn't figure it out, but I'm only a college professor; the police are trained. Please encourage them to take a closer look."

"I'll do my best. Is there anything I can do for you?"

"No, I just need to be alone. Thanks for coming by."

Feeling dismissed, I put on my most convincing face and headed to the door, on my way to a second round with the chief. Bill remained seated, deep in thought. I hadn't known Bill for long, but didn't know how he could appear more depressed.

CHAPTER 6

A career as a corporate administrator had paid my bills; photography was my passion. I'd sold my fine-art photography over the Internet, in galleries, and in juried art shows for years. If I'd had to live off that, I wouldn't be living on the Atlantic coast, but under a highway overpass in Louisville. Fortunately, I had been able to support my passion with my day job.

I heard Charles before I saw him. "Hey, Mr. Photo Man," he yelled. He'd called me that in all but the most formal settings since we met.

I was walking along West Arctic Avenue, the two-lane road paralleling the beach, photographing the setting sun behind the sea oats and wood-slatted erosion fences. The road ended abruptly just past the Charleston Oceanfront Villas, a large, modern condo complex that looked as out of place on Folly as the Eiffel Tower in a desert.

"It's about time I caught you taking pictures," he said as he jogged to my side, stooped over, and placed his left hand on his knee; his breaths were coming hard.

"What do you mean?" I asked. I had more than a good idea but wanted to see if he got it right.

He slowly stood erect and pointed his ever-present cane at my Nikon. "You know you have fun doing this, but you haven't done it since you got here. Remember, you're here to have fun, retire, and live the life of Charles."

I wouldn't have put it exactly that way. Charles was nearly my height and weight, around 160 pounds—not thin, but as we've decided, 160 is the new 150. At least, that's our story.

Part of my decision to take early retirement and move to Folly Beach had been the unique photo opportunities in the Low Country and in historic Charleston. During my month-long vacation last year, my friendship with Charles had grown from our mutual interest in photography; that was about where our mutual interests ended. I had worked full-time since graduating from college more years ago than I'll admit. Charles had worked full and part time—mainly part time—until he reached the ripe old age of thirty-four, moved here from Detroit, and retired. He hadn't been on anyone's payroll in the last twenty years. He was extremely well-read, both in the classics and the comics; I only read a book when I ran out of anything else to do. He quoted United States presidents—usually the more obscure ones—and occasionally *Peanuts*; I can't even quote myself on things I said more than a few hours ago.

Despite our differences, I thoroughly enjoyed his company, and we had spent hours walking around the island taking photos, talking about photography—me mainly teaching, him learning—and talking about the life, times, and people of Folly Beach. The island was small, but there was no shortage of people to talk about.

"You're right," I said, reluctantly acknowledging that he had, in fact, gotten it right. "I've been so busy taking care of stuff, I haven't wandered around like I want."

"Busy with what?" he said.

"Getting moved in, setting up my computer stuff, all the paperwork required to move, selling my house in Kentucky—is that enough stuff for now?"

"I guess when you add putting together a spectacular housewarming party for yourself and helping Bill, you're forgiven."

"Forgiven for what?" I asked, knowing it was a mistake before finishing the question.

"For starters, not teaching me more about photography like you promised. And for sending me this University of Kentucky sweatshirt without even asking if I wanted it."

He hesitated, put his thumb against his chin for a moment, then held up three fingers. "Oh yeah, third, for sending me this really classy Tilley hat. It ruined my reputation as a total bum. And finally—for now, anyway—for your inexcusable lack of progress on finding a location for your gallery, so I can show you how to make it look so great that everyone will want to buy your photos. And …"

"Enough, enough!" I interrupted. "There's only so much forgiving I can take for one day. I didn't realize how much I could have offended one person in such a short time. Tell you what: to make up for it, I'll get with my Realtor in the next two or three days and get started on finding a building. I don't want to deprive you of showing me a thing or two."

"That's better," he said, with the beginning of a smile. "Now, what do you think really happened with Mr. Palmer? Rumors have it he offed himself."

"I've no idea. Bill is convinced he couldn't have drowned himself, because of his water phobia. He makes a convincing argument. So was it an accident?"

"Either way, I'm going to the funeral," he said. "I'd be glad to let you give me a ride."

Only Charles could make it sound like he was doing me a favor by riding with me. Of course, I said okay. We parted ways and I headed home to ponder my future gallery location and what, if anything, I could do to help Bill through his time of need.

CHAPTER 7

Large, ominous clouds, a cold rain, and a brisk breeze off the ocean greeted my morning. Dried flowers and wind-worn foliage were everywhere. It was the perfect day for a funeral.

"Chris, don't you think you need to trade in this fancy Lexus for a good, sturdy, pickup truck if you're going to fit in?" asked Charles as he slid across the leather-trimmed front seat.

Most people would have started the conversation with "Good morning." I didn't expect anything that normal when I picked Charles up at his small apartment on Sandbar Lane. What his apartment lacked in size, it made up in view: just past the gravel and crushed-shell-infused parking area, he had a kitty-corner view of the Folly River and marsh.

Charles was dressed smartly in a dark gray ribbed sweater and a pair of crisp navy slacks that appeared new. Despite the cold, wet weather, he didn't have on a jacket. As always, he carried his digital camera and handmade cane. This was the first time I hadn't seen him in a long-sleeved sweatshirt with some school mascot on the front. I barely recognized him.

"Charles, you look quite appropriately attired today. Sorry it has to be for a funeral."

"'A little flattery will support a man through great fatigue.' James Monroe, long-dead United States president," he said, selecting the appropriate words from his vast vault of presidential trivia.

I never knew whether to believe him about the quotes, but on the scale of life-time communication, it didn't matter; I kept my mouth shut. A byproduct of maturity on my part, I assumed … I hoped.

The cemetery was northwest of Charleston, about thirty miles from the bridge connecting Folly to the forty-eight contiguous states, off the beautiful and historic Ashley River Road. Pre–Civil War plantations competed with a few shopping areas, but the gorgeous plantations clearly won the battle the farther from the city we traveled. The Ashley Oak Memorial Gardens were just a block off the highly traveled road, but well-placed evergreen landscaping provided a peaceful, serene environment. In deference to Mr. Palmer's written instructions, the service would be conducted graveside. He had no family, but a large number of mourners lingered around the funeral home tent.

I walked toward the fourteen-by-fourteen-foot-square structure and the traditional white wooden folding chairs placed under the canopy. The mahogany casket rested on stanchions covered by a material that looked like pliable Astroturf. Bill, dressed in a dark gray wool suit, dark burgundy tie, and black topcoat, was already seated in the second row. He was talking to the officiating minister. Not wanting to interrupt their deep conversation, I walked over to Chief Newman. I was pleased to see him, along with his daughter, Karen Lawson, a detective with the Charleston County Sheriff's Department. We exchanged whispered pleasantries and stood in silence, looking out over the manicured field of tombstones. Small American flags were scattered throughout, along with the occasional urn of faded artificial flowers. Two of the nearby marble stones were covered with weather-faded Christmas decorations, obviously the last resting place of children who left this earth way too early.

Others continued to arrive; I didn't know most of them. I did recognize a few from Folly and assumed they were members of Preserve the Past. A half dozen well-dressed men were standing together and talking in reverent tones; they appeared to know each other. My guess was they were fellow antique-shop owners or others from the King Street retail community. An attractive lady in her late fifties was dressed in black and stood with five younger people. They stood apart from the others, and I had no idea of their relationship to Palmer.

A sad-faced woman about one hundred pounds past petite—the minister's wife, I assumed—waddled to a portable CD player and pushed the Play button. Solemn music began, and we all focused on the lonely casket. Strengthening gusts carried rain into the tent, and the minister, his girth nearly as large as his spouse, clearly was hurrying through the ceremony. No one seemed to mind. As I stood in the light rain, I couldn't help remembering the funerals of my parents. Coincidentally, each had been held in the rain, but several years apart. A few of my tears mixed with the increasing rain.

The ceremony ended as quickly as it had begun. The horizontal rain drove the mourners to the protection and artificial heat of the cars. I wanted to speak to Bill, but he had already rushed to his late-model Buick and was leaving his parking space beside the narrow drive that wove through the cemetery. I assumed he was heading back to class in downtown Charleston.

＊　　　＊　　　＊　　　＊

Charles was in the car when I opened the door. He was rubbing his hands together and blowing on them.

"Where were you?" I asked. "I didn't see you after the service began."

"Good," he said, "then I succeeded in my stealth. I was over to the side, photographing everyone."

"Charles, I gave up long ago trying to figure out why you take some of the photos you do, but I've got to ask: why were you taking photos of the mourners?"

"You surprise me sometime with your ignorance," he said. "Don't you ever watch television?"

I didn't gaze his way. "We have a long ride back home, so I'll be patient," I said. "I know you'll tell me eventually what my viewing habits have to do with anything."

"I won't make you worry all those miles," he said. He sat back as warmth filled the car. "Everyone knows the murderer comes to the funeral of the person he killed. The police hide in the bushes, or behind headstones, photographing everyone, so they can figure out who did it."

"Charles, do I have to point out that you're not the police, that there wasn't murder, and that you wouldn't have a clue what to look for?"

"No need to remind me," he said. "You just did. Now it's my turn. Bill said Julius wouldn't kill himself. Bill is your friend, and you need to pay attention to what he says. He knew Julius; you didn't. I'm your friend, so through you, I'm paying attention to Bill. Now it's a little harder to do, because you're throwing out all those … those doubt waves, I'll call them, but I'm managing to swim through them to believe Bill. See?"

I couldn't think of anything to say to compete with that. Maybe Charles had a point. Maybe I needed to pay more attention to Bill. Maybe I should tell Charles he was a certifiable nut and let it go. Maybe I would just change the subject.

"Are your parents alive?" I asked as I maneuvered through the rain and heavy traffic.

"Strange segue, Mr. Photo Man—am I beginning to rub off on you?"

"Not that strange. I don't know much about you other than you came from Detroit after your brief career in a big Ford plant up there. The funeral made me think about my parents, who are both gone. I wondered about yours."

"Oh, I was beginning to think my illogical mind was having a positive influence. Now you ruined it by making sense." He paused for the longest period, then continued. "Both my parents died when I was young. I was raised by my grandparents with a little help from my alcoholic aunt. That made it fun around the house."

"How?"

"My grandmother was the librarian in the public library in one of the poorest sections of Detroit. She was the most traditional librarian in the universe. For years, I thought my name was 'Quiet!' She brought all the good and bad home from the library. She ran the household like an old-fashioned library: books were everywhere, and we all spoke in a whisper. I almost had to check a book out before looking at it, even if it was on the coffee table." He again paused, as if deciding how much to divulge. "She's the one who refused to let anyone call me Charlie; I resented it when my friends had to call me Charles. What self-respecting ten-year-old is called Charles? I guess she had an influence on me, since I now prefer it. If we were Catholic, she'd have been a great nun."

"What was the deal with your aunt?"

"Aunt Melinda introduced me to most everything Grandma tried to keep away from me. She lived just three blocks from us and would wander over all the time, usually when my grandmother wasn't around. Everybody said she was an alcoholic—actually, they said she was a drunk—but she seemed the same to me all the time, so I couldn't tell. Besides, I didn't know what an alcoholic was, except it must be something fun, since Grandma was always preaching against it. Aunt Melinda taught me there were two sides to everything—maybe even more. From her, I learned that 'quiet' was a bad way to be; checking out books wasn't necessary if no one was looking; having fun wasn't evil; cussing was good for the damn vocabulary; and that work was evil and should be avoided if possible. A true role model."

I glanced over at Charles and observed a faraway gaze punctuated with a smile—a true role model, indeed.

"From what I've seen, other than your name, your aunt had a greater impact on you than your grandmother."

"All except my love of reading," he said. "Grandma thought I got it from her, but it was really a way I could escape. Literature, poetry, history, and an occasional dirty book helped me avoid living in the real world in a librarian's house— a nunnish librarian, at that."

Nunnish? He seemed to also have learned the knack of creating new words as well. *Is that his aunt's influence or Grandma's?* I wondered. *Another conversation, another day.* We pulled up in front of his apartment, and neither of us seemed to have any words left.

"Charles, thanks for letting me take you to the funeral."

"That's better—illogic reigns," he said with a wry grin.

For the sake of our country, I hoped no president had ever said that.

CHAPTER 8

Valentine's Day began with the smiling, friendly face and cheerful voice of Amber as she greeted me and pointed to my favorite booth. I spoke briefly to Jim "Cool Dude" Sloan, an early-morning regular, and headed to my seat by the window overlooking the patio. My near-boiling, black coffee was already there, along with heart-shaped sugar cookie covered with white icing and sprinkled with red candy dots, or whatever they were called.

"Sorry I couldn't get to the funeral," said Amber in somber tones. "I guess you know I had to work."

"No problem. I know you were thinking about us standing in the wind and cold rain. Besides, I had your main squeeze Charles to keep me entertained."

"Not so fast, Chris. Maybe 'main touch' would be better than 'main squeeze.' We just have a good time talking to each other."

"Whatever," I said, not believing her for a moment.

Before I continued playing Dr. Phil and thanking her for the sweet—in both senses—gift, Chief Newman entered and headed my way while giving the "police scan" to the other diners.

"Morning, Chief; join me for coffee?" I asked.

He sat, took off his sunglasses, and waved for Amber. "Not a bad idea. I've been up since three," he said.

"A problem?" I responded, sliding my cookie away from his reach.

"A minor one, I think. Officer Robins was on patrol last night and noticed the side door of Julius Palmer's house ajar. Since Palmer's death, we've been trying to keep a watch on the house. We don't know who'll be taking care of things; I don't think he has any family. Anyway, Robins called me, since it could be a delicate situation. In fact, he calls me about everything."

That didn't surprise me. Robins was one of the long-timers on the force; his waist was about as wide as the door to the police car. "Slovenly" the only word that came to mind in describing him. I suspected he wouldn't do anything to endanger his job or rock the boat; with his size, rocking the boat could be a disaster.

"Someone break in?" I asked.

"Robins was guarding the door when I got there," the chief continued, not directly answering my question. "It'd been damaged—looked like someone kicked it hard enough to break the lock. We couldn't tell much. Nothing else appeared damaged. The television was still there—although I wouldn't have stolen it either, since it's old and heavy. Would've taken two to carry it out ... wouldn't be surprised if it was black and white. It appears someone went through all the papers on the desk in his office, and the drawers were open. But for all I know, Palmer could have left them that way. Who knows?"

"Any way to tell when it happened?" I asked.

"Not really. I don't know if we would've noticed the door earlier. Robins was lucky even to notice it this time. We'll take some prints, but I doubt that'll help. My guess is that someone learned about his death and broke in to see what was there to steal. Sadly, when someone dies, and the obituary indicates the absence of relatives, this is often a byproduct. They could have done it during the funeral—that's how it usually works. I'm always amazed at how many ways the bad guys have of doing their job."

"Chief, you know Bill Hansel is convinced Palmer didn't kill himself," I said while he took a sip. "Could this be connected?"

"Chris, people never think their friends commit suicide. I saw that time after time during my years as a MP. Sorry, but I don't think this break-in—if that's even what it was—has anything to do with how he died." He pushed his half-full cup away. "I have to get to the office and start the paperwork."

I was glad he felt close enough to let me know what happened, but I still had doubts about randomness of the events. *Oh, well. That has nothing to do with me—nothing.*

On the way out, I asked Amber to ask around and see if she could find out anything about Palmer. I shared some skepticism about suicide. If anyone could learn anything, it was Amber. I also thanked her for the cookie. She smiled and gave me a quick hug.

"Happy Valentine's Day," she whispered.

Not a bad way to begin the day.

*   *   *   *

Tammy's job made it difficult for us to see each other on a regular basis. She would be off around six, so we decided to celebrate our first Valentine's Day with supper where we had eaten last year during a daylong walking tour of Charleston. I picked her up at her warehouse loft apartment and drove a few blocks to Tommy Condon's Irish Pub and Seafood Restaurant. Located just a block from the historic market, Tommy Condon's faux Irish pub was a Charleston tradition. Locals frequented it in impressive numbers during the week; tourists flocked there on weekends and during the high season.

Her status as a frequent diner gave Tammy priority on one of the busiest nights of the year. She-crab soup, fish and chips, and a bottle of their finest mid-priced wine met our culinary needs.

Conversation turned to the first time we had eaten here and the difficulties of our nine-month long-distance relationship. She had taken a week of vacation in October to enjoy leaf-changing season in Kentucky, but aside from that, we hadn't spent much time together before I moved nearby.

Tammy had lived all over the country with her parents and in several cities with an ex-husband as he rose in the highly competitive world of broadcast news—during that visit to Kentucky, Tammy had frequently referred to him as a "talking head" in a derisive tone. My marriage to my college sweetheart had ended many years before; I had little to say about it, good or bad. Tammy had sworn Kentucky in the fall was as beautiful as anywhere she had ever been. True or not, it was good to hear.

I had met Tammy when she was the reporter covering a murder that I had the unfortunate displeasure of stumbling upon. I went from a minor player in a story about a death, to the subject of a puff piece of newspaper filler, to whatever I am now. Lovers, yes; in love, maybe. With a twelve-year difference in age, we didn't share much in the way of taste in movies or the social mores of our peer groups—an analytical way to say we didn't really understand much about each other, other than that we really enjoyed being together. We thought that was more important than the trappings of our age groups.

Reminiscing gave way to a more current topic: the untimely death of Julius Palmer, a topic we wouldn't have broached if he hadn't been a friend of Bill.

We had just finished our "famous Charleston" she-crab soup. "You're the crime reporter—what's your take?" I asked.

"Chris, if it weren't for Bill's comments and strong feelings about Palmer's fear of water, I wouldn't see anything out of the ordinary about suicide."

"Don't you think it peculiar he would come from work, make a bank deposit, and then climb over the railing on the pier?" I asked. "Not even considering his fear of water, that sounds strange to me. Who worries about finances at a time like that?"

"Let's take another tack: say someone killed him," she said. "Why? Who benefits from his death? Most murders are committed for money or love."

I nodded agreement, and she continued her analysis.

"You said he was well-to-do, but does he have any relatives? Who inherits? Since he made his deposit before returning to Folly, he didn't even have much money on him, so I don't think we need to worry about muggers."

"True," I said.

"Then there's the question of love. Was he involved with anyone? If not, back to my first question: why?"

"I have no idea who'd benefit," I said. "Bill told me Palmer didn't have relatives, and Chief Newman said the same. If Bill's correct, he didn't even have close friends, much less someone who'd kill for love." I knew I had addressed only a couple of her questions, but her journalistic mind could be tough to keep up with.

"Do you know if he had a will?" she asked.

"I don't, but I'll ask Bill. Maybe by now, he's over the initial shock and will remember something Palmer told him that'll make some sense out of this."

We'd finished our meal and found ourselves too full for key lime pie. Tammy said she was tired and had to be at work early the next day. Still, she offered to share her apartment with me if I wanted to stay in town. I wanted to but caught the reluctance in her offer. Besides, I was meeting my Realtor in the morning. I drove her the few blocks home and headed back to the beach.

Dark came way too early in winter.

CHAPTER 9

At nine sharp, I stepped out the front door. I knew that the best real-estate agent in the second-largest of the three small realty firms on Folly Beach—a dubious professional accomplishment if there ever was one—would be at the curb. Promptness was about the only predictable—or normal—thing about Bob Howard. I wore a heavier coat than I'd normally need and carried my canvas Tilley. The sight of Bob, dressed in a lightweight nylon jacket and a Los Angeles Lakers cap, sitting proudly in his purple PT Cruiser convertible with the top down, reassured me that nothing had changed. This was still the quirky island I'd learned to love. To most people, driving along in the breeze on a dreary, cold, damp day would seem absurd. Those people had never met Mr. Howard.

"Morning, Bob. A bit cool to have the top down, isn't it?"

"Hell, no. If you can't stand the cold, get out of the fridge."

I silently apologized to Harry Truman. Bob could learn a thing or two from my president-quoting friend, Charles.

Knowing I treaded on sacred ground, I said, "I see the purple car is still your Realtormobile of choice."

"Shit, aspiring famous photo gallery owner, I told you it was *dark plum*, not purple. Now put on your hat, cover that rapidly growing bald spot, and get in. I'm a busy man. You've already wasted too damn many of my valuable minutes."

He had the heater blasting, so I knew he hadn't gone completely off the deep end.

"Thank God I won't have to show you 173 properties before you take one this time. There're only two retail spaces available."

"Fewer than ten" would have been a more accurate number of places he showed me during my house search, but facts seldom got in Bob's way. Besides, I enjoyed his banter and knew how much he cared about his clients. Under his gruff, profane exterior was a … well, a gruff and profane interior. But if one ventured another level or two deeper, there was a kind, caring side, buried down somewhere near the center of the earth.

We had driven not more than three blocks when he pulled up in front of a new building less than a block off Center Street, the commerce center of the island. The building was in the final phase of construction. The exterior was fresh and pristine.

"Until a year ago, this was the site of an ancient duplex," explained Bob. "It burned down one Friday night. The owner said the fire was caused by worn electrical wiring; the local wags called it arson. The local police called it one hell of a big fire! Less than a week later, the owner, a damn Canadian, submitted plans for a retail space with an apartment on the second floor. I guess he had the plans ready just in case his duplex burned. Those damn Canadians think of everything. Anyway, here it is. It's almost finished, except for a little paint on the inside."

"So what's the price?" I asked, shivering and feeling a little like we were north of Niagara Falls.

"Chill, prospective gallery owner. I'll tell you after you've had a chance to look inside. All fine Realtors establish value to the client before getting into the nitty-gritty stuff like price. I, being the consummate professional, will follow religiously the time-proven techniques of selling. And don't even think about saying anything about me being such a 'big' Realtor. Your sarcasm is not lost on me. Statistically, my weight is appropriate for my height."

"Sure, if you were eight foot three," I said.

"I rest my case," he continued. "Now, are you ready to look inside, or would you rather waste more of my time analyzing my vital statistics?"

I wasn't very good with space, but Bob said the interior was just over a thousand square feet. The roll of carpet in the corner was a cheap commercial-grade gray with a subtle pattern—the sort of flooring whose sole purpose was to hide dirt. The large front room was as basic as possible—all "frost white," according to the painter cutting in around the rear door frame. There was a small restroom and a larger office area behind what would become the gallery. Everything was fresh, bright, clean, and boring. About the only exciting thing was the temporary propane heater, which was fire-engine red and looked like something that had fallen from a fighter jet. It huffed and puffed, spewing out heat into the center of the room and keeping the workers warm. I didn't think I could make it a permanent feature. Bob finally got around to telling me the rent, which was a little over two thousand a month, plus utilities. He tactfully told me that since there had been no utilities in the past, he couldn't tell how much the *damn* utilities would be in the future. It took a highly trained real-estate agent to tell me that in such a professional manner.

"Okay, let's see the other space," I said.

"Get in the *dark plum* car, and I'll drive you to the next—and don't forget, only other—option."

No more than thirty seconds later, we pulled up in front of a tired-looking, stucco-fronted two-story structure on Center Street within sight of the Dog.

"There she is," said Bob as he nodded toward the aging edifice. "This used to be the town's most expensive and worthless souvenir and T-shirt shop. It was so worthless, it only lasted in this spot for twenty-seven years. The average beach vacationer will choose worthless over anything else nine times out of ten—somehow, good ole United States currency starts looking like play money to people on vacation. T-shirts and stuff they'd never buy at home have to be in their suitcase when they leave. God bless this wonderful country!"

I was receiving a lecture on the clothing-purchasing habits of our fellow citizens from the man who wore his faded gold "Wipe Out Rodents: Kill Mickey Mouse" T-shirt every third time I saw him.

"So why's it gone now?"

"Simple: the owner decided to take his fortune and move to Branson, Missouri. He told everyone that his customers were getting tired of the beach and needed more country music. He said Branson was the new country-music center of the free world. As a student of that fine indigenous genre of music, I can tell you he's full of bovine manure. Nashville was, is, and will always hold that title. I'd say he'll be missed, but I've noticed that the clothing of the vacationers has improved since his move to the ocean-challenged center of Missouri."

"Interesting," I said with little enthusiasm.

The front of the building had two large windows with frames painted a faded ocean green. Peeling paint revealed red as the previous color. The interior was nearly identical in layout and size to the first property. There the similarities ended. Two of the walls had rows of adjustable shelving painted either red or orange. This paint had been applied fairly recently by geological standards—say, in the seventies. Now, the dust and dirt made it impossible to tell the true color. It didn't matter. The floor was hardwood, with paths worn by thousands of feet, sandals, flip-flops, and clogs around where display racks had once stood. The ceiling was tin, and an old, apparently inoperable ceiling fan hung in the center of the room. A strong, musty smell permeated the place. A good airing was a must, along with a good cleaning, insect fumigation, new paint, new lighting, new fan … whew!

"This fine example of beach-aged, quality retail space goes for eighteen hundred a month. That might be a little negotiable, since the owner hasn't managed to con anyone into renting it for over a year. One of the best Realtors in the galaxy—that's me, if you were wondering—might be able to get a better deal."

"Why don't we walk over to the Dog and discuss the *many* options I've been shown? Or would you rather drive?" I asked, then headed out the door.

"I detect a glimmer of an insult in that last statement," Bob called after me. "But a good Realtor gets along with all clients—regardless how obnoxious they might be. So, okay. We'll walk. I could use the exercise."

I didn't disagree, but doubted hundred-yard walk would do much for his waistline. He reinforced my belief when he ordered a large piece of "breakfast pie," which was fancy phrase for "pie you eat in the morning." He would need to jog back to his car—via downtown Charleston—to work that off!

"So, who killed the antique dealer?" he asked after the first bite.

A drastic segue, I thought, from discussing the merits of the two properties.

"What makes you think he was killed?" I said. "The only person who's raised that question is Bill, and he's basing it on Palmer's fear of water."

"I really have no idea," said Bob before stuffing more "breakfast" in his mouth. "I could argue suicide. It seems to me that someone who lived his entire life in the past, with that old stuff he called 'antiques,' would almost have to spend a lot of time mighty damn depressed. I know I'd be."

"But not if that's what he loved," I said.

"True, but he inherited his job—and all that old stuff—from his father. Who says it's really what he liked? I just know all that old crap would make me depressed. Speaking of old crap, what about the two stores?"

"There's nothing to complain about on the first one," I said. "Everything is new and fresh, it's in move-in condition, the price is okay—well, as okay as any price on this overpriced island."

"There's a big damn 'but' coming, isn't there?"

"Not yet. I'll withhold my buts for later," I said. "The second shop would be an illogical choice for anyone. Poor condition, stinks, needs everything—paint, repairs, CPR. The price is okay, but the owner would have to agree to some improvements before I'd consider it."

"I'm patiently waiting—something you know I don't do well," Bob said, thumping his chubby fingers on his right hand on the table. "Lay the but on me … and I sure as hell hope nobody heard me say that!"

"*But*, the first choice is just too perfect."

"Holy moly. Shit, Chris, you're enough to drive even the best Realtor—me, of course—to drink, drugs, suicide, and murder! Crocodile crap, we wouldn't want to put you into something perfect, especially *too perfect*."

"I didn't say I wouldn't take it. I was pointing out my concern. Actually, the perfect condition isn't nearly as big a problem as the location. I like the idea of being this close to the Dog. And tourists wouldn't be able to miss me. Maybe I'll get my hands on some of that play money of theirs."

"Chris, the 'perfect' property is less than a block off the main drag. You, and all those damn tourists, can see it from the sidewalk on Center Street. It's not like perfection is two miles from the nearest clump of civilization."

"I know, and I didn't say I was rejecting it," I said. "I need to think about it."

"Sure," he said. "Remember, I'm the brilliant Realtor who found your house. I do understand something about your warped thought process. Why don't you call me in a few days? I don't think the stores are going anywhere soon. Hell, I'm sure the one across the street isn't."

I wasn't in a hurry to leave, but Bob apparently had to go harass some poor client. He paid for the coffee and his dessert—or breakfast, as he liked to call it.

"By the way, for the record, I think your highly successful antique dealer was killed. Talk to ya later," he said, not looking back as he walked through the door.

CHAPTER 10

I wasn't ready to go home and look at four walls, so I walked the five short blocks to the beach. This was my first winter experience on the coast. It was amazing how a cold, windy morning can make the ocean appear menacing and uninviting—a feeling I've never had in the summer. The beach, littered with vacationers in the summer, ribboned for miles without a human presence. I stood to the left of the signature pier and tried to picture a distraught, well-dressed lone figure purposefully walking to the seaward end of the wooden structure, climbing over the side rails, and stepping off to a cold, painful death. Then I tried to picture the same scenario with someone who was deathly afraid of the water. I tried to picture that, turned away from the pier, turned back, and tried again. I failed miserably.

*   *   *   *

Now I really wasn't ready to be alone. I took the short walk back to the Dog and accepted the good-natured ribbing from Amber about just leaving. This time, I spoke to Cool Dude Sloan. I had seen him in the Dog most mornings during my visits last year, but we never spoke more than a word or two. I had just remembered him as someone who smiled at me each time, waved occasionally, and looked like an aging hippie totally content with his 1960s lifestyle. If I hadn't known better, I would think Arlo Guthrie moonlighted at Folly.

He—Sloan, not Guthrie—shared that for some reason, February was not high season for business in a surf shop on Folly Beach, South Carolina. I speculated it might have something to do with no one being here. He pondered my comment as if I were an economist with the Federal Reserve who may have hit on a previously undiscovered economic truth.

He scratched his chin and said, "Could be."

My regular spot was still available—as was every other table, except for Jim's perch and one occupied by a couple I didn't recognize.

"Who's that?" I asked Amber when she brought my water.

"Oh, I guess you wouldn't know them. They're the Pascals from somewhere in Canada—Quebec, I think, wherever that is."

"The food's good, but isn't this a long way to come for lunch?"

"They usually stay for more than a day, duh," she said. "They own a condo in the Oceanfront Villas. They come the middle of February and leave sometime in March. They're some of the early snowbirds who arrive during the winter; it's much warmer here than at home, they say. Those poor Canadians. You can usually recognize them in here—light jackets and even shorts while the rest of us have on heavy coats, jeans, and boots. They wanted to sit on the porch, but I told them it wasn't open until spring."

We regulars always needed to know who was visiting, using, and abusing our island.

"Chris, I've been thinking," said Amber. "I'm not afraid of much—snakes and men mainly—but if I wanted to kill myself, I'd want it to be in as nice a place as possible. I know it sounds silly; I'd be just as dead. But I'd want some peace near me when I go."

"You're not thinking of killing yourself, are you, Amber?"

"I have no plans to kill myself; Charles may drive me to it some day, but that's another story. My point is, I don't believe Mr. Palmer committed suicide by jumping in the scary, cold ocean. So, if he didn't kill himself, who did him in?"

That was five of us now.

"And if someone killed him, who and why?" I asked.

"Sorry, haven't figured that out yet," she said. "You have a knack for learning stuff others can't, so I thought you'd better know my thinking. Now you do, so … are you going to eat, or just chatter and keep me from my customers?"

The number of customers was up to three, so I let her go.

CHAPTER 11

The sun broke over the horizon but did little to warm the cold, ocean air. Bob had agreed to meet me at the former souvenir store. I told him I wanted to discuss the two sites and commit to renting one. The commitment part got his attention.

He arrived, convertible top down, wearing a light jacket, an old fishing hat that flapped in the wind, and his usual irritated look on a windburned face. I recalled Amber's description of inappropriately dressed tourists. Maybe Bob was from Canada.

"Why in the hell didn't you just tell me yesterday you wanted this damn store? That would've saved me a trip on such a lovely spring morning."

"Sort of pushing the spring thing a bit, aren't we, Bob?" I asked as we approached the vacant building. "It's February, after all."

"Hell, no. The sun's out, I'm still alive; it's spring to me. Adjust, new retiree; you're a resident of Folly Beach now. Burn your damn calendar."

"I didn't say I was taking this space. This is just where I wanted to meet."

"You're taking this one, and I'll tell you why," he said. "The new one would be too easy. It's way too neat, clean, and pristine for you. You want a challenge; the other store isn't one. Plus, the uglier location will be within a nine-iron shot of the Dog, healthy damn food and all. And most importantly, I only brought these keys. You've got to take it."

I didn't think I had that many reasons, but he was right. This space felt right. I wasn't sure why, except it was the same feeling I had when I chose my house over the newer and nicer ones. It felt like Folly Beach, the very place I had chosen to live in the first place.

"Bob, that did it," I said, suppressing a smile. "It would have been horribly rude of me to ask you to go get the other key. So, sure, I'll take this one and live with it for the rest of my life, just because you didn't bring a key."

"That's more like it," he said. "You're finally beginning to understand what's important. If you're available, I'll meet you here Monday with the paperwork, and we'll get it all taken care of. After that, you're stuck with it."

Stuck with it. Quite a sales pitch from such a successful real-estate professional.

*   *   *   *

"Morning, Charles. To what do I owe the privilege of your presence?" I said to the huffing and puffing visitor behind me as I walked along the beach just east of the pier.

"Just lucky, I guess." He moved in lockstep beside me. "Now what are you trying to take photos of?"

"I was getting some images of the sun and shadows of the dune fences. Why are you out so early?"

"I'm helping the guys working on a house over on Huron," he said. "They've got to get the bathroom remodeled before renters arrive in April."

"That almost sounds like work." I was surprised. "Have you turned over a new leaf?"

"Nope, just need a little more money. Cash payment—love it."

"Did you know someone broke into Palmer's house sometime around the funeral?" I asked.

"How'd that slip past the rumor mill? Now where will I get my information?"

"I don't know anything about your rumor mill, other than it's pretty good, but Chief Newman told me." Finally, I was becoming a native—getting information before Charles. Amazing! "The chief thought the break-in was unrelated to the death—just somebody hearing about the funeral and breaking in when no one would be home."

"Sorry, Mr. Photo Man, but it's clear—or in focus, in your terms—that the killer broke in for something. Clear as day; yes, clear as day." He nodded as he repeated the words.

"Why so sure?" I asked as I continued to fiddle with the camera angle, bending low to capture the shadows.

"Chris, you're a handsome fellow, at least according to the ladies, and on the upside of bright … but you can be dense at times. Think about it: How many houses are on this island? Several hundred, right? How many were broken into on the day of Mr. Palmer's funeral? One, right? Everyone knew he didn't have any money in his house; he always made deposits right from work, right?" With each "right," Charles scuffed his right foot in the sand, like Mr. Ed counting with his hoof. "I'll bet the chief told you nothing was stolen, right? The only things worth anything in his house were those big old ancient pieces of furniture—some folks call them antiques. Right?"

I knew two wrongs didn't make a right, but I wasn't sure how many rights made a wrong. I had lost count after Charles reached four.

"So, say you're correct about all your rights; what's it mean?" I asked once he finished his equine counting trick.

"It means he wanted something that was small enough to steal and not be noticed. Most likely, papers, a will, or some of those bearer bonds that anyone can cash. Maybe even a fistful of diamonds … whatever. The point is, the burglar killed him and then got something from his house. See? Clear as day!"

I confess, it wasn't quite that clear to me, but I did wonder whether the death and burglary were related, regardless of what the chief said.

*   *   *   *

By the next day, I'd put Charles's circuitous speculation out of my mind—not really that hard, as it hadn't offered much sticking power from the beginning. Breakfast at the Dog was seldom a boring experience. Just having Amber around made the most miserable of days pleasant. She always shared a cheerful comment with smile on her lovely face. Combine that with the rest of her natural beauty, and how could anyone go wrong by choosing the Dog?

Folly Beach was unusual for a resort-island town; many of its residents were here year-round. Like all beach resorts, the area suffered—er, enjoyed—a large influx of tourists in the summer, but the residents played a dominant role in island activities. The 24-7 residents had their routines. Many of them hadn't fallen prey to the rigors of a daily job and spent much of their time hanging out with others of the same persuasion. Several spent hours each day soaking up the wit, wisdom, charm, and sex appeal of Miss Amber. I could think of far worse ways to spend a few hours.

Two of the city council members held almost daily debates from a corner booth. They were used to me now and spoke freely. The mayor, Eric Amato, dropped in occasionally, so they often nearly had a quorum. If they could ever agree on anything, they could conduct some of the city's business over coffee, the Dog's original breakfast burritos, and jokes. Fortunately for the rest of the council members—and most likely for the citizens of this fair city—they seldom agreed on much.

"Morning, guys," I said as I took my regular booth. "How would someone find out what's in someone's will?"

"Well, if he ain't dead, ask him," said one of the elected officials without skipping a bite of burrito. "If he's dead, it gets more complicated."

Now I knew why the fine citizens of this charming community continued to elect these two scholars.

"Complicated how? Or shouldn't I ask?"

"The executor of the estate has to file the will with the probate court in Charleston. Then there's some legal mumbo jumbo, and everyone splits the rewards."

"Any way to find out who is executor of someone's estate—assuming the person's dead, and I can't ask him?" I asked, trying to cover all bases.

"Guess there's no way to know for sure," said the other elected official. They were tag teaming me, so each could keep eating. "You could narrow it down a bunch, since there are only two law firms here, and one specializes mainly in criminal stuff." He paused to take a bite. "The other's Aker and Long. Sean Aker stays here, and his partner, Tony Long, practices mainly in North Charleston." I knew which office he was referring to; it was on Center, of course. "You've seen Sean in here occasionally—nice guy, for a lawyer. Short, curly hair, thin, late thirties. Athletic cuss—makes me jealous." Come to think of it, I knew who the official was talking about. "He scuba dives, surfs, and skydives. I don't think he's ready to grow up."

"Thanks, that's helpful."

"Then don't forget us come election time: your friendly, helpful public servants."

The only other folks in the Dog were a couple of young guys I didn't know, although they looked familiar.

I was getting nosier by the day. "Amber, who are the guys at the table behind our fine lawmakers?"

"They both work somewhere on James Island. The one facing us is Arnold something, the other is Buddy—don't know if that's his name or just what his friends call him. They come in every Wednesday. Arnold's always trading something with some unsuspecting stranger; he always needs money. Don't know about Buddy."

"Trading things like what?"

"Boats, cars, go-karts—if it has wheels or moves, Arnold will offer to sell you one or buy yours. Buddy doesn't seem too interested in Arnold's hobby." Amber laughed and added, "Buddy did try to sell one of our part-timers a boat and a rototiller once. Don't think he bought them."

"I'll remember that the next time I need a rototiller," I said, suspecting—no, hoping—that day would never come.

"How's Bill?" she asked, her voice lower and more serious.

"Good question," I said. "I haven't seen him for a few days; I need to check. I'm surprised how hard he's taking the death."

"Don't be; friends do that to you. Good friends, that is."

*   *   *   *

It took four knocks before Bill answered. His easy smile had been replaced by a halfhearted effort. He invited me in and strained to make conversation.

"I haven't seen you for a few days and wanted to how you're doing," I said, hopefully masking my surprise at seeing him in that deteriorating condition.

"Thanks for stopping. I guess I'm okay. I still can't get over what happened. If truth be known, Julius was my best friend ... sad, isn't it? I didn't know him well."

Not knowing what to say, I tried to steer the conversation in a slightly different direction.

"Bill, I was talking with Chief Newman the other day, and he said someone broke into Mr. Palmer's house around the time of the funeral. He didn't think anything big was taken. He decided it was someone who'd heard about the funeral and took advantage of the vacant house to see what he could steal."

"It was the killer, Chris," Bill said without hesitation. "See, that's just more proof Julius was murdered. Why doesn't anyone believe me? He would never have gone close to the water—never."

"It's not that no one believes you. The police just don't see any motive. Amber, Charles, and even Bob Howard are leaning toward something suspicious. I'm definitely in agreement with them. We just don't know what we could do about it. You may not believe it now, but several folks on this island consider you a friend and would do anything for you."

I saw the glimmer of a real smile.

"I appreciate that, Chris—I guess all I want anyone to do is find who killed my friend," he said with a little more resolve in his deep voice.

"I wish it was that simple. I wouldn't know where to begin. I just don't see a motive. Do you?"

"Not a motive, but the more I think about it, I remember him missing a few of the lighthouse meetings. He said he had something to do. That's rare—it isn't as if we have much to do here. He had no family, his business closed fairly early, and he didn't have any other outside interests … at least none I knew of."

"Try to think about it more, and let me know if anything comes to you," I said.

We talked a few more minutes about the weather, the heavy snows in the north, and his most recent disagreement with his dean at the college. His spirit rose slightly, but his brighter mood was clearly temporary. I was worried.

CHAPTER 12

"Here're two sets of keys to your run-down, dirty, hole-in-the-wall gallery. Enjoy your new status as a famous photographer."

Bob greeted me with these cheerful and optimistic words as I met him at the Center Street site of my yet unnamed gallery. The keys, one rusty and the other newly minted, were on a "Tidewater Plantation, North Myrtle Beach" keychain. I didn't bother to ask why.

"Morning, Bob. I see I caught you in a good mood."

"Damn right, you did—never thought I'd be able to unload this piece of crap. I should've known to try to push it off on you when I got the listing. Only problem was, I didn't know you then. Now sign these papers before you change your mind or the building falls down."

"Bob, did you ever consider another career—maybe a prison guard, or movie critic, or just a part-time troll living under a bridge and scaring little kids?"

"Yeah," he responded with a straight face, "but none of them, especially troll, pay as well as real estate. At least you're making my job easier on this deal. I hate commercial real estate. That was most of my business in Charlotte for twenty-five damn long years, when I owned my firm."

"Why'd you leave?" I asked. I had known he owned his own realty company before moving to James Island, but the details were fuzzy.

"Didn't you hear me? I hate commercial work. Charlotte is a rapidly growing city—too damn rapid for me. There was a lot of development in the eighties and nineties—tons of money to be had. But commercial real estate is a pain in the ass. You don't just say 'Here's a property, I'll give you this big ol' bag of money for it

... okay, here's your money,' and off to the bar to celebrate. It takes months—at times, years—for the deals to get put together. You have to worry about financing, partners, zoning changes ... problem after problem. Then it seems half the deals fall through, and guess who gets left holding the damn ball—the ball, not the money? Yep, me!"

I signed the papers; he thanked me, sort of, and we walked to the Dog for a celebratory coffee—and for Bob, a piece of breakfast pie.

*   *   *   *

"I've been asking around about Palmer," said Bob as he shoveled in the fresh apple pie. "A few folks I know in real estate in Charleston have dealt with him. Some of the wealthy clients downsize and look for honest antique dealers to work with; my acquaintances refer them to Palmer. They all say he was a nice person—almost too nice."

"Sort of eliminates dissatisfied customers as a possible murder, doesn't it?" I asked.

"I think so," mumbled Bob, pie crumbs falling on his Hawaiian shirt. "One of the guys I know even said Palmer was generous to a fault—would give discounts to those who appeared to need a break. I don't see anyone wanting him dead because of any business dealings." He paused as Amber filled our near-empty cups. "So now what're you going to do to find out what happened?"

"Why think I'd do anything?" I said.

"Easy question—that's just you. I don't know what you were back home, but this is the new you. Adjust."

CHAPTER 13

Now that I had a gallery, I had just one simple task left: figuring out how the heck to start a business. I would need a business license from the city of Folly Beach, along with a tax number. I would need to form a business entity—an LLC or corporation or something that involved using initials after my name.

The walk to city hall took a couple of minutes. A brisk ocean breeze made the air feel colder than the thermometer indicated. The coral, two-story city hall building proudly faced Center Street. It not only housed the city government, but shared space with the department of public safety (or simply the police department), the fire department, and the animal-control officer—a handy arrangement for all concerned.

The clerk's office had the feel of a small-town, friendly, beach-oriented office—which made sense, I supposed, considering it was exactly that. The young staff member, Charlene—at least that's what the nameplate said—greeted me as if she actually wanted to be helpful—a rare approach for government, I'm afraid.

"I'm starting a new business—a photo gallery on Center Street—and need to know what to do."

"Ah, in the old tourist-trap shop," she said. "It's about time someone moved in."

Her response reminded me that I was in a small town, with all its pluses and minuses.

"It wasn't too hard to figure out where I would be, was it?"

"Only vacancy on Center Street ... and unless I'm badly mistaken, you're the guy who made quite a stir around here last year. Now you're a friend of our chief. Go figure!"

"Do I need to fill anything out, or do you already know enough to get whatever paperwork you need from me?"

Fortunately, she laughed. In reality, it was hardly more than a giggle, but it felt good.

"Sorry, Mr. Landrum, but I'll still need more information. The application to do business in Folly Beach doesn't have a place to check 'killer catcher.'"

She handed me a simple, one-page form and said I could fill it out later. And, she asked, did anyone affiliated with the local government not know my name?

"I don't have any pets," I mused, excluding Charles for the sake of simplicity. "Maybe the animal-control officer doesn't know about me. Thanks for the form. I'll bring it back tomorrow. Oh, and could you recommend a good lawyer? I need to get help with my incorporation papers."

"Didn't know there was any such thing as a good lawyer," she said, enjoying our conversation way too much. "If I had to get one, I'd suggest Sean Aker over at Aker and Long. Their offices are just a block from here. Sean's sort of a local character, but I hear he's good at lawyerin'."

I didn't ask what she meant about Sean being a local character. So far, I hadn't found anyone here who wasn't. I thought I'd save my "lawyerin'" errands for another day and head to my new place of business so I could ponder what I wanted to do with the dilapidated space. Would my new business venture be my first major mistake in retirement?

"By the way, Mr. Landrum ..." I was almost out the door, but Charlene wasn't done. "I hear you've been asking around about poor Mr. Palmer. Good luck on finding out what happened. Folks in the building are sticking to suicide."

Way too small a town.

$$* \qquad * \qquad * \qquad *$$

"Where have you been, and what took you so long to get here?"

I was staring at the pointed end of Charles's cane, which had been aimed at my head.

Before I could get the key, I was barraged by questions. I saw why he had been so anxious about my whereabouts. He was in front of the shop, wrapped in a University of Southern California warm-up jacket, sitting on two yellow and white striped boxes containing gallon cans of paint, along with a large black trash bag of cleaning supplies. He looked like a street person who had just robbed a paint store. I almost expected to see a tin can on the sidewalk in front of him to hint for guilt donations. Of course, everyone here knew Charles and would end up stopping and talking rather than dropping change in the can and slinking off. If it hadn't been so cold this morning, he would already have accumulated a conversation group.

"Charles, I should know better by now, but I'll ask. What in the world are you doing sitting here keeping those boxes from blowing away?"

"Chris, 'Take time to deliberate, but when the time for action arrives, stop thinking and go in.' Long-dead United States President Andrew Jackson."

He paused for me to assimilate the presidential wisdom, therefore wasting several seconds of both our lives.

"In case you haven't noticed," he continued, "you have yourself a fine photo gallery behind me here that still thinks it's a run-down, 'grab your vacation spending money and run' tourist trap. I'm a busy man, so if you want my valuable assistance in the transformation, you'd better use it before you lose it."

"And," I asked, "why would you think I'd be here this morning to begin that transformation, as you say? Maybe I'd sleep in, or go to Charleston, or just act retired and do nothing."

He looked at me as if I were a total idiot. "' It's Monday. You've gotten up every Monday for the last ninety-eight years, gotten dressed, and trudged off to your fancy corporate world. Old—ancient—habits are hard to break. Where else would you be today? Enough analysis. Are we getting to work or not?"

"Thanks, I guess. Charles, I don't think I can pay you. It'll take a long time before I'll even be able to break even."

"Did I say anything about pay?" he asked, then stooped to pick up one of the boxes containing the paint. "I think I'll just hang around here and make sure you do everything right. After all, this is your first gallery, right? I visited a gallery once, so I'll be able to keep you on the right path—don't want you to be a failure this early in your retirement."

Had Charles made any sense? Of course not. But his kindness was touching. And on some strange level, he *would* help. I just wasn't sure how. And, heaven may wonder, he was my best friend.

"Okay, Charles. I need your help. Are you ready to get started?"

"Thought you'd never ask."

CHAPTER 14

I didn't have a detailed plan of what needed to be done. Clearly, all the display brackets and shelving had to be removed from the walls; I wouldn't be displaying any trinkets, especially not on those worn-out fixtures. Holes needed to be patched and fresh paint applied. Charles had brought eight gallons of crisp white paint—"snow white," the marketing gurus called it—so I decided that would be the gallery's wall color. He agreed that was a wise choice, especially since he'd have been stuck with it otherwise.

"You know you need to get the locks changed on the doors," he said. "Nobody wanted the junk that was sold here ... but now, with your valuable works of art, this would be a thief's heaven."

"I guess so," I said, although I doubted the 'thief's heaven' part. "Who could change them?"

"Larry at the hardware store. Want me to call?"

Considering I had zero options, I said sure. Besides, I needed to take advantage of my new underpaid help. Not fifteen minutes passed after the call before Larry arrived. I recognized him immediately; last year, he'd replaced a broken window in my rental.

Larry LaMond—whose last name I hadn't known before—couldn't have weighed more than a hundred pounds, was five-three at best, and had eyes that I could only describe as sad, even when they peered out over a smile. I almost expected to see a champion racing horse walking behind the tiny man.

"I remember you," he said. "Had any more break-ins?"

"Larry's an expert on break-ins," added Charles—uninvited, for what that was worth. Then he turned to Larry. "Is it okay if I tell Chris a little about you? Chris is my best friend; no need for secrets."

I don't know who seemed more uncomfortable—Larry or me. I had no idea what Charles was talking about, so I suspected Larry was most unsettled.

"Why not?" said Larry with little enthusiasm.

"Larry bought Pewter Hardware seven years ago from Old Man Hall ... Randolph was his first name, I believe, though no one ever actually used it," said Charles. "You worked there about a year before that, didn't you?"

"A year, maybe a little longer," said Larry.

"Now I'm confused," I said. "You're Larry LaMond; the former owner was Randolph Hall, right? So where'd the name Pewter Hardware come from?"

"Damned if I know," said Larry. "I asked Old Man Hall once. He said he didn't have any idea. He'd never heard of Mr. Pewter. He told me he didn't change the name to Hall's Hardware because it'd cost more to change the sign and all the invoices and stationery than it was worth. I just followed in his footsteps when I bought it."

"Larry, mind if I tell Chris where you were before you took over the store?" said Charles.

"I doubt I could stop you; go ahead," said Larry, palms up in a pose of surrender.

Larry had that right.

"Before moving to Folly, Larry was a guest of the Georgia Department of Corrections for eight years," said Charles. "The fine taxpaying citizens of Georgia paid his room, board, and medical bills."

"Right, Charles," Larry said. "All I had to do was agree to stay in a nice, petite, peaceful cell in the nicest-sounding prison in the country: the Coastal State Prison in—get this—Garden City, Georgia. Always thought that sounded more like the name of a retirement community than a jail. It's north of Savannah."

"Okay." I looked at Charles and then back at Larry. "I'll bite. How did you come to be a guest of the state?"

"It's not something I'm proud of," said Larry. "I'm afraid I spent most of my early twenties trying to figure out how to get something for nothing. I hate horses, so being a jockey was out. So I used my size to take up the honored profession of cat burglar. I grew up in the Atlanta area, and there was no shortage of wealth, large old homes, and old money to go with them. Fortunately, there *was* a shortage of burglar alarms—Southern trust and all."

"Larry, somebody must have had an alarm, or you wouldn't have wasted the tax money of the fine citizens of Georgia," said Charles helpfully.

"Not really. I never had any problems with alarms. I was very good at picking locks. If I wasn't so modest, I'd tell you I was one of the best. All I had to do was open the door, and I could tell if the house was alarmed. If it was, I'd just hightail it out before bells started ringing."

"Then how did you screw up?" asked the diplomatic Charles.

"The bad thing about stealing from houses as opposed to the all-cash career of bank robbing is that you have to fence what you steal. I can assure you the old 'honor among thieves' lore is bunk. The damn fences will turn on you in a second if the police turn up the pressure. That's what got me."

"Then how does one get from being a captive in Garden City, Georgia, to hardware store owner in South Carolina?" I asked.

"I'd like to tell you I saw the light, or found Jesus, or some such admirable revelation. But to be honest, I simply realized—and don't laugh—that crime doesn't pay. I just grew up. Rather than finding Jesus, you could say I found myself. I hope to live to a very old age. The life of crime won't get me there. No IRA, no pension, no 401k, no future."

"Chris," interrupted Charles, "as you've observed, folks you might call quirky, eccentric, or just plain strange tend to gravitate to Folly Beach ... you being the exception, of course. Larry was like the rest of us; he just took a more direct route. Tell Chris what you did when you got here."

"Well, the first thing I did was find out who the police chief was. I went to Chief Newman's office and told him I was a reformed thief. I was just out of prison. I was moving here to start a new life. And I wanted him to know everything about me, so he wouldn't find it out from anyone else. I even gave him my official resume—crimes done, time served, everything."

"What did he do?" I asked, more than a little surprised by Larry's strategy.

"I think it seriously confused him, but he seemed impressed. I also told him that any time there was a crime on the island, especially if it involved a burglary, I knew he would have to come talk to me. Hell, I'd do that if I was the chief. So I gave him my address, phone number, and even my cell-phone number, so he wouldn't have to look too hard to find me."

"That had to throw him," I said with a smile. My respect for my most recent acquaintance was increasing by the moment.

"Guess so," said Larry, looking more at ease with the conversation. "He contacted Old Man Hall and recommended me for a job at the hardware store. He told Hall he couldn't think of anyone with better skills to sell locks and security bars. The chief never told Mr. Hall why he was recommending me. To my knowledge, he never told anyone. And, to beat all, he never questioned me about any crime on this marvelous island. For that, I'll be forever indebted to him."

I answered, "I wouldn't imagine there are many break-ins anywa—"

"No," interrupted Charles again. "That's why the one at Julius's house doesn't fit. I still think it's about his murder."

"Speaking of Mr. Palmer, I hear Preserve the Past is inheriting millions from him," said Larry.

"Where'd you hear that?" I asked, trying not to act too surprised.

"Renee Lewis, the group's treasurer, told me," he said. "Since Palmer didn't have any living relatives, the lighthouse group was given a copy of the will. It hasn't been through any of the legal channels yet, so they can't get the money, but Renee said it was nearly three and a half million dollars. She said she was shocked. Mr. Palmer never mentioned anything to the group about his will or leaving the group anything."

"Where'd they get the will?" asked Charles.

"According to Renee, Palmer's attorney, Sean Aker, gave it to them. That's all I know. Renee was in the store yesterday buying some new house numbers, and she mentioned it."

While I soaked in that startling news, Larry changed the locks on both doors, and Charles and I continued trying to salvage the walls from years of abuse. As I tore out the hanging shelves that had been full of Folly Beach T-shirts and posters and signs, I asked myself for the first time why I chose this store over the new one. I'm sure there were great reasons; I couldn't remember what they were while the drywall dust was flying. "Mostly cloudy" would best describe the atmosphere in the gallery.

"Chris, it was nice getting to know you," said Larry. He had finished changing the locks and was watching Charles and me from the corner of the room. "If you need anything else, just give me a call. It looks like you'll need a bunch of stuff from the store. I'll give you a big discount. I don't want you driving to Charleston and buying your stuff at one of those big-box places."

"Thanks, and you'll be seeing me a lot," I said. "If you hear anything else about the will, let me know. Bill Hansel is a friend of mine, and he's convinced something's not right about the suicide—or, in his mind, murder."

"From what Charles said, I'm beginning to believe that too," said Larry as he grabbed his tin toolbox on his way out the door.

I stopped for a minute to bask in the irony of having my locks changed by a burglar.

The gallery soon looked more like a construction—or more accurately, destruction—zone than an old, worn-out shop. I knew this was a step in its rebirth, but it still was a mess.

"How's Bill doing?" asked Charles as he looked away from the door jambs he was sanding.

"Don't know. I haven't seen him for a few days. I hope he's adjusting better. I wouldn't bet on it. His emotions aren't always obvious, but they're strong and fairly stubborn. I need to check on him."

"From my way of thinking," he said, "we need to do something."

Charles's way of thinking could get a little scary occasionally. "What do you mean by 'do something'—and more importantly, what do you mean 'we'?"

"Chris, it's time for the C&C Detective Agency to take action. Seems to me we have a murder on our hands, and the police ain't doing diddly-squat and don't plan to."

"If C&C means Chris and Charles, you're out of your gourd—even more than usual, that is. Why do you think we can find out anything?"

"Simple: we did it before," he said. "Besides, it's Charles and Chris, not Chris and Charles. You're the logical brains behind the organization. I'm the street-smart and simpleminded, yet complex, Tonto. Seems like a slam dunk. Of course we can do it."

"Simpleminded, yet complex!" I repeated. This expert analysis sounded like a description of an overpriced, pretentious wine. So Charles!

"Charles, if you remember, a murderer came after me last year. I happened to be in the wrong place at the wrong time. My life was in danger. We lucked out by putting one and one together and getting three, then guessing who did it. We operated on luck and the fact that we had no choice."

"So, the way I see it is, now a killer has seriously harmed one of your good friends. Bill is hurting, and you've got to help him. Chris, that's what friends do."

"And how do you, a person who doesn't even know Bill other than meeting him a couple of times, fit into this detective agency?"

"I just told you—weren't you listening? Bill's your friend; you gotta help him. I'm your friend; I gotta help you. Besides, you can't solve this without me. You need someone to bring the 'dumb and doesn't know any better' factor to the job. So where do we begin?"

"We begin by getting this disaster looking like a photo gallery. While we're doing that, I'll think about what might have happened to Mr. Palmer."

I didn't bother to tell him I had no idea where to begin.

CHAPTER 15

Aker and Long was on the second floor of a two-story, nondescript brick building on Center Street (a most unsurprising location, as I had learned), three blocks from the Atlantic. The firm shared the building with a candy shop that took the entire first floor. In the spirit of the idiosyncratic island, the words "Aker and Long, Lawyers," were stenciled in black on a florescent orange surfboard hanging horizontally above the first-floor entry to the stairs.

The second-floor door was more in keeping with the image of a lawyer's office. I entered and was disappointed not to find sand on the floor and a beach umbrella over the receptionist's desk. I was greeted by a pleasant-looking lady in her thirties. She was in a lime green dress with small yellow palmetto trees sprinkled about; her outfit bridged the gap between the beach and a professional office. I wondered idly if she had planned that.

If she was surprised to see a stranger walking into the office early in the morning in February, it didn't show. In my newly christened detective role, I detected her to be Marlene. The name plate in front of her gave me the first big clue. In a most pleasant, professional voice, she introduced herself and asked if she could help me. I told her I wanted to see Mr. Aker if he was available. I told her who I was and that I was opening a business and wanted to take whatever legal steps necessary. I wanted her to know a paying client had entered.

She said that Sean wasn't in, but should be shortly. I could have a seat and wait or make an appointment. I'd wait, I decided, then moved to one of the three side chairs in the small waiting area. Directly behind Marlene was a small room with an oversized wooden conference table taking up most of the space. Along two of the mahogany-paneled walls were rows of the obligatory leather-spined law books—dust covered, without a doubt. Two doors were to the left of the conference room; one had a wood cutout of a Frisbee-sized parachute with "Sean" printed in primary colors on the canopy. Nothing was on the other door. To the right of Marlene was one door with a brass plate inscribed "Tony Long, Attorney at Law." Should I have asked for Mr. Long instead of skydiving Sean?

The blank door opened, and a tall, cute, trim female a little younger than Marlene appeared. She looked vaguely familiar, but I couldn't remember from where. Unlike Marlene, she seemed surprised to see someone in the waiting area.

"This's Mr. Landrum. He's here to see Sean," said Marlene. "Sandy's our paralegal, Mr. Landrum."

Sandy smiled and nodded my way. "And coffee maker, and food fetcher, and errand runner, and person who gets to go to Office Depot when the printer runs out of ink," she said, all in one breath.

"I hope that doesn't interfere too much with all your paralegalin'," I said, hoping to bring the conversation back to her most important role.

"Nope. I get that done in a couple of hours—plenty of time for all the other stuff."

The room really started to get crowded when a short, curly-haired, thin, and well-tanned gentleman entered. This latest arrival, who fit the description I'd heard of Sean, seemed surprised at the crowd.

"Good morning, Sean," said Marlene. "Mr. Landrum is here to see you about setting up his business. Mr. Landrum, this is Sean Aker."

"Nice to finally meet you, Mr. Landrum. I've heard a lot about you," said the attorney, as he firmly—as in, python firmly—grabbed my hand. "Welcome to our charming little island."

"It's Chris, and what part of my reputation preceded me?"

Sean led me into his office, moved a basketball from the leather guest's chair, and waved for me to sit.

"I wouldn't know where to begin." But he did anyway. "Remember, this is a small, close-knit community. Let's see … everyone here knows what happened last year, so that's a given. Chief Newman told me about your fun-filled housewarming party and how trouble seemed to follow you wherever you went. That's good news for a lawyer, by the way," he said, with a grin on his face and dollar signs in his eyes. "Trouble keeps us in business. Then your friend—and Folly's source of news—Amber mentioned how nice you are. For what it's worth, she said it quite fondly … even had a sparkle in her eye. Then there's one of my favorite real-estate agents, Bob Howard. I occasionally handle closings for him.

He said if you show up at my door, I'd better take good care of you or else. I don't want any of Bob's 'or else's,' so what can I do for you today?"

"Anonymity appears to be one commodity in short supply on your island," I said.

"Correction: *our* island. And you're right. To prove what you just said, is today's visit about helping you get set up in business or to find out about Julius Palmer's will?"

"Should your sign out front say 'Attorney and Mind Reader'?"

"Mind reading doesn't pay very well, so I'll stick to lawyering," he said. "Let's just say Bob mentioned that you were curious about who might benefit from Palmer's death. Something about a depressed friend of yours not believing it was a suicide. Actually, I've heard that rumor from a couple of folks I doubt you know."

"Close," I said. "But there's a little more to it than that. Now that you mention it, though, I heard that Preserve the Past was in the will. Could I get a copy without breaking any laws? After all, I might be a member of the group and could see their copy. Since I'm already in your office, it would be more convenient to see a copy here."

"I'm not sure it would be quite by the books, but since Mr. Palmer has no heirs, I don't see the harm in sharing a copy. I'll have Sandy or Marlene run you one before you leave."

Sean practiced some of his trade as we discussed the formation of a sole proprietorship, Landrum Gallery, so I would be official, taxable, and apparently even reputable to all officials who looked at that sort of thing.

All in all, I had made a productive trip to the attorney—a whole corporation for little ol' me, with a last will and testament thrown in for no additional charge. Of the two documents, the will proved to be the more interesting reading. Interesting ... and strange.

CHAPTER 16

I, Julius L. Palmer, of Folly Beach, South Carolina, revoke my previous Wills and Codicils and declare this to be my Last Will and Testament . . .

I sat in my regular spot at the Dog, reading the document Marlene had copied a few minutes earlier. Much of the six-page document was filled with routine boilerplate—describing payment of debts and expenses, liability of fiduciary and beneficiary disputes, blah, blah, blah. I knew Mr. Palmer didn't have any living relatives, so Sean Aker was listed as executor. Consistent with what Larry had said, Preserve the Past was a beneficiary.

The crisp, black Times New Roman typeface took a drastic turn at that point. Under the residuary estate section, the distribution of the estate listed Preserve the Past as receiving fifty percent, with the remaining fifty percent going to Amelia E. Hogan of Folly Beach, South Carolina.

Amelia Hogan's name didn't ring any bells. I'd only been here a short period, so that didn't mean much; time to go to my source of sources.

"Amber, who's Amelia Hogan?" I could tell Amber was curious about what I'd been reading; each time she passed by the table, she had glanced over at the papers. Legal documents were as rare in the Dog as the *Los Angeles Times*.

"Don't know for sure," she said. "Was she that lady pilot who disappeared a bunch of years ago?"

"That was Amelia Earhart," I said. "No, I think Amelia Hogan lives here."

I was shocked by her answer; it shook my entire foundation of beliefs about the all-knowing, all-seeing Amber.

"I have no idea. Don't think I've heard of her. Sure you have the name right?"

"I believe so," I said, still stunned by Amber's response.

"Want me to ask around?" she said. "Somebody here might know."

"Sure, anything would be helpful."

*   *   *   *

I was blessed that night by a visit from Tammy. She managed to get off work around four—unusually early—and didn't have to be back until nine the next day. She arrived with an overnight bag—always a good sign.

We walked three blocks to the Terrapin Café for supper. It was still cold outside, but the winds had died down. The restaurant, formerly Café Suzanne, was on the corner of Center Street and Arctic Avenue, kitty-corner from the Holiday Inn.

"Old-timers say this is the exact spot of a bowling alley that was a prominent feature on the Folly Beach of old," I said in my best tour-guide voice as we crossed the threshold of the nearly empty restaurant.

In the summer, the Terrapin Café opened a nice screened-in dining area facing the Folly Pier. The main dining room was a little dark for a beach restaurant, but the food was outstanding. It was a great winter dining spot, and close.

I ordered a bottle of California cabernet, and we each selected the steak special. We both were fairly good listeners, so neither of us dominated the conversation. Tammy shared some newsroom gossip and a little about the double murder she had covered the last two days. Her work-related stories were seldom pleasant dining fare, but her enthusiasm and animation in the telling served as the antidote for any queasiness her stories might have caused. She loved her work and planned to do it for many years. That was more than a small stumbling block in our short, comfortable relationship.

I was more than ready to share when she asked what had been happening in my life. I told her about meeting a new friend, Larry LaMond—more accurately, inheriting a new friend through Charles. She was interested in what I'd found out about the will. She turned more thoughtful and intense when I shared that Charles thought we should find out what happened to Palmer.

"Chris, have you already forgotten what happened the last time you got involved in a crime?" she asked. "Didn't almost getting killed leave more than a casual memory in your thick skull?"

"Of course it did," I said. "I didn't say I agreed with Charles. I don't have a clue what we could do. Everyone—everyone official, that is—has written it off. I don't see any harm in looking for something the police may have missed."

"I know you well enough to know you'll do what your logical mind says." She reached across the table for my hands; I didn't put up a fight. "I also know Charles will do everything to convince your heart to act," she added in softer tones. "And for Bill ... I don't know if he even could be objective enough to analyze anything—heart or mind—in his current state. Be careful."

Our entrées arrived, and the conversation turned to more pleasant topics. We laughed about my choice of location for the gallery, how Charles and I looked like two of the three stooges during the remodeling process, and how little I missed Louisville. Resisting the temptation of homemade lemon-meringue pie, we ventured out in the cold evening breeze and slowly walked hand in hand a couple of hundred yards on the dark beach, enjoying the sound of the water lapping against the shore. We headed home and basked in pleasurable silence as we warmed ourselves with nothing but blankets and body heat. A great end to a very busy and enlightening day.

Before falling asleep, I wondered what hidden evils I might run into if I followed the hearts of my friends.

CHAPTER 17

I arrived just before nine at the newly christened Landrum Gallery; Charles was already leaning on the front door. The temperature was in the upper forties, but he only had on torn jeans and a long-sleeved sweatshirt bearing the usual college logo. I had learned long ago not to waste words asking why he had all the college sweatshirts or where he got them.

"Late again," he said as he looked at his wrist. His gesture would have been more effective if he had a watch. "How am I going to be able to keep you on if you can't show up for work on time?"

Charles: a true quirk of nature.

"Unless I'm mistaken, Charles, this is my place. What did I tell you about the first sign I'm having made for the gallery?"

"'Open When I'm Here, Closed When I'm Not,' I believe. But you don't have it yet, and you're a long way from being ready to open, so stop jabbering and get to work." He waved his cane in the direction of the door.

"Slow down, Charles; we've already come a long way."

"Ah, as the late, great, far-less-than-famous United States President Millard Fillmore said, 'It is not strange to mistake change for progress.'"

"You looked that one up just for me, didn't you?"

"'No comment'—late, not so great, but much more infamous United States President Richard Nixon."

"Enough foolishness, Charles. Let's get to work." I suspected some president had said that too, but had no idea who.

Regardless of what Charles thought, the gallery looked much better and not that far from opening day. The walls were ready to paint and the floors ready for refinishing.

"I met with Sean Aker the other day," I said. "He was helpful in getting me started on the paperwork to open the gallery."

"Did he say we knew each other?"

"I don't think your name came up—sorry. How do you know him?" I asked as I unlocked the door.

"We're both in the Charleston Skydiving Club. We've jumped a couple of times together."

"Skydiving," I said as I stared at him in wonderment. "Isn't that the sort of hobby you would mention to a friend?"

"Guess not, since I haven't mentioned it," he said with a shrug. "Thought I had, though."

"Aker also gave me a copy of Julius Palmer's will," I said. I assumed our sky-diving discussion was already winding down, although it never got much off the ground. "Who's Amelia Hogan?"

"Don't know. Why?"

That was nearly as big a surprise as his skydiving.

"Oh, no reason other than she just inherited more than three million dollars from Palmer," I said. "She's supposedly a resident of your island. I thought you knew everyone here."

"I do, or thought I did. Is she a year-round resident?"

"All I know is that she's in the will and inherits half of the estate and is listed as a resident of Folly Beach," I said. "Amber's never heard of her either."

"Then she's a ghost, or lives under a rock. She's also likely a gold-digger, and without doubt the person who killed Julius Palmer—case closed," he said, tapping his cane on the well-worn floor. "See? Only two days after the formation of the C&C Detective Agency, we've solved another one. All before this coat of paint's dry."

"Let's continue to paint and ponder," I said. "Remember, you said we had to get ready to open." We made a fairly uneventful transition from drywallers to painters—uneventful if you didn't count the quart of trim paint Charles poured on the floor instead of in the paint tray. For what he was getting paid, I couldn't complain—not too much, anyway.

We adjourned to the Dog for an early lunch and to see if the mysterious Amelia E. Hogan was to be found in the phone book. Amber was glad to see us together—and especially glad to see Charles. I wasn't quite sure about their relationship but knew there was one. Amber wouldn't bring us the phone book until we told her what number we were looking for. One of her primary tools for gathering information was the point-blank question, and she was never afraid to ask. Charles briefly explained, and Amber quickly brought us the frayed, grease-stained book.

There wasn't a listing for Amelia Hogan, but there was A. Hogan on East Erie. The address was less than three blocks from where we were sitting. Three blocks, and neither of my best sources of information and gossip had heard of her. That was a mystery in itself.

"There she is, Chris," said Amber. "Just over on Erie … and a killer, sure as shootin'."

"Sure as drownin'," corrected Charles, grinning at Amber.

"We have no reason to believe Ms. Hogan killed anyone," I said. "For that matter, we don't even know if A. Hogan is Amelia."

"No, but if Charles and I haven't heard of her, she's trying to hide something," said Amber. "Don't you think you should tell Chief Newman?" Amber nodded in the direction of the chief, who was sitting at his regular table in the back of the restaurant. She meant tell him now. Rather than wait until he walked by and surround him—figuratively, of course—with a group of amateur detectives, I decided to take my message and information to his table.

"Afternoon, Chris. When are you opening the gallery?" asked Brian. He had looked up from a recent issue of *Charleston* magazine and seen me standing beside his table.

"Soon, Brian—thanks for asking. Listen, I've got something to tell you. It might mean nothing or … who knows. Mind if I join you for a minute?"

He didn't object, so I sat and walked him through everything I'd learned about the will and the mysterious Ms. Hogan.

"I think I know her," he said. He even took a couple of notes in his well-worn faux-leather notebook, but I could tell he was mainly being polite. In his mind, the death had been suicide, plain and simple.

But plain and simple weren't to be.

CHAPTER 18

The gallery walls weren't self-painting, which was another clear drawback of the property. Charles and I walked back across the street to the waiting paintbrushes. They seemed pleased to see us—a feeling I didn't share.

"Why don't you call your buddy at the hardware store?" I said. "He'd know many folks who you or Amber wouldn't. Maybe he knows the mysterious Ms. Hogan."

Charles called Larry, and after a few pleasantries and a joke about a dull-quilled porcupine, I heard him mention Hogan. After a couple more minutes, Larry had apparently agreed to visit us sometime soon; Charles sat the phone on the floor and began his report.

"Larry sure likes animal jokes, and yes, he knows Hogan."

"And ..." I said.

Charles had grabbed his brush and slapped some paint on the door.

"He doesn't know much about her," he continued. "The only reason he knows her name is because she pays with a charge card. She's in her late fifties, with a friendly smile and demeanor—didn't know Larry even knew the word "demeanor"—and must have some children. She was with a guy once, in his thirties, he guessed. On another visit, she brought a gal who was also maybe in her thirties."

"Could you mind the store for a little while?" I asked. "I'm going to see if Bill's home. See if he knows her."

"Chris, this modern invention—a telephone, I believe they call it—can do wonders. You punch a bunch of these little numbers, and Bill will answer. Folly is strange, but not electronically challenged."

"I need some fresh air and to see Bill firsthand," I said as I picked up my jacket and headed to the door. "He wasn't doing well the last time we talked."

*   *   *   *

The winds were picking up, and the gusts felt colder than the thermometer indicated. Getting away from the strong smell of paint gave me a few minutes to think. I didn't know what I could do, but I owed it to my friend to see if anything would give him peace. Even if Julius had killed himself, proof of that would offer some closure for Bill. I had to try, had to do something.

"And what do I owe the pleasure of a visit?" said Bill.

He answered his door dressed in his professorial finest—cocoa brown corduroy slacks and a white Oxford cloth shirt frayed around the collar.

"Did I catch you at a bad time?"

"No. In fact, it was the best time possible. I have a class in two hours and don't have to leave for another hour. Come in."

Bill looked ready for class but didn't act as if he wanted to be there. Truthfully, he acted like he didn't want to be anywhere.

"I guess you've heard by now that your friend left several million dollars to Preserve the Past," I said, hoping he already had.

"Yes, the grapevine does a fine job," he said, shoulders slumped and looking at everything but me. "No fewer than three members of the group called with that amazing news. The strange thing about it is, no one from the group knew anything about it until they heard it was in his will."

"Were you surprised?" I asked.

"Absolutely. Julius was a fairly active member, but never spoke of money or seemed like the kind of person who would do something like that. To be honest, it has me confused."

"Why?"

"I've been thinking he was killed for his money. But if no one knew anything about it, why would they kill him?"

"Have you ever heard of Amelia Hogan?" I asked. "Did Julius ever mention her?"

"Hogan ... don't think so. Why, who's she?"

"Don't jump to any conclusions, but she's in his will," I said. "In fact, she inherits just as much as your group."

That got his attention; his eyes suddenly were focused on mine.

"You're kidding," he said. "Is she someone he knew in Charleston? I thought I was a good friend of his and don't ever recall him mentioning her."

"My understanding is she lives here, not Charleston," I said. "Larry from the hardware says she is in her late fifties and may have a couple of grown children. Keeps to herself, he said. I believe that. Neither Amber nor Charles knows her. And if they don't know someone, she almost doesn't exist."

Bill sat in silence, staring at his flower-patterned living room wallpaper. I didn't know where his thoughts were, but knew I wasn't in them. I waited. The only sound to be heard was warm air from the furnace rushing through the ducts.

"Chris, that woman killed my friend," said Bill, without interrupting his gaze at the wall. He said it so softly that I wasn't certain I had heard him correctly. "She killed my friend," he repeated.

So much for not jumping to conclusions.

"That's a possibility, but we don't know anything more than I just said. I told Chief Newman about the will, and he said he'd investigate."

"Yeah right, I'm *sure* he will," said Bill.

"Are you certain you never heard Julius mention Ms. Hogan, or maybe say anything about dating someone, or anything else that would indicate he even knew who she was?"

"A few nights, he said he was busy and couldn't go to the meetings; I think I already told you that. He never said where he was going. Sorry, I have no idea what to say. I need to get ready to go to school. Thanks for letting me know."

He was polite but left no doubt about wanting to be alone. I knew he didn't have to leave for nearly an hour and was already dressed.

The walk back to the gallery was much colder than the walk to Bill's; the outside temperature was warmer, but everything in me felt cold … very cold.

CHAPTER 19

"Your paintbrush is waiting patently. Mine's weary—getting a little limp and needing to rest," said Charles as I entered the gallery that was even starting to look like one.

"Then have a seat, and let me tell you what I learned," I said and led him to the back room.

He didn't argue. I rehashed the discussion almost word for word—not difficult, since Bill had said so few of them. I was more concerned about Bill's mental health after the visit, and I told Charles as much.

Charles, who could be amazingly perceptive when I least expected it, reinforced what he had previously said, and what I was beginning to understand.

"Bill will never come out of his funk until he knows who killed his friend," he said, washing wet paint from his brush in the tiny sink in the small restroom. Clearly, his brush was done for the day. "You can talk around it all you want, but that's a fact. And you've got to involve him in the solution somehow. He needs to feel he's doing something for his friend. He'll not avert his gaze from that ugly wallpaper otherwise."

"I think he's got Fridays off," I said. "Maybe he and I could visit the home of one Amelia Hogan to offer our condolences. I don't now what her loss is, but there must be one."

"Now that's a plan ... about time, by the way. Now, get painting."

My new supervisor left his brush in the bathroom and followed me to the gallery.

*   *   *   *

I took Charles's occasional good advice and called Bill the next morning.

He answered with a tentative, weak hello. "You don't go to school today, do you?" I asked.

"No, I don't have classes on Friday," he said, with slightly more enthusiasm than his hello. "This week, I don't have to go to one of those stupid, boring faculty meetings. Chris, last week they argued more than an hour about the length of the new graduation gowns for the master's degree students. If it weren't so stupid and counterproductive, I'd laugh."

It was good to hear him complain about something … something other than murder, anyway.

"I was thinking about going over and paying my condolences to Ms. Hogan," I said. "Want to go?"

"I don't know," he replied. "She doesn't have any idea who I am—you either, for that matter."

"I wasn't planning to invite myself to lunch," I said. "I was going to tell her I had seen a copy of Mr. Palmer's will and noticed that she was mentioned, so I knew they must have been close. You'd be able to talk about your friend."

"I'd be more inclined to go if I didn't know she killed him," he said.

He was trying to be upbeat; he failed.

"Bill, to be honest, that's sort of why I'm going. If she had anything to do with his death, we might be able to learn something."

"Since you put it that way, when are we going?"

*   *   *   *

The A. Hogan residence was on a tiny, shrub-infested corner lot. It was painted light blue, and was small, even by Folly standards. I'd walked by the one-story, cedar-shingled house several times while exploring the island. A 1980s faded red Chevrolet Caprice sat in the sagging carport. Before I knocked, it struck me that this might not even be the home of Amelia Hogan. I would be embarrassed if someone named Arthur answered the door.

"Yes, may I help you?" asked an attractive, thin lady, as she cautiously opened the door only a foot at the most.

She looked to be in her late fifties, but could easily be several years older. Her gray-streaked brunette hair added to her classy appearance.

"I'm Chris Landrum, and this is my friend Dr. William Hansel. We're looking for Amelia Hogan."

I didn't really have to ask; I had seen her at the funeral, with several younger people and standing apart from the other mourners.

"You're looking at her," she said, her cautious facade giving way to a beautiful smile. "Bill, I should have known it was you. Jay spoke so kindly about you. Please come in—and pardon the mess. Things are a bit hectic."

If her house was a mess, I thought, I would love to see it when it was neat. The furnishings, like Ms. Hogan's clothing, were of discount department-store quality, but functional, attractive, and well kept. I was struck by the irony of not seeing anything that could come close to being an antique, despite her apparent relationship with Palmer. Four bankers' boxes were stacked in the corner, near the entry to the kitchen; someone had been packing. The entire house couldn't be more than a thousand square feet, with a galley kitchen on one side separated from the living area by a wood-paneled counter. Everything was so neat, I almost felt guilty sitting down.

"Chris," she said, "I believe I remember you from the funeral. I know Bill was there, but I was so distraught I couldn't speak to anyone except my family."

"Ms. Hogan," I said, "we didn't want to interrupt anything, just offer our condolences. Bill, as you might know, was in Preserve the Past with Mr. Palmer. The group was a beneficiary of his will, and we saw that you were also mentioned."

"We saw" was a bit of an exaggeration, but I wanted to bring Bill into the discussion. Besides, why sweat those details when "mentioned in the will" was one of the grandest understatements I'd ever made?

I continued, "The two of you must have been close, so we wanted to express our sympathy for your loss."

The silence from Bill was overpowering; he was looking at Ms. Hogan like she was a viper poised to strike. Before he blurted out his theory about her killing Palmer, I tried to get her talking.

"I do remember you from the funeral," I said. "I believe you were there with four or five other people."

"Yes, those were my two sons, my daughter and her husband, and one of my sons' friends."

"Do they live here?" I asked, while Bill continued to watch with what could easily be interpreted as a hostile glare. She didn't need to talk to him now.

"One of my sons, Mike, lives on Kiawah Island. My other son, Steven, lives in Charleston with his significant other, Lance. Lance was with Steven at the funeral. My daughter and her husband live here on the island."

"It must be nice, having the children so close," I said, to keep the conversation going.

"I don't see the boys much—I guess that's the way with boys. They're both busy with work. Steven's an interior designer. He and Lance opened their own design firm last year. I know that takes a lot of time, but they manage to visit every couple of weeks. Mike's a stockbroker at Millard Harman and Something-Or-Other, one of the old firms in Charleston."

"What about your daughter?" I asked. I was still carrying the visiting team's end of the dialog. Bill continued his professorial "Who threw the eraser?" stare.

"Sandy's between the boys in age, just turned thirty-one. So she's always trying to please everyone. She works over at Aker and Long as a paralegal. Buddy, her husband, works at a food mart on James Island. Sandy visits almost every day. She's a big help; it's nice that she's so close."

No wonder the paralegal at Aker's office had looked familiar; I'd seen her at the funeral. "I met Sandy the other day at her office. I was there so her boss could help me get a business started."

Bill could wait no longer. "And how did you become acquainted with my friend Julius?" he asked her in his formal, unbending voice.

It was the tone I suspected he used when telling a student he was dumber than a rock and didn't deserve to be in Dr. Hansel's class. I gave him a dirty look while smiling at our gracious host. I've never been accused of being two-faced and didn't pull it off well.

Ms. Hogan handled it better than I. "Good question, Bill. My husband and I—with the kids, of course—moved here twelve years ago. My husband worked for Global Shipping. When they expanded operations in Charleston, we agreed to move from Jacksonville to help with the transition. My husband died six years ago after a fall down the stairs in his office building. No one was at fault; it was just one of those freak accidents that could never be explained. What made it worse … well, it was over a weekend, and Mike was there with him and found his dad's body."

"Sorry," offered Bill in a slightly kinder tone.

"None of us knew how to handle it," she continued. "At least I had the kids here. Both Mike and Sandy were in their midtwenties, Steven a little younger. They were a big help. With a lot of prayer, we made it. God, it was a terrible time," she said as she wiped tears from her face.

"We didn't mean to make you so uncomfortable; we're sorry," I said.

"Oh, it's not you. There's so much going on now, and I guess it's all getting to me. Now, Bill, I haven't forgotten your question." A smile was beginning to show through her dampened eyes.

"I met Jay—that's what I call Julius—a few years ago at church. We both go … *went* … to the Baptist Church. It's a small congregation, so it wasn't too hard to get to know the others, or at least know who they were. Both Jay and I were loners by nature, so somehow we found each other."

"Did you begin dating at that time?" asked Bill, with more kindness than suspicion.

"Oh, no, Bill," she said. "Jay and I never had that kind of relationship; it was nothing romantic." She smiled. "We both liked cooking and good food. We'd try to meet every week and alternate fixing a meal. Occasionally, we went to Charleston to one of the nicer restaurants, but Jay said he had to put up with people over there every day, so he enjoyed the solitude and privacy we could share here. To be honest, I couldn't picture him in a romantic relationship. And at the time, with the death of my husband so recent, I couldn't even fathom replacing him in my heart with anyone."

"You must have been good friends. I'm sorry Julius never mentioned you," said Bill, thawing even more.

"Jay was good at compartmentalizing things," she said. "He seldom mentioned his shop, and that was most of his life. I knew he was in Preserve the Past, but other than telling me some about you, he hardly talked about it. He loved his privacy. To my knowledge, you and I were his only friends. That's sad, because he was such a wonderful man. He should have shared his kindness with others. Oh! Speaking of kindness, I'm being rude." She stood and started toward the kitchen. "Would you like something to eat or drink? I have finger sandwiches I keep on hand for Sandy's visits. I have tea and soda too."

"A glass of tea would be nice," responded Bill—no surprise, since I knew his penchant for the leafed drink.

"The same," I said. "Could I help?"

She of course declined, then quickly brought a small wicker tray topped with two glasses of iced tea and a sugar bowl. "About a year ago, I started dating a gentleman from Mount Pleasant," she added after we had a chance to stir sugar into the tea. "In fact, Jay introduced us. I met him when I went to pick up Jay at the end of his workday. We were going to have supper in the city. Harry was in the shop, buying an antique side table. He was one of Jay's regular customers, and we hit it off immediately. He owns three pawn shops: one in Charleston, one in North Charleston, and the other in Mount Pleasant."

"Did that bother Julius?" I asked.

"Heavens, no," she replied, a faint glimmer of a smile showing. "All he ever said was that he wanted me to be happy. He joked if I ever married Harry, I'd still have to fix supper for him every other week. I told him he could count on it." That memory seemed to cheer her.

"What did your children think of Mr. Lucas?" Bill asked, less studious and more friendly.

"Another good question, Bill. No wonder Jay thought so highly of you. Mike couldn't care less if I dated anyone. If it weren't for holidays, I'd never see him—I'm not on his radar. Steven was happy for me. He said I needed someone. He said he and Lance 'just complete each other's lives' and wanted me to have that kind of happiness. To be honest, I'm of the age to still have problems with my son's—what's the polite term for it these days?—alternative lifestyle, I suppose. But he and Lance appear happy, and that's the important thing. Lance is like a member of the family."

"What about Sandy?" I asked. "What does she think of your dating?"

"Sandy's having the most trouble with it. Being the only girl, she was her daddy's favorite. She's never gotten over his being gone; she harbors a lot of anger. But I think she's finally adjusting to my need to move on."

"From what you've said, I doubt the boys have had much contact with Mr. Lucas," I said, before taking another bite of a pimento cheese finger sandwich.

"That's true, and maybe one of the reasons Sandy has been affected the most," she said. "Harry is a few years older than I."

After several minutes of silence that seemed like hours, Ms. Hogan began crying. She grabbed a lacy, white cloth napkin from the tray to wipe her face.

"Last month, Harry asked me to marry him … I can't." With both hands covering her tearstained face, it was difficult to hear her. "And now Jay's gone … I just don't understand how Jay would kill himself—especially now." She mumbled something else.

"I'm sorry, Ms. Hogan, I didn't hear what you said," I said.

"Oh, I'm sorry; I said Jay said he would always be here for me. It just doesn't make sense. Two days before Christmas—my birthday—I learned I have brain cancer. They only give me six months to live."

And I had thought the room was quiet before. All I did was look at Ms. Hogan. Bill made an audible gasp, then nothing. For a second, I thought I could hear his and Ms. Hogan's hearts beating. I knew I heard mine.

I think I said "I'm so sorry." God, I hope I did. Bill didn't speak. The silence—the strongest, deepest silence I'd ever experienced—was broken when Ms. Hogan looked up and apologized for hitting us with such terrible news.

Here we were, two strangers sitting in her living room, looking for evidence to prove her identity as a murderer, and she's apologizing to *us* after sitting there and telling us she most likely wouldn't see the end of summer. I unmistakably saw what Julius had found so attractive in this lady. I knew beyond any doubt that she couldn't have had anything to do with his death. And now I was convinced—truly convinced—that Julius couldn't have killed himself.

I have little idea what any of us said after that. I remember exhausting my vocabulary of ways to say I was sorry. For the first time since I'd known him, Bill was speechless. What I do remember unmistakably was that Ms. Hogan walked us to the door, hugged both of us, and asked us to come visit anytime. We said we would.

How much longer would that be possible?

CHAPTER 20

The gallery was only a few days from being ready to open. Most of the painting was done; the floors looked as good as they were going to. My larger images were in Charleston, being framed; a dozen already framed works were ready for hanging. Nearly seventy other prints in varying sizes were attached to foam board and encased in clear plastic to sell unframed. I just needed to install spot lighting for the side walls, apply touch-up paint, clean the place up, post an announcement about the opening, prepare wine and cheese, and then wait for the art-starved throngs to arrive and buy all the photos. All but the last item were under my control. My control with the help of a few good friends.

Speaking of friends, I was still shaken by what Bill and I had learned earlier, so I called Charles and asked if he wanted to come to the shop for some food and drink. As usual, he said yes before I finished the question—immediately after the mention of food as I recall. He asked if I'd mind him inviting Larry. Why not? Being less—far less—than a gourmet chef, I'd be calling for pizza; it would feed three as well as two. I had plenty of wine and beer to add to the mix—all the ingredients for a well-rounded guy meal.

I would rather have spent a romantic Friday evening with Tammy, but that was occurring less often. Her work took more hours and energy than ever. I didn't blame her; she had a fantastic job and did it well. I was just selfish.

Charles arrived around seven wearing a gold and black University of Wisconsin-Oshkosh Titans sweatshirt, his hat, and red gloves. Thank goodness we weren't opening a clothing store. Larry arrived a few minutes later. He didn't share Charles's propensity for outlandish attire. He simply wore a fleece coat with the Pewter Hardware logo on the front.

"So, Chris, when are *we* having a grand opening?" asked Charles as he looked around the room as if he'd never seen it before. "I'm getting tired of painting and cleaning. I need to use my extraordinary retail-sales talents to sell your pictures."

"What skills would those be?" asked Larry between bites of pepperoni pizza. "If I remember correctly, I tried to get you to work at the store, and you said you couldn't sell anything."

"I knew I shouldn't have told you that," said Charles. "As Calvin Coolidge said, 'I have never been hurt by anything I didn't say.'"

"And that has what to do with what?" I asked, looking first at Charles, then Larry.

"Well, I did tell Larry that. What I really meant was, I didn't know anything about all that stuff you sell in the store. What's the difference between a Phillips head screwdriver and a regular one? And while I'm on that subject, Larry, I guess the Phillips screwdriver was named after someone named Phillips. Who was the flat-headed one named for?" Charles asked in total seriousness, his arms spread as if to grab the fleeing answer. "Why isn't his name on that handy-dandy tool? See, how could I answer that question if a customer asked? And don't even get on the topic of nails. I walked down your nail aisle—or whatever you call it in the hardware business—and there are bins filled with millions of different kinds of nails. Beyond me … way beyond me." His half-empty beer bottle rapidly approached his lips.

"Back to your retail skills," said Larry, either unwilling or unable to answer the mystery of the flat-head screwdriver. "What would those be if hardware wasn't your forte?"

"Last fall, I almost sold my classic Saab convertible."

"But you didn't," I said. "What happened?"

"This guy from the other side of Charleston was ready to buy it sight unseen; then he asked if it ran. I knew he'd get around to that, but since I was asking so little, I thought he naturally assumed it may not be quite roadworthy."

"And …" prompted Larry, fidgeting in his chair.

"And I was completely honest. I told him it ran the last time I went anywhere in it. But that was more than a year ago. He said he wanted a classic, but preferred one he could drive home. It takes all kinds."

"So let me understand," I said. "Your aborted car-salesman career is the extent of your sales experience."

"Up until now, yeah. But I'm still in the prime of my life and have many more years as a successful salesman left."

Larry and I had at least one thing in common: we knew not to question Charles's view.

"Back to your original question, Charles," I said, hoping I could remember back that far. "I think we're about a week or so away from opening. Then we'll need a way to let folks know we're here and ready for their visits."

"That'll be easy," responded Charles. Hopefully, he was finished with his used-car-salesman story. "First, there aren't that many people around this time of year. And you know, one of my other talents is delivering packages for some of the shops—via United Parcel Charles. All you have to do is come up with a hand-out, and I can deliver it door-to-door to the houses where folks are staying, and to the stores and restaurants. And don't forget: tell Amber, and everyone else'll know."

"If you put it that way, we could plan for a small opening next Saturday," I said.

"Good. While I'm thinking about it, why are we calling it Landrum Gallery?" asked Charles. As usual, I ignored his liberal use of the pronoun "we." "Seems like it's a store—a store that sells photos. Larry doesn't call his store the Pewter Hardware Gallery. The Surf Shop's a shop and not the Surf Gallery. You ought to consider Landrum Photo Store ... or maybe the Landrum/Fowler Photo Store."

"Charles, that's an insightful observation," I said. "For now, I think I'll stick with gallery."

At least he hadn't suggested the Fowler/Landrum Photo Store!

"Hardware Gallery doesn't sound that bad," commented Larry. He was sliding lower and lower in his chair. "Maybe I should change the name."

It appeared that Larry and Charles—and possibly I—had traveled one or two drinks past sensible. Hopefully by the next day, "the Landrum Gallery" and "Pewter Hardware" would sound better than they did right then.

"Okay, enough about this place," said Charles. "When did you plan to tell Larry and me what you found out about the Julius Palmer—killing, blood-sucking, greedy Amelia Hogan? You know that's the real reason we're here."

I filled them in, as well as I could, on our visit to Ms. Hogan, even though I wasn't sure they'd remember what I said. They weren't very interested in Ms. Hogan's life until she met Julius. Other than Charles calling her an "insincere ingrate" when I mentioned that she called Mr. Palmer "Jay," they listened attentively when I told them about her description of a nonromantic relationship.

I was surprised that when I told them about her three children, Charles—the person who knew everyone and everything on the island—still couldn't place them. He thought he remembered seeing the daughter, Sandy, going and coming from her job at the law office. He said he avoided lawyers whenever possible, so he wasn't sure. Larry remembered Ms. Hogan coming in the store, but had never had any significant conversations with her.

"I did help her find a toilet plunger," he said—more than we needed to know. "But she didn't mention planning to kill anyone."

I was sure that what I had learned about her health clouded my description. I tried to be as objective and factual as possible in describing our visit. I wanted to get their objective opinions. I left out the part out about her cancer—for the time being.

"So, what do you two think?" I asked.

Charles stood, then pointed his cane at me and Larry in turn.

"Just what we thought," he said at a much higher decibel level than necessary. "She found out about Julius's will, lured him out on the pier, and pushed him off. She needs money. She has herself a new boyfriend. Either the new guy doesn't want his new beau to share the dinner table with another man, or she's getting tired of fixing food for the antique dealer. Doesn't matter which; she did him in—case closed." A solid rap of his cane on the wood floor punctuated his declaration.

All this was said between sips of his fifth, sixth, or maybe fifty-sixth beer. Charles was short of many things, but opinions were not among them.

Larry remained in his seat, slouched as low as possible without melting into the fabric. Charles's cane in his face didn't seem to faze him.

"I really don't know enough about it to judge," said Larry. "But if we assume Mr. Palmer didn't take his own life, I'm afraid Charles's analysis makes as much sense as anything."

"There's one more thing you need to know," I added, suspecting that the next fact would change a thing or two. "Two months ago, Ms. Hogan learned she has terminal cancer. She has less than six months to live."

"Oh, damn. Shit, shit, shit," Charles whispered before falling back into his chair, his cane falling to the floor. The analysis was not quite as articulate as usual, but got his point across.

"Did Julius know?" asked Larry. He had scooted back up from his resting place, his head higher than the back of the chair.

"Yes," I said. "He told her he'd stick with her and take care of her and her family."

"Shit, why didn't you tell us this before I accused her of being everything but a dog tick?" asked Charles.

"Sorry. I didn't want to jade your opinion before you heard about her situation, her relationship with Julius, and her family."

"You've had a few more hours to think about what you learned," said Larry. "What's your take?"

"After hearing Ms. Hogan, I feel confident that Julius didn't kill himself. If what she said is accurate—and there is no reason to doubt it—I can't see him killing himself and leaving her to deal with her last months without his support."

"Why so sure?" asked Larry.

"He told her he'd be there," I said. "From everything Bill said, he was a man of his word—and one with a big, sympathetic heart. What's more cruel than deserting a longtime friend in her situation?"

Getting over the initial shock, Charles added, "It seems to me that every time you hear of someone killing himself, all the loved ones and friends say he never would have done it and he would never leave them, or something like that. Why would this be any different?"

Charles never ceased to amaze me. Within a matter of an hour and a few beers, he had gone from making no sense (or less than no sense, if possible, when he described his supposedly extraordinary sales ability) to perfectly good sense (or whatever is better than perfect) with his observation about suicide survivors. Maybe his wisest and most astute comments came after some beers. Or perhaps he sounded wiser to alcohol-influenced ears.

"Good point, Charles," I said. "To be honest, you may be one hundred percent correct. But after sitting with Ms. Hogan and hearing her story, I simply can't see suicide."

Then Larry, the man of few—and mostly logical words—said, "So now what?"

So far, this had been a night of very good questions. If only the answers were of equal quality. Maybe after a few more beers.

✳   ✳   ✳   ✳

Larry's question wasn't addressed for about an hour. It had been easier to move some boxes around and pretend we were readying the gallery (or store, or shop, or whatever) for the opening.

"Larry, you've been a model citizen and upstanding resident for several years," said Charles.

I wasn't certain where Charles was headed, but his use of the phrases "model citizen" and "upstanding resident" made me want to slink to the back of the room.

Charles continued, "I know you brought with you a grand career in what many would consider to be the wrong side of the law."

"Yeah," said Larry, "I'd guess that the police, the prosecutors, the judges, the juries, the media, and even my mother—who said she would love me no matter what—would tend to agree with you. What's your point?"

"Simple," said Charles. I could almost see the wheel spinning behind his shiny eyes. "As Gerald Ford, deceased United States president, said, 'Indecision is often worse than wrong actions.' Guys, the police believe Julius killed himself; most everyone else don't give a warm gargle of spit about what happened; and a few of us care a great deal. Now, add Ms. Hogan to the minority who care, and care deeply. If we don't act to find out what happened, who will? Save your breath. I'll answer that myself: a big, solar-system-sized no one!"

"So what're you suggesting, and what's Larry's ancient history have to do with it?" I asked, although I wasn't certain I wanted to hear the answer.

"We have to find out what happened," Charles said. "We could put a big-ass ad in Tammy's newspaper asking the killer of one Julius Palmer of Folly Beach, South Carolina, to give our fine chief of police a call and confess. Or we could ask Amber to use her gossip-collecting talents and rumor us up the murderer. Oh, here's even a better idea: I hear there are some mighty fine fortune-tellers in Charleston—none here, since fortune-telling's outlawed. We could pool our limited resources and ask Madame Know-It-All who killed Mr. Palmer."

"I assume you'll get to your point eventually," I said as I tried to look serious through an emerging smile.

"Yep, I'm almost there. Hang on. God gave each of us unique talents; I read that in a fortune cookie, but maybe a dead president said as much at some point. We need to use them. For example, I was given the talent of being able to live the life of a bum and not need much money or fine things, although I sure like this classy, expensive Tilley hat you gave me. I digress. I also have the talent of stumbling on things and usually come out smelling like a rose. I also hate injustice and want to do whatever possible to right wrongs."

"And?" I said, feebly attempting to keep him on track—wherever that led.

"And," he continued. "You have a talent for logical thinking, courage to do what you believe is right, and most importantly, a knack for choosing friends—with me as a prime example. You've only been here a few weeks, and you've accumulated a group of friends that includes Larry, Bob, Amber, Tammy, and even the chief of police. We all see something special in you … although it's hard to figure out what sometimes."

"And?" I tried again.

Larry nodded his sad-faced head in agreement.

"And Larry has the God-given talent for breaking into and entering some of the finest, and most secure, homes and businesses in these great United States. It's time we use our talents to solve this murder."

I had known I wasn't going to like the track Charles was heading down. I doubted Charles or Larry would remember much of this evening in the morning, so rather than running home and avoiding Charles for a few days, I asked him what he had in mind.

He then outlined one of the worst, most ridiculous, and most stupid plans I've ever heard.

Lord, please let him forget it before you give us another day, I silently prayed after they left.

CHAPTER 21

The weekend, not unlike the previous few days, was cold, windy, and damp. I had been assured by the natives that not all winter days were this miserable; I hoped they were right.

It wasn't the perfect day for a stroll on the beach, so I headed to the Dog for a beverage, some banter, and a little breakfast. There I was greeted by the smiling, pretty face of Amber.

"Chris," she said, "check out the board. Cute, huh?"

I surveyed the latest Amberism: "If a dog could talk, it would take a lot of fun out of owning one."

I giggled appropriately and agreed it was cute. Before reaching my booth, I stopped to speak to the Arlo Guthrie look-alike, Cool Dude Sloan, from the surf shop. He asked if I thought the weather would keep the surfboard-buying public away. This was the second time he'd asked, or mentioned, the lack of customers in February. It was also the most he had said beyond a couple of words in all the times we'd exchanged waves and smiles. A breakthrough?

I asked how long he had owned the shop. I assumed it had been years but didn't know. He nodded toward the chair across the table. I interpreted that as an invitation to sit.

"Bought it in eighty-eight, you can do the math," he said. "Had surfed for many years. Didn't know anything about the business end of the wave."

"So why'd you do it?" I asked.

"Needed a job; liked the area. Couldn't cook; didn't have any skills. Saw ad in the Charleston paper, went to the bank. They made a dumb decision and lent me the money. Rest is history." This very efficient manner of speaking didn't even require a breath in the middle.

Doesn't believe in full sentences either, I thought.

"So, Jim, after all these years owning the store, has February ever been a busy time—good weather or bad?"

"Nope. Just thought I'd ask to see if you'd get it right," he said.

"Did I?"

"Yep," he said before looking back down to his newspaper.

"Oh, by the way, Jim, do you know Amelia Hogan?"

"Nope," he said. No surprise; no one else seemed to either.

"I know her son, Mike," he added. "Why?"

Now, I was surprised. Finally, I had found someone who knew the family existed. *Progress,* I thought. I asked what he knew, telling him I'd run across the name and was curious.

"Mike's an a-hole—seriously stuck on himself. Can't surf, but thinks he can. Acts rich, don't know if he is or not. Lives on hoity-toity Kiawah. Don't come around much … glad of it. That's it."

Amber had my coffee on my table by the time I finished my highly enlightening, sentence-challenged—and by far, longest—conversation with Cool Dude. When she returned to take my order, she was laughing.

"He likes you, Chris. That's one of the longest conversations he's had with anyone."

"He seems nice enough; I've never been in his shop."

"Dude serfs to the beat of a different wave," said Amber. Despite the baffling mental picture, I understood what she meant. "I've heard he does a killing in the summer and has socked away tons of money. All he does in the winter is sit here for hours, then open the shop and read books on astronomy while he wonders where all the shoppers are. Rough life."

"Amber, is there anyone here who doesn't … surf to the beat of a different wave, as you put it?"

"Yep. Law of averages says there is. I just don't know who," she said and turned, with my order for a Belgian waffle committed to memory.

*   *   *   *

I didn't remember everything Charles, Larry, and I had talked about, but vaguely recalled that we were supposed to meet at the shop at five. Beyond that, all I remembered about Charles's grand plan was that it could result in incarceration. That should've been enough to make me realize it couldn't have been the best plan ever created.

"Do you remember what we're supposed to do tonight?" asked Larry as he opened the door just before the designated hour.

Regretfully, I told him that the previous night's wine had erased some of my memory. Larry nodded all too sympathetically. We decided that if Charles failed to bring the details with him, we would spend a couple of hours talking about nothing and go our separate ways. To be honest, that had to be the best plan.

Just as I was completing that thought, Charles bounded through the door. If I had a cuckoo clock in the shop, it would have been crowing five times. He was dressed in a blue and gold University of Delaware Fighting Blue Hens sweatshirt; a black, logo-free, ball cap; black jeans; and black tennis shoes. If it weren't for the signature cane, a little gold on his shirt, his red gloves, and his pasty white face, I would have missed him.

"Well, guys, are you ready?" he said.

Larry looked at me; I stared at Charles.

"Ready for what, exactly?" said Larry. "We were having trouble remembering the details."

I thought Larry was being exceedingly generous; we were missing a lot more than the details.

"Simple," said Charles. "We're just going to take a nice winter walk."

"And?" I asked, performing my usual tooth-pulling dentistry.

"And then we'll visit Julius Palmer's house. And then, since I seriously doubt he'll answer the door, we'll have to invite ourselves in, using one of Larry's many talents. And then, since we're already in the house, we'll look for evidence about who killed him. And then ..."

"And then, we'll go directly to jail, without passing go," I said.

I was pleased to see Larry slowly moving closer to me. Two against one, I hoped.

"Guys, come on. Unless we grab the bull by the balls, we'll never solve this crime. We agreed last night—now let's go," said Charles.

And I had always thought you were supposed to grab that sucker somewhere else; live and learn.

"Charles," said Larry, breaking the awkward silence, "assuming we go along with this harebrained plan, why do you think we'll be able to find anything about the killing? Especially after his house was already broken into."

"See, Larry, that's the reason we need to do this," said Charles. "How else'll we know what's there? Besides, we're much smarter than the average killer; we'll find what he missed. Doesn't that make sense?"

Not knowing which part Charles was referring to, I simply said sure. That's was the only response he would hear anyway.

"Okay, let's hurry," said Charles, pointing his cane at me. "We want to get there just before sunset, so you can stay outside and be the lookout. If anyone comes by, you say you're taking pictures in the area with your big camera while giving them your innocent look. Everyone will believe that. Larry and I can go through the house, and when we find something, we can either borrow it, or I can take its picture."

✳   ✳   ✳   ✳

The three of us, collars pulled tight around our necks to block the cold winds swirling around the island, traipsed six blocks to Palmer's house. I was in my warmest, down-filled coat and Tilley; Charles, dressed in almost all black with his camera strap over his shoulder, looked as if he were headed to a Halloween party at the University of Delaware; and bundled-up Larry looked like a jockey who had lost his mount in a snowdrift. No one would mistake the three of us for the three wise men headed to Bethlehem—especially the wise part. I was also burdened with my heavy tripod and camera. Most wouldn't have noticed, but I wouldn't be able to convince a knowledgeable photographer that I was taking photos without the aid of a tripod in this light—or more accurately, lack of light.

Palmer's house had been built in the 1930s. No stranger to hurricanes, it had been beaten down by weather and age. The color was a faded pink—not an uncommon color in older resort areas along the coast. Thick wooden legs held it above the high tides that accompanied most tropical storms. I knew it was deceptively sturdy, despite its outward appearance, and would stand up to most extremes that Mother Nature threw its way.

"Here we are, crew," said Charles. "Are we ready to execute our well-thought-out and brilliant plan?"

Clearly, I had forgotten a great deal of last night's planning; my foggy recollections seemed far from brilliant.

"Charles, this better be worth it," said Larry. "I've stayed on the right side of the law for many years. I'm about ten seconds from backing out now."

"I understand, Larry," said Charles as he took off his red gloves. "If this weren't so important to my friend Chris, we wouldn't be here. He'll make sure we don't get caught."

Yep, I had forgotten more than I thought.

I found a rotting fence post framed by a stand of decorative grasses in the corner of Palmer's front yard nearest the road. The winter brown of the grasses contrasted nicely with the white paint peeling off the decommissioned post. I set the tripod in plain sight and prepared to photograph the post and its surroundings while performing my chief task as lookout. If necessary, I could communicate with the "inside crew" via Larry's cell phone. Charles said cell phones were the work of the devil and refused to entertain the thought of getting one. Most likely, cost was the reason.

The lack of vehicles in the neighbors' drives or lights in any of the windows reinforced our belief that there were no prying eyes close enough to notice the odd couple climbing the stairs to the wraparound porch on Palmer's home. The cat burglars, pro and amateur, were in the house before I had a chance to look around. I saw how Larry made a successful living in his pre–hardware store, pre-incarceration days.

The good thing about most of the roads on Folly was unless you were going to a house on them, there was no reason for much drive-by traffic. And in February, there were seldom reasons to drive down the more remote roads. West Ashley Avenue wasn't that remote, but it would have been surprising to see traffic. Besides, I had a good, legitimate reason for staring at the rotting fence pole. In fact, I was doing such a good job photographing it, I didn't notice at first that I had company.

The distinct sound of a car door closing jarred me out of my concentration. From my peripheral vision, I noticed the sound came from a white Ford Crown Victoria. That jarred me more, especially since this particular Crown Vic had a blue light bar on top and the distinct logo of the City of Folly Beach, Department of Public Safety on the side. Off the top of my head, I couldn't think of a vehicle I wanted to see less.

"Officer Spencer, good evening," I said, as I tried to keep my voice sounding opposite of how I felt.

"Hi, Mr. Landrum. I see you're at it again. What're you shooting this time?" asked the young member to the department.

Good beginning. "Oh, this time of year, around sunset, you get a unique quality of light; it reflects the weather, cold and lonely. This old fence post exemplifies that feeling for me. It's one of many mundane landmarks on the island I like photographing."

I hoped that explanation sounded mundane enough so he would decide quickly to move on—surely there was crime on the island he could pursue. Other than the one being committed a mere few feet away.

"Did you know that's Mr. Palmer's house?" he said as he closely scrutinized the exterior of the house currently inhabited by my two felonious friends.

"I knew he lived around here. Speaking of Mr. Palmer, someone was talking about you the day after he died," I said, redirecting the topic and his gaze.

"Who?"

"Diane, the desk clerk at the Holiday Inn. She said you were there early that morning. Said you were the cute officer."

"She's a real sweet kid," he said. "She'd be even more attractive if she'd lose a little weight."

The real sweet kid in question was, most likely, older than Officer Spencer, but that was the way police officers talked. At least he was talking about her instead of wondering who might be in the closest house.

Spencer was facing me and looking away from the late Julius Palmer's house when the door opened, and Charles started out. Larry, digging deep into his years of experience, was more astute about exiting a house where he had not been invited and looked around first, then grabbed Charles by his belt and dragged him back in the house. I took a breath; it had been a while since I had one. It was sorely needed.

"I'd better get back on patrol," said Spencer. "Have a good evening, Mr. Landrum."

I didn't tell him my evening was getting better by the second. After he turned the cruiser and headed back toward town, my two friends scampered down the stairs and toward me. I removed my camera from the tripod in record time and rapidly walked with Larry and Charles the same direction Spencer took.

"Chris," said Charles. "Have we got a passel of stuff to ponder."

Charles shared this insight within shouting distance of the crime. The sun had just sunk below our vision, but I suspected it was going to be a long, interesting night.

CHAPTER 22

Charles and Larry were in stiff competition to see who could tell me the most about their adventure. By the time we entered the gallery, I had had enough of the contest and finally yelled "Time out!" More calmly, I then asked if they wanted something to drink—hot or cold. The introduction of drink into the conversation slowed them momentarily. But it didn't take long for them to say "beer, a bunch of them" before moving back to whatever they had been trying to say in unison.

Charles was pacing back and forth, his mouth moving as quickly as his cane. The ancient furnace churned out warm, dry air. It felt great.

"Chris," he said, "that was one spooky casa. Palmer had to be the newest thing in there—when he was in it, that is. Everything, and I mean everything, was ancient. He had more antiques in his house than some of the larger stores in Charleston—hell, more than the antique mall. And, that doesn't even count the stuffed parrot and something that looked like a stuffed beaver, and ..."

"Don't forget to tell about the man who attacked you," said Larry, sporting a huge grin. He was leaning against the side wall, watching Charles pace.

"He ... it ... didn't attack me. I went around the corner into the living room and was surprised to see a suit of armor standing there."

"Is that why you yelled 'Larry, run, before he catches you'?"

"I just said 'Larry, run.' I was startled. You don't often see one of those huge sardine-can people in a dark room. Besides, I was looking out for you and trying to save your life. Is this how you repay me?"

"I wish I had been the one holding Charles's camera," said Larry, still leaning against the wall. "He did stand up to that silent, completely motionless attacker."

"Enough about that," said Charles. "I've got photos I need to download. I think I found some interesting stuff but didn't have time to read it all. Besides, it was dark."

The three of us moved to the back room and the computer that was on an old card table in the corner. There were only two chairs, so I stood while Charles took the memory card from the camera and attached it to the computer. He rapidly downloaded thirty-four images.

"The first bunch is just an overview of the house," said Charles. "I didn't know what I was looking for, so I shot everything."

He was right: the rooms were filled with antiques. I was surprised there was enough space to walk around, particularly in the dining room and what I guess was an extra bedroom. Most of the pieces appeared European, and though I didn't know much about antiques, they looked expensive. The kitchen was the neatest room in the house. I could picture Julius cooking supper for his dinner guest, Amelia. What I couldn't picture was them wandering through the rest of the house without bruising their legs on the corners of the highly experienced furnishings.

"The office is a mess," said Charles as he pointed to the image on the screen. "I understand why the police said they couldn't tell if this is how he usually left things or someone went through the papers and left them like that."

"What're these?" I asked as he clicked on a half dozen images of what looked like handwritten notes and bank statements.

"These are what's going to tell us who killed pack-rat Palmer," Charles proudly proclaimed.

The first photo was of a copy of a cancelled check made out for five thousand dollars to Amelia Hogan.

"I found three bank statements beginning with November," he said. "I didn't go through each cancelled check—Larry told me not to dally, and he's the expert on break-in etiquette. Each showed a five-thousand-dollar debit around the tenth of the month. Since the last one was made out to Ms. Hogan, I assumed the others were too."

His next two photos showed the page from the statements where the checks were recorded. Not a bad job of evidence gathering, I reluctantly admitted.

"The next picture is of a note he had in the desk tucked behind old maps of London and Bath, England. Bath is a stupid name for a town, even in the country of stupid-named towns." He looked up from the screen. "Don't say it—I'll move on. Okay, the note was sort of hidden, so I thought it might be important. It's a love letter to Mr. Palmer."

Charles was right. In her letters, Amelia had addressed Palmer as "my dear Jay" and "dearest Jay," signing them "Always, Amelia." But, when read closely, the words were of a caring person thanking a "dear friend" for the "finest meals I've ever eaten" and that she'll "always be indebted" to him. The last paragraph was the most telling: "I can't even begin to think of the words to express my feelings. Your promise to take care of my children is the greatest medicine I could ever receive. You're the answer to my prayers."

"Charles, you're partially right. It's a love letter, but not a letter between lovers."

"Yeah, I guess. You know what it also does, don't you?" he asked—rhetorically, I assumed, since he was going to tell me regardless of what I said.

"It reinforces everything Ms. Hogan told you and Bill. It sure seems she would want him alive. She didn't have anything to do with his death, did she?"

"No, Charles, she really didn't," I said." I knew that after our meeting; this confirms it."

Larry, who hadn't said boo since Charles began showing the results of his clandestine photography, finally chirped in.

"So, other than me risking my entire future by breaking into a stranger's house, and Charles showing he could hold his own against a suit of armor, what've we accomplished in this little adventure?"

"Charles, help me if I leave anything out," I said. "First, we learned you haven't lost your touch getting past locks. Second, we learned Officer Spencer isn't as observant as he should be—thank God. Third, we learned Palmer has a house cluttered with antiques—most very valuable, I assume. Fourth, we learned he was an extremely kindhearted person. That was no surprise. And fifth, and most important, we relearned he wasn't killed by Amelia Hogan."

"Sixth," said Charles, "We learned I'm getting to be a pretty good photographer—you could read the whole letter. Besides that, the visit was a failure."

"I'm not nearly as good as you are with quotes," I mused. "But I seem to recall something Thomas Edison said when asked if he was disappointed when so many materials he tried to use as a filament in a lightbulb failed … something like 'I have not failed; I've succeeded in finding ten thousand things that won't work.'"

"Point for you, Chris," said Charles. "I believe Mr. Edison also said, 'Opportunity is missed by most people because it is dressed in overalls and looks like work.' So, let's get to work. We need to finish this gallery and to find a killer. Any more beer?"

I reminded myself never to get in a quoting match with Charles.

Larry offered, "The only quote I can remember is from Fat Louie, one of my suitemates a while back, who said, 'Get off my fuckin' bunk or you're hamburger.' That inspired me to be very, very careful where I treaded. Do we really want to be in this hunt?"

"Hell, yes," said Charles.

Excellent question, I thought. "I'll get more drinks."

CHAPTER 23

The shrill ringing of the phone rudely interrupted my deep sleep. I had hoped I was dreaming, but after sitting up, I continued to hear the irritating sounds of modern communications. The clock on the bedside table read 3:45. My addled brain couldn't think of any positive possibilities for why my phone was ringing at this ungodly hour.

"Chris, I'm sorry to wake you. This is Chief Newman."

Another bad sign. This wasn't my new friend, Brian Newman, but Chief Newman.

"I knew you'd want to know," he continued. "Our ambulance just took Bill Hansel to Charleston. They ..."

"What happened?" I interrupted. "Is he okay?"

"I think he'll be okay; we have no idea what's wrong. About a half hour ago, Officer Robins found Bill in his pajamas, standing in the middle of the street in front of his house. He was disoriented, shivering, and mumbling something about how there was no point in being positive. Robins asked him to sit in the patrol car with the heat on full and called for the ambulance. He said Bill wasn't hurt as far as he could tell, but he had no idea who Robins was or why they were in the street. When the ambulance got there, they put him on the stretcher, wrapped him in thermal blankets, and started an IV. Even then, he just stared at the ceiling of the ambulance and seemed resolved to whatever was happening."

"Was anyone else around? Did Officer Robins go in the house to see if everything was okay?" I asked.

"Everything seemed fine in the house, Chris. Robins looked around, didn't see anything disturbed, and didn't find anyone else. As soon as the ambulance headed for the hospital, Robins called me. He knew Bill had some connection to Palmer's death and that I'd taken an interest."

"Most likely," Brian continued, "my guys have already left the hospital. My guess is the docs will keep him for observation. If you want, I'll have dispatch call the hospital and have them call us when he's to be released. I'd be glad to have one of my guys bring him back."

"Thanks, Chief." I was still trying to wake up and get my mind around the news. "I'll go over in a few minutes and see what's going on. I can get him when they release him. And again, Brian, thanks for letting me know."

The trip was not exactly how I wanted to spend my Sunday morning, but Bill had been there for me in the past, and now it was my turn. I didn't rush; I knew regardless of what was happening at the hospital, they would take hours to sort it out. I swung by Bill's house. The chief had said Bill was in his pajamas, so I doubted he had his wallet—no identification, no insurance card. Now if only Officer Robins had left the door unlocked.

He had.

✳   ✳   ✳   ✳

One of the main selling points of Folly Beach was its proximity to Charleston. Charleston Memorial Hospital was located on the edge of the city and only about twelve miles from my house. The road from the beach to the hospital was nearly deserted. South Carolinians were smart enough not to be out at five in the morning in February—present company excluded.

Finding the hospital had been easy. Finding somewhere to park was a challenge. The hospital shared two things with nearly every hospital I'd ever visited: hard-to-find parking and eternal construction. I saw the parking garage as I approached the main hospital, but then had to drive past the front, down one side, and around the back before entering the garage. Construction barricades were everywhere. Temporary fencing, construction trailers, and heavy construction equipment were as much a part of modern health care as emergency rooms, patient rooms, CAT scan equipment, signs banning cell phones, and insurance co-payments.

Entering the lobby and finding Bill Hansel within the maze that permeated most hospitals was another challenge. The helpful, and sleepy, security officer at the door directed me to the emergency room. There I learned why more people weren't on the streets at this unnatural time of the morning: they were all gathered in the emergency room.

Another friendly member of the hospital staff asked me if I was a member of Mr. Hansel's immediate family. I'm guessing she hadn't seen Mr. Hansel. I confessed no, so she said I would have to wait in the nearly full waiting room for someone to update me on Bill's status.

Without question, I was the healthiest person in the room. My bad-hair morning couldn't compete with the young man with his hand wrapped in towels with blood oozing out the side or the elderly gentleman leaning against the side of his chair, moaning about pains in his head. Thankfully, only forty minutes passed before a young, male nurse asked for anyone waiting for a William "Hanset." That was close enough, so I followed him out of the waiting room. In the quieter confines of an off-white, sterile-looking corridor, I explained my relationship with Mr. Hansel and that he didn't have any family within five hundred miles. The nurse hemmed and hawed until I showed him Bill's wallet and insurance card. Then this helpful employee asked me to wait and headed toward the bowels of the emergency area. Ten minutes later, he returned and explained that he wasn't able to release any information about a patient without his or her permission, but Bill told him to tell me anything.

With the legal hurdle overcome, he shared that physically, my friend was in stable condition. He was dehydrated, which had caused much of his disorientation. The IVs were helping, and within a day, he'd be physically able to leave.

His psychological condition was another question.

"Your friend keeps telling us we can stick all the food we want in his arm, but he doesn't care. He keeps repeating there's no use trying to be positive."

"What'll that mean to his stay—any idea?" I asked.

"Our psych resident will be in to see him in the next half hour, but from what I've seen, most likely, they'll keep him a few days. We're affiliated with the Medical University of South Carolina, and they have a great institute of psychiatry."

"Could I see him for a few minutes?"

"We'd rather keep him isolated for now. We have no idea what's going on in his head, and we need to control the environment."

"Should I wait?"

"I don't think so. Give me a phone number; I'll call you or have the resident call you once we know something. If we discharge him, which is unlikely, we'll take good care of him long enough for someone to pick him up. Let me have his insurance card and driver's license, so we can get the paperwork started."

Feeling helpless and with nothing more to do, I headed home.

CHAPTER 24

"What do we owe the privilege of such an early visit?" asked Amber, sitting near the door and looking up from the morning paper. "You don't look very spry."

I had needed to see a friendly face after my depressing visit to Charleston. What better spot than the Lost Dog Café? I was the first customer—no surprise since the door had just been unlocked, and it was Sunday. Amber had coffee at my table before I took off my jacket.

"Belgian waffle?" she asked, more softly than usual.

I nodded. Words were hard this morning. I kept thinking of words from a Kris Kristofferson penned song: "there's something in a Sunday, makes a body feel alone."

Along with the hot, golden brown waffle came the question, "Hey, where's your cheerful, endearing, and—if I might add—handsome smile?"

I gave her an abbreviated version of the last three hours and my concern for Bill's mental health. She leaned over and gave me a kiss on the cheek, then said something about how wonderful I was to care so much about Bill. All I felt was helpless.

She obviously sensed a need to cheer me up—mainly by changing the subject. She sat down across from me. "I can't see any reason to stand until another customer arrives," she said, in response to my surprised expression. "When we met last year, I was thinking how nice you were to me. You'd be surprised how many people come in here and treat me, and the other gals, like dirt—maybe not quite dirt, but at least dust ... like we don't exist."

"What do you mean?" I asked.

"They think they just sit down, say some words about food, like 'two eggs, scrambled, wheat toast, tomato juice,' and it magically appears. There's no recognition of who takes the order, who prepares the food, who brings the food, and who cleans up after them. Just flat-out rude. You listen; you really care. And you really are nice."

Without knowing what to say, I smiled. She smiled, stood, leaned, kissed me on the cheek again, and walked to the door to greet the next customers.

Amber had such a wonderful way of making me feel good. The more I got to know her, the more I realized her beauty was more than skin deep. Those "flat-out rude" customers didn't know what they were missing. For a minute, I forgot about Bill ... but only a minute.

I was working my way through Charleston's hefty Sunday *Post and Courier* when Chief Newman appeared.

"I figured if you were back, I'd find you here. How's Bill?" he asked as he slid into the booth and faced me.

I knew he was off most Sundays; his jeans and a bright orange hunter's jacket furthered my theory. He was here to find about Bill. Despite the situation, it was nice to know so many people cared. I gave him a similar version of what I told Amber.

"I've known Dr. Hansel for several years," he said. "He's always been a quiet, respectful, and kind person. I've never seen any strange behavior in him. Any idea what's up?"

"I know you're getting tired of hearing it, Brian, but Bill believes—strongly believes—Palmer's death was not suicide or an accident. For whatever reason, Bill felt close to Palmer. It's eating at him."

"I understand," said Brian. "I know the reasons for your suspicions, but the evidence doesn't support it. We really didn't have any choice but to lean that way. Unless something else can be proven, my hands are tied."

I wanted to say I'd have to find something then. Instead, I smiled, thanked him for caring and talked about the weather—still cold, not as windy, and dry for a change. He told me to tell Bill he was thinking about him, then left.

The restaurant was still nearly empty; only a couple of the regulars were seated near the doorway to the restrooms. Amber returned to the table and sat down again.

"Chris, this may not be the best time, but I've got to tell someone, and you already know what I think about your listening abilities. We both tried the last few months, but I don't think Charles and I are going to remain an item."

I was surprised. Knowing both of them, I thought they'd be a nice couple. Both were great people, cared about others almost to the point of harm, were dedicated to being lifetime residents of the island, and were far enough off kilter to be entertaining.

"I can't put my finger on it," she continued without looking up. "He'll always be my friend ... maybe even my closest. He gets along with Jason. I think they both think like ten-year-olds. The spark just isn't there."

"Amber, I'm sorry."

"Thanks," she said. She kept looking at the checkerboard-painted concrete floor. Then she jerked her head up as if she had been startled out of her sad memory by something. "Oh, by the way ..." She paused for a beat, then said, "I hear someone from Preserve the Past killed Julius Palmer."

Fortunately, I did usually listen to what she said; otherwise, I would have tuned out somewhere around Jason and Charles thinking alike and missed the nugget about a killing.

"Whoa, Amber—what's that about someone killing Palmer? Who said it? Any names?"

"Chris, that'd be too easy. I've been asking around about Palmer. Cool Dude told me he overheard one of his customers on a cell phone tell someone that one of the group did Palmer in. He didn't remember who the customer was and didn't know who was on the other end of the conversation."

"Arlo Guthrie Sloan?" I asked.

"Arlo who?"

"Never mind," I said. "When did he say that?"

"Yesterday morning, or maybe Friday. I usually don't pay much attention to what he says. To tell the truth, I'm not sure what planet's language he's speaking most of the time."

"And that's all he said?" I nudged.

"Yeah, I didn't ask too many questions. If I did, people would think I was snooping and stop telling me things. Then what would happen to my nonpaying career as a gossip?"

"Good point," I said, then excused myself to head home and get a shower. I was beginning the feel the grunge of my early wake-up call, trip to the hospital, and wait in the depressing emergency room. Before I left, Amber thanked and kissed me again, still on the cheek.

I wasn't sure why I received the thanks ... and was equally unsure why the kiss felt so good.

*   *   *   *

Many of the island residents had gotten dressed in their finest and were taking seats in the pews of Folly's handful of houses of worship while I dried off from a refreshing shower and talking to Dr. Hoolili (or something like that), a psychiatrist with an extremely broken foreign accent that I couldn't place. He had called to update me on Bill's condition. The good doctor was a bit difficult to understand, but patient and concerned. He said Bill was stabilized and was being transferred to the psychiatric unit for "acute crisis stabilization." I said that sounded more serious than stable.

"Not really," he said—or at least I thought that was what he said. "Mostly, it's a precaution, but Mr. Hansel does need some attention, and he could best get it there."

Bill wouldn't be released for at least three days, the doctor explained, and visitors were discouraged. Dr. Hoolili said he would have someone call when it was okay for a short visit.

I walked the few cold blocks to the shop. I was surprised to see that Charles wasn't there. I had finally given him a key—after all, he was 100 percent of my workforce. I didn't want to inhibit his work habits by locking him out. For what I was paying him, I wanted to get all the help possible.

I was pleased to see the gallery was coming along; all it needed now was a good post-construction cleaning, a few odds and ends, some framed images on the walls, and some customers.

The door opened, and I was greeted with a loud, "When in the hell is this damn photo gallery going to open—especially with a fancy-dandy grand opening? I need to know when I'll get some free food and booze and when I won't be buying any of your overpriced photos."

"And a good morning to you too, Bob," I said without having to turn to see who it was.

"Yeah, whatever," he said. "Now, with all those damn pleasantries out of the way, are you ready to walk over and buy me some homemade apple pie for brunch?"

"How can I resist such a nice offer? Of course. Are you ready to go, or would you rather help me clean the windows first?"

Call me psychic, but I saw his answer forming in his rough-hewn, profanity-laden brain.

"Hot damn! Just what this town needs: a comedy club slash photo gallery," he said. "Let's go."

We beat the church crowd by just one verse of "Just as I Am" and got a table near the rear. It wasn't my regular seat, but it was still one of Amber's stations. It'd do.

"Amber, Amber, good morning," said Bob. "How's my favorite Dog chick?"

"Fine, Mr. Best Realtor," she replied. "What brings you here on a Sunday morning?"

"Came to see my entrepreneurial friend to let him buy me some of your fine pie. I also wanted to see if he was broke yet, so I can get the listing on his gallery."

Amber giggled—the worst thing she could do. It would only encourage him.

"So what's the latest on your efforts to find the killer of your friend's friend?" Bob asked when Amber left to get his pie and my coffee.

"Have you heard about Palmer's will—the three and a half million to Preserve the Past and an equal amount to Amelia Hogan?"

"Not a damn thing," he said. "Where'd he get so much money? With that kind of bread, he could have used a good Realtor."

"Well, regardless, I don't think he'll need a real-estate agent now," I said as he shoveled the pie into his mouth. "Besides, I suspect his housing is paid for. Even if it wasn't, I doubt you'd be able to get in to work with him. Think you'd be able to pass the entrance exam?"

"Well, my judgmental friend, you must not have looked closely enough to see my damn spiritual side," said Bob. "All you can see is my charm and warm personality—look deeper, and I'm almost growing angel wings."

"Sorry, Saint Howard—I missed the wings. Do you want to hear more about Mr. Lucas or continue this discussion about your nonexistent chances of getting through the pearly gates?"

"We can come back to my spiritual side later; let's hear about the potential killers. And who the hell's Amelia Hogan?"

Over the next twenty minutes, I filled Bob in on everything I knew about the will, the Hogan family (including Amelia's cancer), and Bill's sudden turn for the worse. Surprisingly, he listened without interruption—not many interruptions, anyway.

"I don't think I know any of the Hogans or Ms. Hogan's boyfriend. You say the boyfriend has some pawn shops and a house in Mount Pleasant? I can do some checking and see what the public records show. At least I can find out what his financial situation is. Way too much information is available in the courthouse and even on the damn Internet. Sometime it helps, though."

CHAPTER 25

The rest of my "employees" arrived for work around four. I asked Charles where he'd been all day, and he mumbled something about honoring the Sabbath and keeping it holy. If I had believed him, and Bob's earlier comments, I'd have to apologize to my friends for doubting their godliness. I may not have known either of them long, but I knew they weren't on the short list for sainthood.

"So, Charles, while you were keeping the Sabbath holy, what else were you doing?"

"Don't tell anybody," he said. "I was reading the biography of Bill Howard Taft, dead United States president, who served our great country from 1909—1913."

"Collecting quotes?"

"If I were harvesting quotes, he wouldn't qualify as fertile ground," said Charles. "Best I could come up with is, 'Politics, when I am in it, makes me sick.'"

"Your reading habits are admirable," I said. "Most of us could learn from you."

"Guess I'd better not tell you I fell asleep and didn't wake up until a few minutes ago. Go on believing the good things about me," he said, head bowed slightly. "So, what've I missed today?"

I shared my day, starting several hours before sunrise. Charles was visibly irritated that I didn't wake him to go to the hospital. He got more irritated when I told him I didn't want to bother him that early. If he had had a presidential quote handy, he would've stabbed me with it.

We touched up some paint and did some minor cleaning, but spent most of the evening talking about Bill and Julius Palmer. We rehashed all we didn't know and bemoaned not having a clue how to learn more. Thanks to his long nap earlier in the day, Charles would have talked all night, but I had to get some sleep. He said he'd lock up. I nodded and left.

*   *   *   *

I hadn't realized how much my long and traumatic day took out of me until I opened my eyes the next morning and saw it was nearly eight thirty. That was the latest I'd slept in months. I also appreciated how pleasant it was to be retired. Here it was, Monday morning, and I didn't have to be at work or anywhere else. That pleasant thought was short-lived; I began wondering what Bill must be thinking, waking in the psych ward. Flexibility was not one of his strengths. Such an experience had to be frightening. Should I ignore the doctor's advice and try to visit? Deferring to the psychiatrist, I decided to wait until the hospital called. My best contribution was to see if I could dig up any information to give to the police; then I could feel I was doing something.

I had debated buying a second computer, so I could have one at the house in addition to the one at the gallery. Now I regretted not making that purchase. I took a quick shower, bundled up, and walked to the gallery to see what the Internet had to offer.

The search engine was both a fantastic and frustrating tool. It seemed to know everything about everyone and everything; the trouble was, it knew too much. There were nearly four hundred thousand references to the name "Amelia Hogan"—and more than two million for Harry Lucas! Narrowing down the search by adding other keywords helped, but took time. Adding the keywords "South Carolina" to the search for Harry Lucas yielded more than a million references. This was going to be a long morning.

Regardless how many words I added—"South Carolina," "Folly Beach," "Sandy Miller," "Mike Hogan," or "Steven Hogan"—Amelia remained a mystery. There were a few references to her sons, primarily about their professional accomplishments, but nothing about her.

The search for Lucas was more fruitful. The logical keywords, such as "Charleston," "pawnshop," and "chamber of commerce" narrowed the search. I thought about adding "killer" to the list, but doubted even the search engine knew that.

I needed a break and called Tammy and caught her taking an early lunch.

"Just thought I'd call to see when we can get together," I said.

"I don't know; work keeps getting in the way," she replied, sounding preoccupied.

"No problem," I said. I hoped I didn't sound as disappointed as I felt.

"Maybe I'll get a break in a few days," she said. "Sorry."

"If you get a few minutes in the next day or so," I said, "could you do a little research on the two Hogan boys—Steven and Mike? Find anything you can about them."

She hesitated. "I'll try, but no promises," she finally said. "I'll check the paper's morgue and, if I get a chance, call a couple of folks."

I thanked her and reiterated that any information would be helpful. All in all, our exchange had not been the pleasant telephone conversation I'd hoped for. Tammy was my first serious relationship in many years. I wasn't sure where we were going, but it hurt to think of it ending.

Break over—back to the computer. I learned on one Internet site that Mr. Lucas had four pawnshops; on another site, three were listed. They were called Harry's Pawn Shop—I had to give him one for creativity! I learned, but wish I hadn't, that his slogan was "Top Bucks for Your Trucks. Great Prices on Everything Else!" His Web site said that in addition to the traditional pawned items, he was a "title-only" pawn shop for vehicles. The fine print explained that you didn't have to leave your car or truck when you pawned it, just give Harry the certificate of registration. There must not be enough room in his glass jewelry cases for vehicles.

About the only thing I learned that I couldn't easily find in the telephone book was that Harry enjoyed partying. One brief article from a local weekly newspapers talked about a party he had had on his forty-five-foot classic Chris-Craft during Charleston's annual Spoleto Festival and another party at his "stately Victorian home" in Mount Pleasant. Both stories were a few years old and clearly society puff pieces, filler in the weekly paper. There were candid photos of some of the guests but none of Mr. Lucas.

By noon, I'd given up finding anything else about Lucas or Hogan and spent a few minutes looking at the extended weather forecast. I was pleased to see warmer weather heading our way from the west. "Cold," "windy," and "damp" were not words I liked to hear at the beach. On second thought, "cold" followed by "drink" wasn't so bad.

*   *   *   *

I was in the back room trying to decide what to say in the flyer Charles promised to deliver to every occupied house on the island when the front door opened. Expecting to see Charles, I was surprised to see the best Realtor in the second of the island's three largest realty firms coming through the door. *Two visits in as many days—I must be living right*, I thought.

"How the hell can I browse and not buy anything if there ain't anybody in the front when I come in?" my visitor cheerfully asked.

"Well, Mister Un-Customer, spewer of double negatives, you know the gallery isn't open. Besides, why should I rush out here when I know you aren't going to buy anything?"

"Mister New Gallery Proprietor," countered Bob as he plopped his ample rear on the metal card-table chair, "let me give you a tip that'll help you get as rich as your Realtor friend." He paused until he knew he had my full attention. "I learned a long time ago that you never know when someone—usually least suspected someone—will put down hard cash and buy. Treat everyone who walks in the door as your best customer. You're so damn pitiful and need all the help you can get; I won't charge you anything for that sage advice."

"Good point, Mr. Potential Customer. Could I interest you in any of these fine photographs?"

"Shit, no!"

"So, to what do I owe the pleasure of a second visit in two days?" I asked.

"Two things," he said. "First, believe it or not, I'm showing a beach house on East Arctic to a family from Columbia. They have more damn money than sense. There's a good chance they may fall for my extreme Realtor charms and make an offer."

"Good—if they have more money than sense, perhaps they'll buy some fine-art photos to improve their walls. The other reason?" I asked.

"A far less potentially profitable reason. I made some calls about your friend Harry Lucas. Got a few tidbits."

"Does he have a long history of killing the friends of his lady friends?" I asked, perhaps a little too optimistically.

"Gosh, Chris, no one mentioned that. See, I don't know how to ask the right questions like my photo gallery owner detective friend. Thank God I'm good at selling real estate."

"Okay, Bob, I understand your limitations. I assume you found something, or you wouldn't be here pestering me."

"Mr. Lucas is in his midsixties. According to my contact, he owns three pawn shops. The interesting part is that until November, he had four. He had to close a shop in Georgetown. He's been telling everyone he did that because it was too far from home. It's about fifty miles away, but he was never there. His manager—or more correctly, former manager—said they were six months behind in rent, he hadn't been paid for two pay periods, and he thought the federal withholding taxes hadn't been paid for months. In other words, a big, fat shitload of financial troubles closed the store, not the long and lovely ride to the idyllic community of Georgetown."

"Interesting," I said. "How did your contact know the former manager?"

"'Don't ask, don't tell' was his response when I asked the same question. Regardless, facts are facts—don't matter where they came from. Another acquaintance, someone I'd never consider a damn friend, told me Lucas had been divorced for three years, and it'd been a highly contested divorce. Typical: both parties lose, and only the tight-assed, shyster lawyers win."

"Anything else?"

"Shit, Chris, do I look like Leslie Stahl on damn *Sixty Minutes*? I thought I did a good job getting you all the dirt I did."

"Thanks, and Stahl doesn't have much to worry about from you. Have time for a piece of pie? I'm buying."

"You're damn right you're buying. But no, I've got to meet my way-too-rich clients."

Before the echoes of Bob's wit, wisdom, and information about Mr. Lucas had stopped reverberating off the bare walls of Landrum Gallery, the door opened, and the balance of my staff arrived.

"Hey, Chris, I got us some valuable information that may break the solution to the crime wide open."

Charles rushed into the room, eclectically dressed, as usual.

"Then take your jacket off, help me move a couple of these display racks to the gallery, and share your newly found clues."

He threw his jacket in the corner but left his gloves and hat on.

"Charles, what's with the dog?" I asked, meeting the stare of the strange-looking dog on his sweatshirt.

"Chris, I often wonder what rock you came out from under. Don't you recognize Scottie, the mascot of Agnes Scott College?"

"Not only don't I recognize that bizarre-looking canine, but I've also never heard of Agnes Scott College. Where is it, and do I dare ask where you got the shirt?"

"First, my cultural ignoramus, Agnes Scott College is a women's college in Decatur, Georgia. And you best not ask where I got it. Some things are better left unknown."

I agreed completely. "So what can you tell me—not about Ms. Scott and her college, but about the murder?" I asked.

"Before I get into that," he said. "Let's get this dang trim painted. I'm sick of that strong, yucky paint smell around here."

He, of course, was right. I hated to take orders from my entire staff, but I agreed we could paint and talk at the same time.

"I occasionally deliver packages for Dude at the Surf Shop," he continued, paintbrush in hand.

"I know—United Parcel Charles," I said.

"This morning, he had me taking some surfboard wax to a customer over at the Oceanfront Villas—one of those seasonally challenged Canadians who think forty degrees is warm. They're real nice folks—funny accent, French I guess—who even wanted to tip me. I told them they wouldn't tip the UPS driver, so I wouldn't take one either. They didn't understand."

"Charles, you learned what this morning?" I asked patiently, having heard more than I wanted to about the tipping habits of French-accented Canadians.

"Oh, yeah. When I was in Cool Dude's shop, two guys were making fun of northerners, Chinese tourists, Chihuahuas, and gays—and they weren't that politically correct in their descriptions, if you get my drift. I agreed with them about the Chihuahuas."

"And?" In my rapidly aging state, I wasn't as patient with off-track and convoluted stories as I had been in my younger and more foolish years.

"And," said Charles, "One of them lives next to the late Julius Palmer."

Now, I began to pay attention. I balanced my paintbrush on top of the can and waited for Charles's revelation. The fumes from the paint were distracting, but we were getting used to them by now—after all, we had been living with them for a week or so.

"He was telling his friend about the dead guy's 'queer interior designer.' The 'dead guy' part perked up my ears. He was saying this swishy, prissy, well-coiffured designer—his words, not mine—was hilarious trying to carry a rack of fabric samples from his car to the house. Apparently, the rack was overloaded, and he kept dropping samples. I guess the hilarious part was when he was trying to pick them up without dropping more. It doesn't take much to entertain some folks."

"Is that all he said?" I asked. "When did this happen?"

"Chris, I was just eavesdropping." Charles whispered that last word. "I wasn't having a conversation with our intolerant fellow islanders. I don't know this for a fact, of course, but was thinking the designer was son Steven. And, no, he didn't say when it was. For some reason, he just thought it was a funny story. Go figure."

Charles's new eavesdropped-upon acquaintance knew Palmer was dead, so the "humorous incident" must have taken place a few weeks ago or longer. *Brilliant detective work*, I thought. I found it interesting that Steven—if in fact the designer in question was Amelia's son—had been in Palmer's house.

"So, what did you get from that conversation?" I asked.

"Several things, I guess," replied Charles. "Let's see … most everyone makes fun of northerners—at least, we southerners do."

I didn't feel it necessary to point out that Charles was from Detroit—not quite considered southern, except perhaps to Santa Claus.

"I concluded that everyone," continued Charles, "except those strange folks who own one of those rat-related dogs, makes fun of Chihuahuas. I also learned three new names homophobes call our alternative-lifestyle-living friends—I won't repeat them."

I began wondering if the paint on my brush would be dry before I could get anything worth hearing from him.

"Is that about it, Charles?"

"No. I deduced—or detected, because that's what we detectives do—the same thing you did; you just haven't said it yet. Steven had been in Palmer's house and could have found out about the will that made him one generation detached from a multimillion-dollar inheritance. That appears to be a humongous clue, if you ask me."

"I agree," I said. "But the only thing we really know Steven is guilty of is clumsy fabric juggling. And even then, we don't really know for sure it was Steven."

"Even what we don't know for sure is more than we didn't know for sure yesterday, right?" asked Charles.

"If it takes bazillions of grains of sand to make a beach, and if the journey of a thousand miles begins with the first step, I guess we're on our way to solving a crime," That was the most profundity I could muster.

Charles was so wrapped up in his story that he had forgotten about his painting and was sitting on the floor. He stared at me. Finally, he appreciated my words of wisdom—or so I thought, until his eyes fluttered and finally closed.

"Chris, Agnes Scott was old … Indians lived … ham and cheese …"

His words, nonsensical as they were, stopped. We hadn't had anything to drink, but I was beginning to feel light-headed.

"Wake up … let's call it a night …" I said. I wanted to say more, but was distracted by Charles floating around the room.

That couldn't really be happening. For one thing, Floaty Charles wasn't speaking, which proved he was a hallucination.

The next thing I knew, I'd fallen off the chair and was leaning against the side of the desk.

"Charles, we gotta get out of here," I mumbled and kicked him in the leg.

"Damn, did you spill the paint?" he asked drowsily. "What's that smell?"

He tried to stand and fell hard, his cane failing at its job.

The answer to his question struck me harder than any hammer: *Gas … we've got to get out of here …*

I was only four feet from the back door; it seemed farther. Did gas rise like heat or fall to the floor? Did we need to stay close to the floor or not? Was Charles still alive?

I was gasping for breath while knowing each one could be deadly. I held my breath and crawled to the door. I reached up, turned the knob, and pushed. Nothing happened.

This couldn't really be happening. My head was throbbing so much that I knew it couldn't be a dream.

The knob was turning; I'd opened the door earlier, so it had to work. Why not now?

"What happened? Where's Agnes?" asked Charles, finally answering my question about his condition. He had crawled up behind me and was trying to stand.

"Help me with the door; we don't have much time," I said, as I got more and more dizzy.

We helped each other stand, moved to about two feet from the stubborn door, and lunged at it. Despite our effort, it didn't open, but the lock was beginning to separate from the door jamb.

"One more time, Charles!" I screamed as loud as my lungs would allow.

"I'm not sure …"

"No choice! Let's go!"

We hit the door with everything we had, which wasn't much by then.

It was enough. The door flew open, and we flew out—more accurately, out and down. I hit the concrete step; Charles hit me. We both sucked in fresh, pure, lifesaving air.

We would live another day.

CHAPTER 26

Charles got his legs back under him first. He stumbled, then walked, then ran to the fire department. It was only two blocks away. I was slower to regain enough equilibrium to slowly stand and move fifty or so feet from the building. I imagined it exploding in front of me. I had no idea how to turn the gas off. The back door was wide open; with any luck, enough of the flammable gas would escape to prevent a larger disaster.

At the same time I heard the sirens, Charles was returning with two firefighters. It was quicker for them to walk than to wait for the truck. One carried a large, red wrench, the other a hatchet. The older of the two—the wrench bearer—went directly to a rusted steel pipe that ran down the side of the building. I assumed it was the gas line. He put the wrench on the rusty valve about a foot from the ground. It turned easily. This took less than ten seconds and made me feel like an idiot. I'd never noticed the old pipe before. That answered one of the most basic questions a tenant should ask when moving in. Now I wondered where the water cutoff was … but not for long. My head was throbbing too much to think about anything.

Chief Newman's unmarked car arrived at the same time as the fire engine. Two more firefighters jumped from the large tanker truck and asked if I was okay. I finally said yes. They ignored Charles—figured if he ran to the station to get them, he must be fine. The firefighter with the hatchet grabbed a gas mask from one of the compartments on the side of his truck, walked through the gallery, and opened the front door. One of the others placed a three-foot-high box fan in the back doorway to begin sucking out the polluted air.

Charles and I sat silently in the rear seat of Brian's car, watching the efficient first responders go about their business.

The entire on-duty Folly Beach Police and Fire Department stood behind the gallery. Fortunately, few other bystanders were there to witness the hubbub. You could almost feel the excitement of something, anything, happening. I had contributed more than my share of excitement opportunities to the fine employees of Folly Beach.

"Guys," said Brian Newman as he climbed into the front seat. "It looks like the pilot light went out. When the thermostat called for heat, the gas started pumping but wasn't igniting."

"Doesn't a furnace have something to prevent that from happening?" I asked.

"Yeah, but remember, your furnace is more than fifty years old. From the looks of the filter and the dirt around the door, it hasn't been serviced since the last decade, if then. It was a disaster waiting to happen. They put chemicals in the odorless natural gas, so you could smell it. The paint fumes probably masked the smell."

"Chris," added Charles. "You got workers' comp on your employees?"

The firefighters were right: he was back to normal … or rather, abnormal.

"I think that's all we can do here," said Brian. "Get someone to work on the pilot light before turning the gas back on. I'll leave the fan here; just bring it to the station in the next day or so."

"Thanks, Brian."

"Chris, have you always had that dark cloud over your head?" asked Brian as Charles and I were getting out of the unmarked Crown Vic.

He left before I could answer. The answer was no, but it seemed I had entered a different weather pattern when I crossed the Folly River. It could just be an age thing—nah.

The gallery must have been safe to enter, or our visitors in red helmets wouldn't have left. Charles entered ahead of me and was already on the phone, calling Larry. I stared at the furnace as if I had a clue what I was looking at. The chief was right: it was old, rusting around the bottom edges, and filthy—and you could barely see light through the dust-clogged filter.

Larry was slower than usual; it took him a whopping fifteen minutes to show up. He was carrying a large, silver toolbox in his left hand. His entire body listed to the left; the box must have contained every tool known to man. He said he was glad we were alive, announced a hardware store owner disclaimer by telling us he wasn't an HVAC expert, and proceeded to light, turn off, light, and turn off the pilot light.

"Chris, it doesn't look like there's anything wrong with the pilot or the furnace. You can have someone from Charleston check it, but all they'll say is it needs cleaning. I'll do that for you now and bring a new filter from the store."

"I've been thinking." This was always a frightening proclamation from Charles. "If there's nothing wrong with the pilot light, it wasn't an accident. Guys, someone's trying to kill us."

"How do you figure?" I asked.

"Hold on a second, Chris," he replied, turning his attention to Larry. "Larry, how could someone do this?"

"Simple. This is an old a furnace," said Larry, as he walked back to the furnace and began fishing dirt from some of the hard-to-reach corners with a screwdriver. "All someone had to do was to cut the gas off outside for a couple of minutes. The pilot light would go out. Then, when the gas was turned back on, without the little doohickey in there that's supposed to prevent the gas from starting, the gas would come into the room."

"There you go, Chris," said Charles. "You just heard how. The why's simple. We've been asking too many questions about Palmer's murder. In fact, aren't we about the only folks here who are pushing the issue? Of course we are."

"Assuming that's true, who decided to shut us up?" I asked.

"Chris, I can't do all the work. That part's yours."

"Charles makes sense," said Larry. He was still cleaning and had already gone through a roll of paper towels. "If the two of you had been asphyxiated, it would have looked like an accident. No one would have given it a second thought."

"And," added Charles, "why in the hell was the door so hard to open? It hadn't ever stuck before, right?"

He had already put on his coat, grabbed his cane, and headed out the door. By the time Larry and I caught up with him, he was inspecting the exterior side of the heavy wooden door. The only light was from a bare seventy-five watt bulb in the fixture immediately over the door— hardly adequate illumination for a close inspection of anything.

"Look at this," said Larry who had moved about nine feet from the outswung door and was bending over something on the gravel-covered alley.

There was no shortage of trash and other odds and ends interspersed with the gravel, but he was focusing on a triangular piece of wood that was about an inch wide and an inch high, tapering down to nothing.

"That's just an old doorstop," said Charles. "Nearly every building and store around here has a couple to prop open their doors to let fresh air and customers in. Wouldn't want to put a doorknob between themselves and all that tourist money."

"True," said Larry as he inspected the small piece of wood.

"So what are you thinking, Larry?" I asked.

"I'm not saying anything for sure; I really don't know," he said. "But this could have been wedged in the door like this." He demonstrated by pushing the wedge into the narrow space between the door and the jamb.

He had our attention.

Charles took a step forward, looked directly at me, and said, "See."

Larry ignored Charles's brilliant observation and said, "The wedge wouldn't keep the door from opening, but would have made it much more difficult. If you were already weak, it could make a difference."

And almost did, I thought.

"See," Charles repeated.

"Then, if you did get out," said Larry, not to be deterred, "the doorstop would've landed on the ground, along with the other trash—nothing suspicious."

"And if we didn't get out?" asked Charles, varying from his repetitive "see."

"Simple," said Larry. "He'd wait awhile to make sure you wouldn't be coming out, then pull the wedge out—accidental death, so sad."

Our evening ended on that frightening note.

CHAPTER 27

"Morning, Chris. I'm on my way to a murder down by the docks. I wanted to let you know about Steven Hogan."

Tammy's early morning call had roused me from a restless sleep. Realizing someone might be trying to kill me had a way of ruining a perfectly good night.

"I talked to two people who have contacts in the business world and the gay community," she said, in a just-the-facts tone. "The paper's morgue yielded squat."

"Learn anything?" I asked.

"You already know most of it," she continued. "Steven lives with his significant other, Lance Branson, in an apartment near the Battery. Damn, now I'm stuck in traffic—hold a sec while I try to get around this truck."

All I heard was a smattering of horns and the heating fan from Tammy's bumble bee—colored Mini Cooper.

"Okay, I'm back. Both guys are interior designers. They worked for Renaissance Design, one of Charleston's premiere outfits. They left last year and opened their own place just off King Street. It's called the Design Shop. Renaissance caters to the bluest of Charleston's blue bloods. My contact said that Renaissance isn't a firm that takes kindly to designers leaving. They spend a ton of money and time schmoozing potential clients and are ruthless when an employee bolts. They spread rumors about the former employee and do whatever necessary to ruin his reputation so he won't take clients."

"Interesting," I said. "I suspect they'd pull out all the stops when two designers leave to start their own shop."

"Supposedly, they tried to smear Steven and Lance's names by hinting at embezzlement and even spreading rumors of them stealing from the homes of clients. Nothing concrete ever surfaced, just hints and rumor. But that's all it takes. I have no idea if it's actually affecting the new business; I'd guess yes."

"Seems like that'd be reason enough to take a strong interest in his mother's potential inheritance," I said.

"Sure, but he'd have to know about it," she said. "On the other side, my friend with gay-community tentacles paints a different and more positive picture of the two, especially Steven. He says Steven's a great guy—always has a smile on his face. He's well liked among his colleagues and friends. He also said Steven's cute, sort of short and cherubic—I doubt that'll help with what you're looking for. My contact hadn't heard any of the embezzlement rumors about Steven, but said if he had, he wouldn't believe them. He says Steven is top-notch, honest, and fair. I see police lights and crime-scene tape, so I'd better find somewhere to park. Talk to ya later."

She was gone before I had a chance to say anything about last night's experience. Truth be known, I didn't know if I wanted to mention it. I also didn't ask when I'd see her. I wondered if she didn't want me to ask. Even if that wasn't the case, I wondered why I was even wondering such a thing. I also wondered what, if anything, the information about Steven Hogan meant—all in all, a lot of wondering for early morning.

After my near overdose of wondering had subsided, I walked to the Dog with coffee and oatmeal on my mind. The cold snap—at least cold for this part of the country—was supposed to break, warming the temperature to the low sixties. Regardless, it was cold now.

Unfortunately, it was Amber's day off, and one of the other waitstaff, Temple, was there to meet my culinary needs. Everyone who worked in the Dog was exceptionally friendly and helpful—they just couldn't compete with Amber.

Before I could make it through the morning paper and half of the generous portion of oatmeal, I was surprised to see Bob ambling through the door—some would call it a waddle.

"Morning. This is your lucky day," he said. "Not only do you get to see me again, but I've also reconsidered yesterday's offer and will let you buy me a piece of breakfast pie ... maybe two. Just lucky for you—damn lucky!"

"Bob, didn't I tell you yesterday's offer expired at midnight? I assume your wealthy clients want to see the property again or make an offer."

"I'm hurt," he said with mock exasperation. "What makes you think I didn't get up this morning, get dressed, drive twelve miles out of my way, and waste a couple of hours of my valuable time just to see someone who isn't going to make me a damn dollar?"

"If you put it that way," I said, "it's apparent you came only to see me."

"Yeah, that and to get you to buy me a healthy breakfast," he said. "Since I'm already here, I might as well meet my clients and prepare their written offer. Now, are you going to continue jabbering or let me order my damn pie?"

"Multitasking ... guess that's why you're such a successful Realtor."

"Yeah, now you know another one of my secrets. Speaking of secrets, I did some checking on the real-estate databases for information on your friend Harry Lucas, former resident of a huge house in Mount Pleasant, now residing in a tiny condo in the same city."

Temple finally gave in to Bob's charming, sweet, unshaven smile and asked if he needed anything. As was his nature, he gruffly asked for a piece of the damn cherry pie—heated and "with vanilla ice cream on top, while you're not doing anything else." She put on her best "I have to smile, but you can't make me mean it" look and left.

"Sweet kid. Where's Amber?" asked Bob as he threw his coat on the adjacent seat.

"Off today. Now, what'd you find about Lucas—and he's not my friend. I've never met the man."

"First, he and his lovely wife of thirty-one years—clock stopped ticking three years ago—lived in a fantastic Victorian mini-mansion overlooking the bay over in Mount Pleasant. It's surrounded by a high wrought-iron fence with impressive stone gates, as I would tell any clients looking at it. If I had it listed, it would be in the four-mil range."

"In what real estate database did you find all that?" I asked.

"Actually, none. My curiosity got the best of me, and I drove by it. Thought maybe the ex wanted to sell; I didn't ring the damn bell but will give her a call. Now, do you want to hear what else I learned or quiz me about my driving habits?"

After I assured him I wanted to hear the rest of the valuable information and wasn't concerned about whose house he cased, he continued.

"After the divorce was finalized, Lucas transferred his portion of the house to her," said Bob. "He had to refinance and borrow an additional 1.5 million to pay her off. Apparently, there wasn't a large amount of equity; he'd taken second mortgages a couple of times to put money into his pawnshops. I called a broker friend last night. Believe it or not, I do have friends ... sort of."

"Law of averages," I interrupted. "Meet enough people, and someone'll be desperate enough to call you a friend."

"He told me Lucas was one of the more shady characters in Mount Pleasant," he said, ignoring my comment. "The pawnshops are in financial trouble, and there'd even been rumors of drugs being sold out of two of them. Nobody was accusing Lucas directly, but everyone suspected he had knowledge about it."

Bob's breakfast pie arrived, and he spent all of thirty seconds devouring it before continuing. Correction: devouring, belching, and then continuing!

"Lucas moved to a small condo with a large mortgage beside the bridge to Charleston. My friend—okay, you win, my acquaintance—said the hot gossip during the Lucas divorce case was who would get possession of his two pride-and-joy boats, a forty-five-foot classic Chris-Craft and a thirty-foot speedboat. Eventually, Harry got the damn boats, since his ex got the mansion."

I told him I remembered seeing the photos of the Spoleto party Lucas had had on the Chris-Craft. Bob waxed philosophically and told me Charleston and the surrounding wealthy communities were saturated with the most smiling, unhappy people in the universe. I didn't ask how he conducted his survey—especially the universe part—and before I could ask anything else, he said he couldn't keep his paying clients waiting and got up. As he walked away, Bob called over his shoulder that he would talk to some more *acquaintances* and see if anyone could shed light on the less-than-stellar citizen Harry Lucas. I didn't have time to tell him about the previous night; I'm not sure I would have anyway. If I didn't talk about it, maybe it didn't happen.

I finished breakfast, said a few words to two city council members, and walked across the street to the gallery and site of my near demise.

✳   ✳   ✳   ✳

I stood in the center of the room and stared at the empty walls, walked around the near-empty space, and realized that hanging photos was the only task left. I decided it was time to finally address reality. The only thing slowing me down was fear. And if Charles were here, he would quote one of his long-dead presidents with something like, "The only thing to fear is fear itself." I didn't totally agree. I had a fear of falling off a cliff. It seemed that the fear wasn't of fear itself, but of falling and the abrupt and quite fatal encounter with the ground. Regardless, Charles would tell me to get on with it, overcome my fear of possible failure, and get the gallery opened. It was even more scary to be guided by the WWCD system: What Would Charles Do!

I also realized we weren't getting closer to a leading candidate for the murder of Palmer. To the contrary: the list was increasing. Steven Hogan, someone from the Preserve the Past gang, and now Harry Lucas. At least Amelia Hogan's name had been removed, I supposed.

Was last night really an attempt on our lives? I wondered. *Is my headache real or imagined?* I hung two photos and headed home.

CHAPTER 28

The next day began as a mirror image of the one before it, with an early morning call from Tammy.

This time, she reported on another of Amelia Hogan's children, Mike. It seemed Mr. Hogan, thirty-three, was single and considered himself God's gift to women. And as he gallivanted around in the social circles as a successful stockbroker, he allowed many women the opportunity of getting to know him. According to Tammy, his good looks, sharp features, slicked-back black hair, tall thin frame, and impeccable attire attracted a bevy of beauties.

"The interesting thing about Mike," said Tammy, "is he appears to be living over his head—way over his head. He definitely considers himself successful, but he hasn't been in the business long enough to accumulate the kind of wealth needed to join the expensive clubs in Charleston, play golf regularly on his home course at Kiawah, and drive a new Jaguar XK convertible. I hear that baby starts at more than eighty grand. Mr. Hogan's headed for a collision with the debt collectors."

"Sounds like we have another suspect," I said. "Anything else?"

"Now that you ask, yes. I thought I'd save the best for last. I was told by someone who attended two parties at Mike's condo that his rooms are chock full of antiques. My friend knows antiques, so she asked Mike where he found such exquisite pieces."

"From Julius Palmer," I guessed.

"You got it."

Amazing coincidence.

"Your information gets more and more interesting," I said. "Anything else about Steven?"

"Chris, I do have a job. I can't spend time helping you and your friends chase wild geese."

I was pressing my luck. "No, of course not. You've already been helpful."

I resisted the temptation to ask if either of the Hogan boys were experienced in furnace repair.

"Any idea when you'll have some free time?" I asked. I regretted it before I finished, but once I had started, I couldn't stop. "When you do, I'll come over. We can do whatever ... whatever you have time for."

"I really don't know," she replied after a noticeable hesitation that reinforced a couple of recent discussions—more accurately, mild arguments—we had had about her job interfering with us spending time together. "Got to run," she continued. "If I hear anything else, I'll let you know."

The recently forming hole in my stomach—or maybe in my heart—was beginning to grow.

Fully awake and in need of positive reinforcement, I headed to breakfast.

"Morning, Chris. Temple tells me you and your lovable, crude, loud Realtor friend were in yesterday," said Amber before I could be seated.

"If you mean Bob Howard, you're correct. We missed you."

More mindless small talk and good food filled my stomach and distracted me from the uneasy feelings I had about the state of my relationship.

"I heard a couple of things you might be interested in," Amber said between serving other customers. "Another one of our Canadian friends with a condo said he was looking for a designer to help with spiffing up his unit. Said he couldn't even pick out a tie to go with his coat, so he was clueless about fabrics and that other designer stuff. He asked me, of all people, if I could suggest someone. Can you picture me knowing many interior designers? Everything in my apartment came from Target, K-Mart, or Goodwill."

I was already zero for two in telling my friends about the "accidental" gas leak. Amber broke the streak. She listened patiently as I blurted out the story, right in the middle of whatever she was trying to tell me. I wouldn't have gone into so much detail if she had told me that she had already heard the story from two police officers, one city council member, and Cool Dude Sloan. Clearly, I had suffered a mental lapse about where I was and who I was talking to.

"So why didn't you tell me that before I told you the whole story?" I asked.

"Wanted to hear it from the horse's mouth—your version wasn't as exciting as most of the others," she said. "Speaking of parts of a horse, you're now the other end for not telling me sooner. I've been mad at you for two days, and I wasn't even here yesterday."

She finally smiled, gave me an awkward hug, and said she was glad I was okay. I reminded her she was telling me something about a Canadian.

"Oh, yeah," she continued. "He said he heard about one guy who was good, but someone said the designer had worked on another house, and some jewelry turned up missing afterward. No one could prove the designer was responsible, but who knows? I asked him if he could remember the name of the designer. He said no, but that he was obviously gay. Sounds like that Hogan guy to me."

I asked if she'd have a chance to talk to him again. She doubted it—thought he had gone back to Toronto over the weekend.

I changed the subject. "So, what did you do on your day off?"

I was surprised when she said she went to Charleston and walked through the historic market.

"I don't get out much," Amber explained, "and wonder about all the stuff my customers are talking about. Working six days a week and being with Jason after school doesn't give me much free time. I had a nice lunch at a cute little restaurant and just enjoyed being by myself. You know what I really liked?"

I shrugged.

"Having someone wait on me," she continued.

That glimmer of insight made me feel even better about Amber, and I had already been firmly ensconced in her camp to begin with. Before I left, she gave me another hug and said to take care of myself. I agreed that would be a good—very good—idea.

✳   ✳   ✳   ✳

Some piddling around the gallery, hanging a few more framed images, and walking over to the Folly pier to see if there were any winter photo opportunities had left me with the need for some human interaction. In my search for a couple of brackets to help manage my computer cables, I walked the few short blocks to Pewter Hardware. Larry's orange, late-model Ford pickup truck, with the Pewter Hardware logo proudly adorning the driver's door, was the only vehicle in the small, shell-covered parking lot.

"Hi, Chris. What can I do for you this afternoon?"

It was a nice feeling, being greeted by name in so many shops and restaurants. I kept thinking how often that happened in Louisville—less than once was my best estimate. I told Larry what I needed, and he showed me two options. I also asked if he'd seen Charles lately.

"No, but interesting you should ask," he said as he took my cash. "I expect him here any minute. We're going to order pizza, share a beer or two, and shoot the breeze about all the goings-on on Folly. This time of year, that'll be tough. Basically, nothing's going on. My business is nearly dead, at least until the middle of next month. You're welcome to join us. I don't close until six; Charles is bringing the pizza a little earlier. Have you got that furnace checked yet?"

I confessed I hadn't.

"Well, you should," he said emphatically. I agreed.

It was nearly five, so I couldn't come up with a single good reason not to participate in their party. I didn't try too hard.

Two hours later, it was dark along the eastern seaboard; Pewter Hardware had been closed for business; and Charles, Larry, and I were feasting on a second pepperoni pizza, the fifth or sixth bottle of beer, and the second half of a bottle of Cabernet. We had solved all the local governmental issues (throw out all the incumbents), listened to Charles's solution for bringing more tourists to the island in the dead of winter (open a Presidential Library for all the forgotten and ineffective dead United States presidents), and how to decrease the nation's dependence on cell phones (okay, we didn't solve that one).

The conversation turned more serious. Larry asked if we had made any progress on identifying who might have killed Palmer and tried to do Charles and me in.

"Larry," said Charles, "you're the expert on the criminal mind in this group. What do you think?"

"Thanks, Charles," he said. "I'm glad you keep reminding me of my ancient past."

"Not so ancient, if my memory serves me correctly," interrupted Charles, as he pointed his cane roughly in the direction of the Palmer house.

"Whatever," responded Larry. "From my limited—thank you, Lord—experience with convicted killers, they're not the brightest rats in the cage. While your tax dollars were providing my living quarters, I knew three of them. All three said—or tried to say, I guess, because I couldn't understand *what* they were saying most of the time—that they killed simply because it sounded like a good idea. No premeditation, no well-thought-out plan, and not even much interest in not getting caught."

"That's not the case with Palmer," I mused. "Someone knew his routines, knew enough not to be captured on the surveillance cameras at the bank when he made his daily deposit, knew how to make it appear to be suicide, and even knew enough about his fear of the water not to just take him to the end of the pier and push him off. Palmer would have resisted mightily and been in worse shape when they found his body."

"So the killer ranks somewhere between the putty-brains Larry shared living quarters with and a Rhodes scholar," said Charles after deep thought.

"Who are the most likely suspects?" asked Larry.

"Of course, Amelia would have been the top choice, if it weren't for her health," I said. "She claims she didn't know about the will, but we don't know that for sure."

"She wouldn't have had much to gain by killing him," added Charles. "Her days are numbered. Mr. Palmer promised to take care of her. And besides, she's a nice lady."

"Then her children have to be considered," I said. "Sandy has the most contact with her mother. She could easily have known about the will before anyone else; she works in the law office that drew it up. I don't guess any of us know much about her."

"There's gay Steven," said Charles. "Most likely, he'd been inside Palmer's house on more than one occasion, where he'd have easy access to the will. He may be the designer who is tied to the rumor about stolen jewelry. Not a ringing endorsement of his character."

"And we can't forget Mike," I added. "From what Tammy said this morning, he's living over his head and had been in Palmer's store. Again, someone with access to the will."

"In other words," said Larry, "we can't rule out any of the children."

"Add two more suspects to the entire Hogan family," I said.

"I suppose you mean Harry Lucas," said Charles. "He seems slimy enough to be the killer."

"Yes, that's one. I wouldn't think the entire case could hinge on his sliminess, but when you couple that with his budding relationship with Amelia and his seemingly dire financial straits, he moves to the top," I said and looked at Larry for his thoughts.

"Let me guess the other candidate," my new friend said. "The entire membership of Preserve the Past. They inherit more than three million dollars."

"That's who I meant ... but who would directly benefit?" I asked. "They get the money, but no one person will have access to it, and it seems unlikely the entire group would be involved."

"You say unlikely, but I say between likely and improbable," said Charles.

That sounded like something one of his dead presidents would have said … or someone in *Peanuts*.

"Those Preserve the Past folks occasionally act like tree huggers on water," he explained. "They're against development and most anything new, so I wouldn't exactly trust them to always do the right thing."

"I'll ask around some and see if any of my customers can tell me anything about the group; some are in it," said Larry. "But before we put the suspects in a lineup and convict one, there's another possibility that hasn't been mentioned. Over the years, I was in prison with hundreds of convicted felons. All but about ten said they were innocent—swore it almost daily. Assuming about two percent of those professing innocence were telling the truth—the first time for many of them—that meant there were five or so guilty people running around loose—"

"And your point?" interrupted Charles.

"My point is there's just as good a chance it was someone that we don't know a whit about. That's more likely. There are seventeen zillion people it could be, and we've only identified a few."

Mathematically, Larry was correct. But since we couldn't talk about each of those seventeen zillion people, we needed to concentrate on those we knew.

"Larry," said Charles. "I think you need to be an honorary member of the C&C Detective Agency. Your thinking as a criminal—retired, mostly—will give us a heads-up on the others, especially the police."

"I know you meant that as a compliment, but it didn't sound like it," said Larry.

The pizza was gone, and we'd dissected the suspects about as much as we could.

"Charles," I said, "I'm going to Charleston in the morning to pick up the framed photos. Want to go?"

"Sure. I think my calendar's got a hole in it," he said.

I thought his calendar through next February was one large hole; maybe he knew something he wasn't telling.

"I'll pick you up at nine. Now, gentlemen, I think we're all about three drinks beyond being able to solve this tonight."

CHAPTER 29

The mild weather continued. In fact, the forecast predicted unseasonably warm temperatures in the upper sixties, along with plenty of sunshine. As usual, Charles was ready and waiting for me outside his small, weather-beaten apartment. For someone who didn't wear a watch, he was always prompt—a trait I appreciated.

"So, what's our agenda?" Charles asked. "Looks like a great day. How about skydiving, or perhaps scuba diving, or maybe just visiting some dives?"

"Charles, did I forget something I said? I believe my offer was to go to Charleston and pick up some framed photos. I don't recall using the words 'diving' or 'dives.' I take it you want to do something other than play delivery person for Landrum Gallery."

"Look at the weather—can't get better in February," said Charles, making a point of gazing out each window. "I'd hate to waste a nice day on something as boring as a trip to a frame shop."

"Good point," I conceded. "Let's get the photos, then figure something out. You have your camera; surely we can find something to shoot ... without having to jump out of a perfectly good plane or go swimming with the fishes."

The frame shop was on the outskirts of Charleston, so we were there in minutes. I had already had several midsized photos framed, but I wanted eight of my best large images matted and framed.

We carefully loaded the eight frames, placing four in the trunk and the others in the backseat. I gulped as I paid the hefty invoice but was pleased with the work.

"Okay, Chris. What're we doing?"

I had hoped he had forgotten my promise; no such luck.

"I've never been to Fort Sumter, have you?" I asked.

"If you mean the historic fort off the Charleston coast named after the South Carolina Revolutionary War patriot Thomas Sumter, the one where the opening shots of the Civil War were fired in 1861 … no, never been there."

"And how many other Fort Sumters are you familiar with?" I asked the walking encyclopedia of trivia.

"None, but I hate to make assumptions," he said.

I assumed he was kidding.

Combining our collective ignorance, we figured the boat tours to Fort Sumter must leave from the Charleston Harbor somewhere near downtown. After a couple of dead ends and wrong turns, I pulled to the curb, and Charles asked a bread-truck driver for directions. This request was a blow to the male ego, but necessary.

Charles powered his window up. "Did you know Charleston has been named the best-mannered city in the great United States for the last umpteen years?"

"Did some president say that?"

"Nope, some chick named Marjabelle Young Stewart. She was some intergalactic expert on manners."

I was ready to comment about how unmannerly it was to refer to Ms. Stewart as "some chick," but I was busy pulling into the parking lot of the Fort Sumter tour boat building, near the aquarium at Liberty Square. Luck remained on our side: only a handful of tours ran each week during the winter, and we were thirty minutes away from one of today's two. Three families already waited. The difference was, they had actually planned to be there.

The boat providing the transportation for the two-and-a-half-hour tour had both an open and closed deck and looked as if it could carry a hundred or so sightseers. The weather was warmer than previous days, but the inside deck was the only place to be as we headed out in the choppy, windy bay. It was a bit strange sharing such a large boat with seven tourists.

Constant narration over the tinny speakers educated us about the history of the fort, the battery, and the Civil War in general, making the thirty-minute trip go quickly. I casually listened to what was being said; Charles took notes. No wonder he had so many quotes.

No sooner had we exited the boat than Charles began telling me about the fort. He spoke with the confidence of a tour guide, gesturing to the various points of interest with his handmade cane. I knew he was regurgitating what he had learned minutes earlier. The National Park Service owned and maintained the historic national monument. Some of the more significant areas had been carefully restored, but many nooks and crannies appeared as they had more than a hundred and fifty years ago. The pavement was uneven in large sections, and we had to be careful walking. For a half hour or so, Charles and I appeared to be competing to find out who could take the most photos. I focused on many of the small architectural details and rusting hardware on the oversized doors. Charles, in his customary fashion, spent more time photographing discarded ticket stubs on the cobblestone path.

One advantage of visiting historic and popular tourist sights in the winter was the lack of crowds. Often, I spent most of my time waiting for my fellow humans to move out of my viewfinder. The more I wanted them to move, the slower they walked. With only seven others touring, that was one problem I didn't have today. I didn't count Charles; he knew how to stay out of the way when I was concentrating on a subject. I tried not to step on his fascinating discarded ticket stubs and the highly photogenic empty Milk Duds box.

We boarded the boat for the trip back to Charleston and quickly moved to the enclosed—and heated—deck. We had on heavy jackets, but it was still cold. The wind washing across the bay seemed to pick up every degree of cold from the air and salt water.

Charles acted preoccupied for much of the trip back, then shared the conclusions of his deliberation. An interesting thought it was.

"Chris, Julius Palmer was thrown from a boat and not off the pier," he said, as he looked at the rough water passing beneath the tour vessel.

That had come out of left field—or, more correctly, out of starboard … or maybe port. I didn't know anything about boats.

"What makes you say that?"

Charles's eyes never shifted their gaze from the cold, dark waves. "If he had as much fear of the water as Bill said, no one could have gotten him to the end of the pier without being seen; he would've raised a ruckus, unless he was drugged. And there were no drugs in his body."

"What if he was restrained before going to the pier?" I asked, trying to shoot holes in his theory.

"He was a big guy, Chris. Don't you think someone would have seen two or more people carrying a body near the Holiday Inn and out the pier?"

"Makes sense."

"The only logical answer is a boat," he said, then finally looked my way. "Palmer could've been knocked out and put in a boat at countless locations; most docks would've been deserted. No one would have paid any attention to a boat a little ways offshore in the area of the pier. The killer could have easily pushed him overboard on the side facing Ireland. No one notices anything unusual, and the murderer is home in bed before the body is found. Yep, had to be how it went down."

Charles's crime narration was interrupted when the tour boat gently bumped the dock. He continued to stand by the rail and stare at the water.

The drive home was fairly quiet; we were mainly interested in getting warm. As we approached the island, Charles looked out the passenger window and asked if I knew the history of an old boat sitting along the side of the road.

He had finally caught me with a little local knowledge. "Sure. It was left there when hurricane Hugo devastated the island in the eighties," I said. "You and your strange fellow islanders just left it there and are constantly painting messages on it."

That part didn't take any brilliance, since the dilapidated vessel in question currently was emblazoned with "Happy Birthday, Donna!" It appeared to irritate him that I knew something—albeit only a little something—about Folly Beach that he hadn't told me.

"Well, speaking of boats," he said. "Since we detected that Mr. Palmer's killer threw him from a boat, all we have to do is figure out who has a boat."

"Wouldn't it be easier to figure out who doesn't?" I asked. "About everyone here has a boat, big or small. Look, you folks have so many boats, you leave them strewn along the road."

He hesitated longer than usual before speaking. "Do you have a boat? No. Do I? No. Does Larry? No. Does Amber? No. Does Bob? ... Well, I don't know if he does or not. If you want me to go on, I could name a flock of other landlubbers who don't have a boat."

"You're right, as usual. Shall we concentrate on the known suspects?" I asked, not wanting to hear his entire list of boatless residents.

"You're the detective."

Without debating my faux detective status, I continued. "First, we know Amelia's son Mike has one. I don't know for a fact, but if what Amber says is correct, most likely, her daughter Sandy has a boat. We know from the newspaper and what Bob said that Harry Lucas has two we know about. We don't know about Steven Hogan. And finally, we don't know exactly who, but I'd bet at least half the Preserve the Past gang have boats. How's that for a start?"

"Chris, I didn't say who did it, just how it was done. Do I have to do all the work? I'm only the *C* in C&C."

It was already late in the day; sunset rapidly approached, turning the sky from bright orange with rays of red to pink with streaks of gray. We decided to see if Larry wanted to join us back at my house for pizza. We stopped at the hardware store, and Charles ran in to ask. There must not have been much debate; he was back in seconds.

"He'll be over as soon as he coses—said he hasn't had any customers in three hours."

*   *   *   *

Two slices into the bacon, green olive, and pineapple pizza, Larry asked, "So now that we have all these likely candidates, what're we going to do about it?"

We were sitting around the old table in the kitchen over an extra large pizza box, beer cans, and an empty bottle of red wine.

"Since it's now *we*, what do you suggest? After all, Larry," said Charles, "you have the most experience with the criminal mind."

"I'd debate whether criminals actually have minds," said Larry. "But from my experience with law enforcement, we have a huge advantage."

"That being?" I asked, feeling the need to contribute something more than pizza and beer.

"That being, their hands are tied. They can speculate all day on who committed a crime but can't do anything more than ask questions and look for evidence. They can't just say, 'I think Kenny did it, so let's go beat a confession out of him, or let's break in his house and find the gun.'"

"So who do you suggest we go and beat up?" asked Charles, showing an unhealthy amount of enthusiasm.

"I think we should skip the beating-up part, but nothing's stopping us from some unorthodox snooping," said Larry.

I had been clearing the table and gathering the pizza box and beer cans to take it outside to the trash; Larry's comment halted me in my tracks.

"Would unorthodox snooping mean something like we—more correctly, you and Charles—did at Mr. Palmer's house ... B&E, you called it?" I asked.

"Exactly, except I would prefer to say 'slightly invasive investigation.'"

"I doubt that's what the judge would call it," I said. "Need I remind you what nearly happened at the Palmer estate when our friend Officer Robins stopped to chat?"

"Nearly happened, Chris," said Charles, scooting to the table as if he were ready to pounce. "What nearly happened when a huge meteor nearly destroyed all of us a few years back, what nearly happened when that tractor trailer came close to us in Charleston last year, what nearly happened, what nearly happened, what nearly happened—the fact is with all near happenings, what happened?" Charles continued without taking a breath. "I'll save you figuring it out: nothing. Nothing happened!"

"Charles," I said. "Other than being able to say the words 'nearly happened' a handful of times without breathing, I'm not sure that your argument is all that impressive. What's your point?"

"You don't have to write this down, although it's fairly profound: the point is, 'nearly happened' is another way of saying 'nothing happened'—nothing bad, anyway. So, since nothing happened, it seems like a good idea to carry out Larry's insightful, and maybe legally marginal, strategy. See?"

"Which part of breaking into someone's house or office would you consider to be only legally marginal?" I asked. "Never mind—I don't think I want to hear. So let's say I go along with this plan, gentlemen. Who do we consider to be the prime suspect?"

The debate on whom to address first continued through a bag of Doritos and half a package of Oreos—not counting liquid refreshments. The "final answer," as one television personality used to say, was Mike Hogan. I doubted we would be able to remember the reason we chose him when daylight arrived, but our plan was to visit—a euphemism for "break into"—his condo on Kiawah Island tomorrow while he was at work.

We didn't realize that this plan would change all of us. Whether we changed for the better or worse remained to be seen.

CHAPTER 30

As a seagull flies, Kiawah Island was less than a couple of miles from the end of Folly. Unfortunately, flight was not an option, so we had to wiggle over man-made roads for more than thirty miles to reach the bridge to the island of Kiawah.

Both Folly and Kiawah were small barrier islands separated from the mainland by narrow waterways. Kiawah Island was as similar to Folly Beach as oil to lemonade. Kiawah was best described as a controlled-growth, well-maintained, and beautiful enclave for the wealthy and wealthy imitators. Such a controlled environment was possible because the entire island had been owned by an individual, then sold to a development company in the 1970s. Kiawah had world-class golf courses; Folly didn't even have a miniature golf course. Kiawah had white-tailed deer in the woods; Folly's largest four-legged beasts were canines leading their owners around the streets. Kiawah had mansions on the ocean being torn down to build larger mansions; Folly had dilapidated garages torn down to build mid-priced resort duplexes.

I'd take Folly Beach any day.

The three of us left just after nine Friday morning. Charles had donned a blue and gray sweatshirt with a pirate on the front. It didn't identify itself, but the consummate sweatshirt collector told us it was the official shirt of the Seaton Hall Pirates. Heaven forbid Charles wearing anything unofficial! I asked if he couldn't find a shirt that had a burglar mascot with his hands cuffed in front of him. He mumbled something about state prisons not being able to use state funds for promotional clothing. Needless to say, he had his camera and cane.

Larry was more inconspicuous in a tan, down-filled jacket—no Pewter Hard-ware logo to be found. I had followed Larry's lead and tried to be unnoticeable in my dark brown winter coat.

Larry slid into the backseat of my Lexus.

"Now, remind me again," he said, "why we decided Mike was the killer."

Good question, I thought. I couldn't remember either.

"He needed the money more than the others," answered Charles. "Love or money, remember? The reason for most killings."

I hoped we had identified more solid reasons last night.

After the forty-minute drive through a rural countryside interspersed with small shopping areas; we crossed the waterway separating Kiawah Island from the rest of the United States. It was no more than a narrow creek. I felt self-conscious and anxious as we went through a security checkpoint. "Guilty" may have been a better description. I told the guard we were going to one of the hotels, rather than sharing our plan to break into the home of one of his protectees. I wasn't com-fortable lying, but both Larry and Charles said I'd made the right decision.

"Now that we're here," said Charles, "any idea where our young killer friend lives?"

"You should have asked the guard," deadpanned Larry, slipping down more than usual in the backseat. "You could have said, 'Excuse me, sir, where would we find Mike 'the Murderer' Hogan? We want to break into his house.'"

I was having a hard time keeping my sweaty palms on the wheel, so I appreci-ated Larry's dark humor. It broke the tension.

"Good suggestion, guys," I said. "But before we left the friendly confines of Folly, I did some keen detecting on my own: I found Mike Hogan's address in the phone book."

*   *   *   *

Mr. Hogan lived in Oceanview Villa—unit 223, to be exact. According to the map of Kiawah that the helpful, and duped, guard had given me, Oceanview Villa wasn't far from the security checkpoint. It was toward the ocean, off the main road, just past one of the island's pristine golf courses, and within easy walking distance to a small shopping area and the beach. I parked in the Straw Market Shops' lot to look as normal as possible—as normal as one could look with Charles, red gloves and all.

"Are we sure we want to do this?" asked Larry, sliding even farther down in the seat than before. He appeared to be having second, third, and fourth thoughts about our plan.

"Yep," said Charles with enough volume to have been speaking for both of us.

We sat in the car and reviewed our extensive and highly complex plan. Larry—reluctantly—was going to use his God-given talents and open the condo door. Then we were going to enter and find unequivocal proof that Mike Hogan killed Julius Palmer—preferably, photos of the murder and a written confession. The plan had made more sense last night; it must have been the pizza speaking.

Hogan's condo was on the second floor of an attractive, cedar-shingled structure. The entry to each unit in the three-story building was on the exterior walkway. The landscaping—overlandscaping to me—made it nearly impossible to see other buildings in the area. Good for a burglar.

We approached Mike's unit, and it was clear Larry wouldn't have to use his well-honed skills. It looked as if someone had already taken a crowbar to the door jamb at the lock. The door was almost completely closed, but a glimmer of darkness could be seen between the door and the frame.

Larry, the pro, told us to stand back, then rang the bell with his knuckle (to avoid leaving prints, I assumed). There was no answer. He pushed the door open about six inches with his left foot, then reached around the corner and turned on the light switch before going in. He then casually entered the door like he was home.

Casual abruptly ended.

"Damn, oh … holy damn! Damn! … Guys, come in slowly, don't touch anything, and close the door with your elbow. Don't touch anything … damn!"

To me, Larry's voice was slightly louder than a tornado warning siren, surely heard by everyone on the island and possibly as far away as Folly—as the crow flies. My imagination was running nearly as fast as my heartbeat.

I didn't know what Larry's expletives and instructions meant, but nothing about them sounded good. Charles and I moved from the safety of the balcony to the unknown of the condo.

The smell hit me before I saw anything out of the ordinary. The rancid smell of death struck my nose with a nearly physical blow. The blinds on the only window into the space were closed; I could barely see. Larry was about eight feet away, in the dining area of the open living space. He stood motionless, his arms pushed tight against the sides of his diminutive frame. Bile began rising from the pit of my stomach through my throat. I had to fight to keep from losing it. Thank God I was successful, because my next sight was of Mr. Hogan, on his back, eyes wide open, staring into oblivion; he was lying in a huge puddle of coagulated blood. It looked black in the dimly lit room. For some reason, I kept staring at the Lacoste crocodile logo on his light blue polo shirt.

"Oh, damn," said Charles, echoing Larry's observation. "What the hell happened?"

Charles had the wits to close the door behind him; the three of us kept looking from the lifeless form of Mike Hogan to each other, as if to say "Why me, Lord?" The silence was almost more frightening than Larry's expletives had been.

Larry walked through each room to be sure we were alone.

Looking around the room, I saw a couple of drawers open in the antique secretary in the corner, papers strewn on the floor. I offered, "Looks like a burglary interrupted by Hogan."

"This isn't exactly what I had in mind last night," said Charles, who slowly backed away from the blood pooled on the light hardwood floor.

Duh, I thought; repeating it out loud didn't seem necessary.

"As the Good Book says," offered Larry, as he returned to the scene of the crime, "for everything, there is a season. This is the season to get the hell out of here."

"Bible scholar Larry's right," said Charles, already turning toward the front door.

"You two leave slowly and go to the car like you were on a leisurely stroll," directed Larry. "I'll be there in a couple of minutes."

I took one last look at Hogan, the Lacoste logo, the antique secretary, and my freedom, then slowly left the condo.

Our journey on the wooden walkway through the small shopping area was as leisurely as walking barefoot on burning coals. We made it to the car, started the engine, and prayed for warm air from the heater. The smell of death was still in my nose, in my mouth, and all over my body. I hoped it was my imagination. Charles and I sat staring out the windshield; we prayed no police car pulled up beside us. We didn't speak for the five minutes it took for Larry to return—a near-record silence for Charles.

"Let's get off this damn island as quick as we can—driving slowly," said Larry as he delicately closed the rear door, almost as if he were afraid the noise would resurrect a migraine.

The rapid, slow drive back to the security checkpoint didn't take more than two minutes; it felt much longer. I could picture us being surrounded by police, sirens blaring, guns pointed at us, police helicopters overhead following our trail, and maybe even a Coast Guard gunboat waiting for us at the bridge off Kiawah.

At least that frightening fantasy got my mind off the smell of the condo that permeated the rest of me.

Much to my delight, and shock, we drove past the security checkpoint without so much as a glance, never seeing a single police car or helicopter. And the waterway separating Kiawah and the rest of South Carolina was so narrow and shallow, the Coast Guard gunboat would have been a canoe carrying someone with a bow and arrow.

What had we gotten ourselves into?

CHAPTER 31

We exited Kiawah and slowly drove into Freshfield Village, a modern retail and office complex rising out of the Low Country farmlands within minutes of the guardhouse. The relatively new resort shopping area was nearly deserted—not unusual in winter. Fortunately, several vehicles were littered about, so we weren't overly conspicuous. Larry suggested we would draw less attention in one of the restaurants rather than sitting in the car. We went into Newton Farms, a grocery and restaurant that resembled a Disney version of a European market. The last thing we wanted to do was eat, but we went our separate directions to the various food areas and got sandwiches and drinks.

I had hoped we didn't look it, but I felt we were more nervous than weeds at the Roundup factory.

"Any thoughts on what we should do?" asked Charles after we settled at a table far from the other diners.

"Chris, do you still have the map you got at the checkpoint?" asked Larry, who appeared cool, calm, and collected. "It should have a number for Kiawah Island Security."

Charles grabbed the edge of our small, polished aluminum table and looked at Larry. "I don't suppose we're going to turn ourselves in, are we?"

"We didn't do anything wrong—not too wrong, anyway. But I don't think that's the wise thing to do," replied Larry. "I'd suggest we drive to Charleston and find a pay phone to call the security office. They can call the police."

"Larry," I said, as calmly as I could manage, "you're the expert. What happened?"

"First, here's what didn't happen," he said, before taking another bite of his fish sandwich. He was the only one of us eating. "I don't think it was a burglary. Someone worked hard to make it look like he broke in the front door. The last few years, I've become an expert on nuts, bolts, shovels, and other hardware-store stuff. Before that, I was—and when needed, still am—an expert on locks, particularly door locks. There are several ways to unlock the one on Hogan's condo. It wouldn't be easy; it's really high quality. But of all the ways to beat it, the crowbar would be the least effective."

"So he let someone in," said Charles, his gaze moving slowly from left to right toward the few remaining shoppers.

"Yeah. The door wasn't the only indication of that," said Larry. "I know you saw the drawers open, and I don't know what was taken. I do know the bottom drawer wasn't opened. It still has a Cartier watch sitting there, plain as day: Roadster model, eighteen-carat gold with diamonds, lists for more than twenty grand."

"Whew!" said Charles with a slight smile. "Not something you sell in Pewter Hardware, is it?"

"Nope … learned that in a previous life."

"How long you think he's been dead?" I asked.

"From the looks of things and the smell, I'd guess a couple of days—definitely longer than twenty-four hours," said Larry.

*   *   *   *

"Charles, give me those sissy red gloves," said Larry as we pulled up to the side of a convenience store just north of downtown Charleston. He said he didn't want to leave fingerprints on the phone and promised his request had nothing to do with denying Charles his fashion statements. We had driven around for the last hour, trying to find a phone booth—more accurately, a phone booth without a surveillance camera nearby. I didn't realize how difficult a task that was in the age of cell phones. Phone booths were going the way of the American Motors' Javelin and the dollar gallon of gas.

Larry called the security department at Kiawah—a brief call. He said he told them, "Dead body, unit 223, Oceanview Villa, hurry."

I asked if he had been taking speech lessons from Dude, but my friends were a little too busy worrying about a stint in prison to get the humor.

I had always been happy to see the sign "Welcome to Folly Beach, the Edge of America," but never more so than today. I also had never been more anxious to take a shower. I dropped Larry at the hardware store, then Charles at his apartment. Little was said at either stop.

I stood in the shower, trying to wash the smell of death from my body. I wondered how a peaceful retirement plan that included buying a wonderful home (or home in a wonderful location), opening a modest photo gallery, enjoying the last third (I hoped) of my life, could be overshadowed by a murder, a close acquaintance in a mental hospital, and a whole passel of stranger than strange friends counting on me to solve a crime the police say never happened.

Something seemed wrong with that picture.

CHAPTER 32

"Chris, I'm over on Kiawah," said Tammy without preamble. "The police found the body of a white male in his midthirties. They said he'd been shot several times. That's all they're saying. PVA records show the condo belongs to Michael Hogan."

The call from Tammy had not come as a surprise. I'd rehearsed my surprise and shocked reaction. She bought it … I hoped.

"Detective Lawson caught the case," she continued. "All she said was she'd talk to me later. I'll let you know if I learn more. Hogan is Amelia's son, isn't he?"

I told her I knew she had a son named Mike living on Kiawah. All true, nothing but true—just not all the truth.

It was almost eleven before she called back. The body had indeed been Mike Hogan, son of Amelia. Detective Lawson had said it looked like a burglary gone astray. I didn't think it was prudent to share Larry's wisdom, so I listened as she said some valuables had been left behind, probably when the burglar had been startled by Hogan. His computer was gone, and so was his wallet and possibly cash.

I asked who'd found him. My fingers were crossed and my breathing erratic as I waited. She didn't know, but a couple of Hogan's co-workers had come to the scene. They told the detectives he hadn't been to work since Tuesday, but they weren't particularly worried. He had taken an occasional "extra few days off" to entertain lady friends. Karen—Detective Lawson—had said that no one from his office had seemed too distraught at his demise.

"Any idea when we can get together?" I asked Tammy, the question coming from the part of my brain that hadn't learned how to take a hint.

"No," she replied, followed by silence—a very powerful, telling silence.

After what had happened, I was blessed with a sleep-filled night.

✳   ✳   ✳   ✳

Saturday, the day most working folks looked forward to, and just another day for those of us among the unemployed, began as did most others. I knew I'd have to resort to deception when the topic of Mr. Hogan's death surfaced. On Folly, that shouldn't take long. I bundled up and headed to the Dog; might as well hit it head-on.

"It's good to see you so early," said Amber. Only two tables were occupied, so she had time to linger. "The usual?"

She knew me well enough to know the answer, but had extended the courtesy of asking. I nodded as I removed my jacket and moved into my home away from home.

"Have you seen the paper yet?" she asked. She leaned close, wearing a serious look on her face; sad words were soon to follow. "Amelia Hogan's son, Mike, was killed. They found his body yesterday."

I was surprised she had seen the story. She arrived at work long before the papers arrived on the island. I asked how she knew.

"The food delivery truck was here before we got the first edition of the paper. Apparently, it's big news, so the driver had to share. Don't tell anyone," she said. "He's one of my best sources."

"Of gossip, you mean?" I suggested before smiling.

"Why, Chris, you know better. If it's a fact, it can't be gossip. Isn't Mike one of the heirs-to-be of the Palmer estate?"

"That's my understanding. Did the paper say what happened?"

"Burglary, they believe. The article didn't say much more, and neither did my delivery man. Ask your girlfriend; she wrote the story."

Hoping to get off that topic, I asked Amber about Jason. She said her son was doing great in school. "You'd be amazed what doing some homework will accomplish," she said.

She added, "What's with you and Tammy? I haven't seen her around lately. You seem a little less feisty … almost a little sad?"

Amber was one of the most perceptive individuals I knew—frighteningly so. Fortunately, my breakfast was ready before I could answer. I didn't have a clue what my answer would have been.

She had returned with my traditional weekend waffle, and I deflected the conversation by asking if she had heard Charles's theory about a boat in the Palmer murder. She hadn't heard—hadn't seen Charles much the last week—but agreed his theory made sense.

"You know, Chris, it doesn't matter how much sense it makes. It still doesn't narrow the list of suspects much. We don't have boats, and neither does Charles, but about everyone else does."

Before she started listing everyone with a boat, our conversation was interrupted by Chief Newman, who entered, his professionally trained eyes surveying the diners. Looking for bad guys, I surmised.

"Morning, Brian," I said. "Have time for coffee or breakfast?"

"I have a minute," he said, and sat. Amber had seen him enter and brought him black coffee. She knew she didn't have to ask; if he wanted food, he'd let her know.

"Any news about the murder of Mike Hogan?" I asked. "Amber just told me about it."

"I've talked to Detective Lawson twice since late last night. I had to tell Mr. Hogan's mother," he said as he stared out the window. "Coming on the death of Julius Palmer, that was a tough assignment. Chris, I've done death notifications for years, going back to my career in the military; it never gets easier."

Chief Newman had always maintained a strong professional relationship with Detective Lawson, even though she was his daughter. In fact, their true relationship hadn't been known on Folly until last year. Folks had suspected for years that he had been having an affair with the young, attractive detective from Charleston. That had made better gossip, to be sure. More than a few people were disappointed when they learned the truth.

"Detective Lawson told me they're treating it as a burglary," he said as he turned his attention back to me and his coffee. "Hogan surprised the perp and lost his life for it."

"Any possible connection between his death and that of Palmer?" I asked, knowing his response.

"Course there's always a possibility, but I sure don't see any. Mike Hogan was seldom over here. Oh, and don't forget, Hogan was shot; Palmer committed suicide! You seem to keep forgetting that."

I was able to steer the rest of the conversation to the weather. I realized when I got home that enough time had elapsed to allow me to visit Bill. Visiting hours weren't until afternoon, so I called Bob Howard to see if he was available for lunch. I thought it would be interesting to meet him on his turf for a change.

"Chris, I'm mighty damn busy—trying to make a living, you know," barked the "lovable" old crank. "But as a favor to an old client, I'd allow you to buy me lunch."

I agreed to buy; he agreed to eat—a lot. We settled on a restaurant near the hospital. I'd never heard of it, but if it was Mr. Howard's recommendation, an interesting experience was sure to be had.

Al's Bar and Gourmet Grill was only a block off Calhoun Street, the main road to Charleston from Folly, and three blocks from the hospital. Calling it a hole in the wall would have elevated its status far beyond what it deserved. It was located in a concrete-block building it shared with a Laundromat. At some point in ancient history, the building had been white. The lower half of the restaurant's large plate-glass window had been painted black to provide privacy for the diners. The neon sign wasn't on at that time of day; I bet it wouldn't be on after dark either.

I saw Bob's car on the street just past the building. It wasn't hard to spot; the purple color was the first hint, and the retracted convertible top was just a bonus clue. After all, it must have been a sweltering fifty degrees.

I entered and stood in the doorway for a few seconds to allow my eyes to adjust to the lighting—more accurately, the lack of lighting. The illuminated ambience was provided primarily by a Budweiser and a Budweiser Light neon sign behind the bar. The unapologetic country sounds of George Jones telling someone he stopped loving her today sweetened the air. The luncheon crowd consisted of Bob, seated in the only booth, two elderly black gentlemen, at one of six tables, a bartender, and me.

I had complete confidence the "Al's Bar" part of the name was accurate. The "Gourmet Grill," I suspected, was considerably less literal. I told my taste buds I'd withhold judgment until I partook of these supposedly gourmet delights. After all, Bob wouldn't be here if Al didn't have good pies, and maybe food.

"That's the best damn country song ever written. The Possum sure knows how to wring every tear out of a note," said Bob—not the normal welcome, but I'd never said Bob was normal. He had a Bud in his left hand and a French fry in his right as he leaned heavily against the torn, black vinyl booth back.

Truth be known, I agreed with Bob about the song. One of the few things Tammy and I shared was a love for country music, particularly classic country.

Bob seemed slightly disappointed that I knew what he was talking about. I had finally learned that most of his repartee was to keep people off guard, so he could stay in control.

"So, Bob, other than a large portion of possum, what would you recommend at this fine dining establishment?" I slid into the booth opposite the disheveled, lounging Realtor.

"Cheeseburger. Not only would I recommend it, it's required. Everything else tastes like shit. Don't even think about any of that vege-fuckin'-tarian stuff or rabbit-food lettuce crap. Better order the cheeseburger well done—that botulism stuff isn't out of the question either. French fries are good too; these are the big fat ones, not those skinny-ass faux fries the fast-food restaurants push off on you."

See, Bob *did* know Charleston's finest eating establishments. And with such an extensive menu, there'd be something for everyone.

"The beer helps keep the germs at bay," he continued. "For you, they have some of that fine wine in a box."

He didn't wait for my decision between cheeseburger, cheeseburger, or cheeseburger—all equally attractive options. He yelled to Al over George crooning about someone being carried away, "Cheeseburger and fries for my scrawny friend here. All this on one check—his." His arms were spread so wide, I feared I was buying lunch for everyone in Al's!

While Bob shared his charm with Al, who appeared more intent on wiping something off the ancient bar, my eyes were finally adjusting to the red neon glow of the room. I looked around at the cheap pine walls that displayed faded nature prints. From the age of the dark wooden frames, I knew they couldn't have come from the nation's largest retailer. Ol' Sam Walton probably hadn't been born when they were bought. I wondered where one bought cheap art in those days. It was my first visit, so I decided not to ask Al. Besides, I didn't care.

Al looked as well-worn as his yard-sale tables and chairs, with his gray hair; skin the color somewhere between dark brown and light black, if that was possible; and a coffee-stained smile earned over his seventy or so years. If I had been in a generous mood, I would have said this bar—and hopefully grill—had character.

"When you stop your damn surveying of the restaurant, you can tell me what I did to deserve the lunch invitation," Bob said, interrupting my appraisal of the near-antique furnishings.

"Bob, why do I need a reason? Couldn't I just call and want to spend an enjoyable lunch with a friend?"

"Of course you could, but you damn sure didn't. Do I look like I just fell off a camel? What's with the invite?"

Bob looked more comfortable than I'd ever seen him, and that was saying something. The bartender/chef paid attention to him when he spoke. His beer was readily available. And he didn't have to impress anyone in this island of casualness. Al delivered my well-done cheeseburger; on the jukebox, John Wesley Ryles was lamenting the loss of his girlfriend "Kay," who had found success in the world of country music while he was stuck in Music City, driving a cab. And Bob was patiently—for Bob, anyway—waiting for my explanation. I loved every second of it.

"Nothing complicated," I confessed. "I was coming over to visit Bill and realized the only time I'd ever seen you was on Folly. Just thought it'd be nice for us to have a casual meal."

"In other words, Tammy wasn't available." Bob began laughing heartily, his abundant stomach peeking out between two buttons of his bright yellow, almost florescent shirt.

He had me; I shrugged and tried to say his company was also important. I didn't want to sound mushy—I knew I'd regret it if I did.

"Well, whatever your damn reason, thanks for calling," he said after his laughing subsided. "Besides, I have a little information for you about Mr. Lucas. Did you know I met him once?"

"Harry Lucas?" I asked, slightly confused—a state that Bob had instilled in many.

"Shit, Chris, pay attention. Not Lucas, Roy Acuff." He tilted his head toward the jukebox, hinting for me to pay attention to the music.

Excuse me, I guess I had fallen in the trap of actually listening to Bob, thus missing the jukebox telling us to listen to the jingle, rumble, and roar.

"So, you met Roy Acuff."

My counseling training many decades ago allowed me to make such profound statements.

"Yep, one of the most memorable moments of my life. Back in the seventies, Betty and I went on a vacation over to Nashville. She hates country music and was angry most of the trip, but she put up with it and went. She spent her day shopping in the humongous Opryland Hotel. I went next door to Opryland USA. It was in its heyday. The idiot bean counters from the damn megacompany that bought the complex later ruined it by turning that fantastic park into a giant outlet mall." Serious irritation, bordering on anger, began to show in his eyes—much more than from his mouth.

"Remember, Bob," I soothed, "I'm from just up the road from Nashville. Opryland was one of my favorite vacation spots."

"Damn, Chris. This is my story—not about you!"

Now I knew who put all the money in the jukebox and chose the country classics. *Wonder what Al thinks of the selections?*

"You know," continued Bob, calming slightly. "Roy Acuff was the king of country music—brought it to the music-illiterate northerners. Opryland thought so much of him they actually built a big ole brick house for him to live in right in the middle of the theme park."

I knew that—I'd even seen it once—but I didn't want to interrupt again. It was Bob's story.

"I had mixed feelings about that—didn't know if Mr. Acuff was being treated as a legend or a resident in a damn zoo. Regardless, I was walking around the park and saw him just standing by a wall. He was as casual as all get out, just leaning there watching the people. No one else was around." Bob paused and stared out the half-covered front window, clearly gazing at the past. "I walked up and told him it was an honor to meet him, and that I'd enjoyed his songs for years. I told him what he meant to his genre of music. He gave me his world-famous grin and said thanks. He asked if I wanted an autograph. I said no, just meeting him was enough. It was like meeting God, and I wouldn't ask for his autograph either. Truth be known, I had tears in my eyes."

I was triply surprised: first, that Bob knew the word "genre"; second, for his sharing such a personal story; third, that we shared a love for country music. Of course, I couldn't tell him I was impressed—much too warm and fuzzy for the burly curmudgeon.

"Rumor on the street has it, he's trying to sell two of his three remaining shops," mumbled Bob through a mouthful of fries.

He must have meant Lucas and not Roy Acuff. If railroad tracks were as disjointed as Bob's train of thought, Acuff's "Wabash Cannonball" would have derailed long before reaching St. Louis, Chicago, or any of its other destinations.

"Where'd you hear that?"

"I may not be a detective—and neither are you, by the way—but I have contacts," he said. "People just love to talk to me and tell me stuff."

I'd love to meet some of these folks, I thought; *I wonder what planet they immigrated from.*

"He's telling people he wants to concentrate his energies on one pawnshop—the one in town," Bob continued. "Complained about the management at the other two. I don't believe it for a damn second; it's about money, always about money. He ain't making enough of it—not enough to meet his payroll, pay rent, and buy diamonds and other baubles from poor folks who can't keep their lights on, so he can sell them for obscene prices. If pawnshops weren't in buildings, and I sold buildings for a living, I'd classify them as the bottom-feeders of the retail trade. But I'm too damn nice to say that."

I shared Charles's theory about Palmer being thrown from a boat somewhere near the pier to make his death look like a suicide. Bob said that would rule out Lucas's two boats; both had been too large to go unnoticed that close to shore, even at the semideserted beach front. He reminded me that the large Holiday Inn sat near the pier, with each room overlooking the beach. Even with a handful of rooms rented, someone could have seen something. And if they didn't, Palmer would have wondered anyway and not risked bringing one of his large crafts. He might be broke, but he wasn't stupid. Once again—a streak by now—Bob made sense.

"Tell you what I'll do," Bob offered. "Tomorrow, I'll find out if he has any smaller boats."

"Tomorrow?" A puzzled look surely appeared on my face.

"Yes, tomorrow, my detective-photographer friend. I thought I'd save the best for last," he said. He sat erect, hands on the table; ignored the French fries (finally); and spoke in a low, conspiratorial tone. "I'm meeting with Lucas to try to get the listing on his buildings. He wanted to meet with me on a day off so his staff, as few as there are now, don't find out about the sale. Of course, they already know; everyone else does. I consider it my duty to the world of trade to get two more damn pawnshops off the face of the earth. I'll sell the two shops to some Asians or Mexicans to open restaurants. Shortage of those, you know."

"What's your plan?" I asked, giving him my full attention. "Ask him if you can have the listing on two buildings, and then say, 'Oh, by the way, have any small boats I can sell for you?'"

"Thought about being more subtle than that, but that's not a bad idea. Want to go into the real-estate racket?"

In the spirit of sharing, I gave in and told him about the gas leak and Charles's theory about someone wanting to do us in. Bob said he wasn't surprised that someone would see us as a "pain in the ass," but thought the chief's theory made more sense.

I paid for our lunches and left a substantial tip for waiter/bartender/owner Al. If for nothing else, he deserved it for having to listen to all the country music; although, it was his jukebox. He could have changed it whenever he chose. He must not have wanted to lose Bob as a customer—right!

We walked out together to the sounds of Patsy Cline's accurate summation of my luncheon experience: "Crazy."

CHAPTER 33

Meeting Bob had been the perfect warm-up to visiting a mental hospital. To say I was anxious about visiting Bill would be an understatement. Even finding him was a challenge. He was housed at the Institute of Psychiatry, part of the Medical University of South Carolina. The facility was several buildings away from where Bill had been admitted.

I hadn't been sure what to expect, but I was pleasantly surprised by the institute. My only experience in psychiatric institutions was in the midsixties, when I was a psychology major. Visiting the local facility, which was still called an insane asylum back then, was not unlike stepping into the 1970s movie *One Flew over the Cuckoo's Nest*. Orderlies in dirty white uniforms had appeared to care nothing about the hundreds of "patients" who roamed aimlessly around in dirty rooms and who uttered words and sentiments in the loudest incoherent voices possible. A few hours in those facilities would have turned the pope suicidal.

I knew my friend was in good hands from my first contact with a receptionist, to Bill's caseworker, to the cheery, bright, spotless visitors' center.

My second pleasant surprise after stepping into the uplifting environment of Bill's involuntary home was Bill.

"Chris, it's great to see you," he said, exuding cheerful sincerity. He was followed into the room by his caseworker, Anthony, who said we could have some privacy and quietly left us in a small interview room.

Our conversation was awkward, but pleasant. Neither of us knew what to say or how to address the situation. We talked about the food (good), the contacts with the staff (very helpful), and the contacts with other patients (strange). Bill hesitated slightly longer than I had been used to between my questions and his answers.

The tenor of the conversation had turned sad when he talked about how much he missed his students. He had lived to teach and didn't know how much longer he could stay away from them. With tenure, the college had to keep him on, but he worried they may take him out of the classroom. I encouraged him not to think about it and concentrate on what the therapists asked him to do.

"The psychiatrist—a nice fellow once you figure out his strong accent—says I should be ready to leave by the end of next week," He sat up straighter and looked more alert. "After seeing some of the folks in here with real illnesses, I feel fortunate to only have a little bout of depression."

His logic was impeccable, as usual—his usual, from what I remembered. He looked forward to discharge and said he'd need to continue therapy on an ongoing basis, something he could do after class. He thanked me two more times for visiting before we ran out of conversation. I said I'd be back sometime during the week to take him home. We shook hands, his grip strong, his back more erect—good signs. I had almost made it out of the room without any mention of what put him there in the first place—almost.

"Chris, have you found who killed my friend?"

Before I could answer, he said there was no need for me to say anything. He knew I'd let him know when I "solved the murder." When—not if. *Pressure?* I thought. *What pressure?* I chose not to mention the death of Mike Hogan. Besides, I had no idea where it fit.

✳   ✳   ✳   ✳

I was usually quick out of bed in the morning, so I was a little surprised when I spent more time looking at the ceiling than at the coffeepot, paper, or outside world. I rehashed the conversations with Bob and Bill. If one of my colleagues in my former life had told me six months ago I would be spending a day at a bar—excuse me, bar and grill—with a nutty real-estate agent talking about Roy Acuff and at a psychiatric hospital talking with a clinically depressed friend about a murder, I'd have suggested he seek psychiatric assistance himself. Was this what I'd looked forward to in retirement? Oh, well; they said one should keep busy. No chance of me withering away—getting killed, maybe, but not withering away.

I walked into the Dog after forcing myself to get out from the security of the covers and was greeted by one of the warm feelings of retirement—or any age, for that matter. Amber presented me with her best smile (quite beautiful, I must add), an offer of coffee, and a comfortable seat at my favorite booth. I waved to Dude, who was seated in his regular spot, and nodded to Buddy Miller and his friend Arnold, who was looking through the want ads in the paper—no doubt looking for items with wheels to buy. Life was good.

I ordered "The Loyal Companion," more famously known as bacon, eggs, toast, and orange juice back in landlocked Kentucky, and someone's leftover issue of the Charleston newspaper. One advantage of arriving a little later on Sunday was not having to contribute eight quarters to the profits of the conglomerate that owned the paper. I didn't see Tammy's byline on the front page, so I skipped to the sports section.

I was greeted by Chief Newman before I was able to get through most of last night's college basketball scores; I offered him a seat, and he accepted. This exchange was sometimes a good sign because of our growing friendship, and occasionally a bad sign, especially when he took on his professional police chief voice.

This was one of those days.

"I keep hearing a rumor around town," he started, without any friendly preamble, "that you and your merry band of misfits are nosing around in the murder of Julius Palmer."

He stared directly in my eyes without blinking, and his tone of voice combined with the cold stare made it abundantly clear he wasn't pleased.

"Chief, I don't exactly know what you've heard, but I would agree my acquaintances could easily be construed as misfits."

I had tried to add my best smile after "misfits." It failed to impress.

"You know exactly what I mean," he said, still maintaining his gaze and ignoring the coffee Amber gingerly placed in front of him. "Chris, first, there is no murder. How many ways can I say it? And second, even if there was, you're only asking for trouble trying to play detective, especially with the likes of Bob, Charles, and Amber. And if I hear you've recorrupted Larry LaMond, you'll be spending the rest of your retirement anywhere but here—that's a promise."

His tense, rigid body relaxed slightly after he made his official warning; he slid into his role of budding friend and asked about Bill. I shared I'd seen him yesterday. Brian was pleased, even relieved, to hear the positive prognosis.

He also asked if I'd had the furnace checked by a professional. I said yes—not quite a lie. He hadn't specified what kind of professional. Larry's previous career might qualify.

We talked about the chief's favorite college basketball team, the University of South Carolina, and I countered with statistics on the most winning program in history, my University of Kentucky Wildcats. He had heard enough on that touchy topic and changed the subject.

Chief Newman had been hard to get to know, but once the cracks in his facade opened a little wider, he was a kind, caring, and highly competent police chief. I hoped he didn't know everything my "merry band of misfits" had considered.

To be honest, I wished I didn't know either. The future was best left to fortune-tellers; I doubted mere mortals could handle it.

CHAPTER 34

"It's time you taught me more photo stuff," said Charles as he sauntered into the gallery as if he owned it. He was carrying his cane in his left hand, camera in the right. "I looked for you at the Dog, but Amber told me you just left. I told her to worry not—I'd find you, because we needed to walk around this fine island and shoot the breeze ... and some photos."

Charles had been persistent in asking for lessons. I'd accumulated enough knowledge about photography to teach him basic techniques and composition; he'd been a quick study.

The winter sun scooting along close to the horizon heightened the intensity of the afternoon coastal blue sky; the temperature hovered in the upper forties. With the proper clothing and motivation, it was quite comfortable.

"Afternoon, Charles," I said as I began layering jackets. As the British said, there was no such thing as bad weather, just inappropriate clothing. I planned to remedy that. Charles was already tapping the old wood floor with his heavy cane—probably expressing impatience in Morse code. I locked the gallery, and we walked toward the Atlantic, then west on Ashley Avenue. Even in midafternoon, the low source of winter illumination provided interesting shadows and pockets of light. In other words, it was a great day to take photos.

"Charles, I'm still amazed at how quiet and serene Folly is in the off-season."

"Yeah," he replied. "In a couple of months, these streets will be jammed with tourists and folks from Charleston looking to spend time at our alluring beach." He picked up his gait, the rhythm of the tapping cane on the pavement interrupting the silence.

Charles, of course, continued to take advantage of the quietness to share his wisdom and experiences—all slightly off kilter from most I had had over the years. I learned more about his skydiving experiences; he described them as moments of "great weakness" or "great strength." I learned he had become friends with attorney Sean Aker during these jumps.

"Chris, I'm sad things aren't working out with Amber … I'm beginning to think that'll always be the case with my love life."

"I'm sorry," I said.

"We're better wired to be brother and sister," he concluded as he diverted his gaze away from me and acted as if he were photographing a discarded, frayed, brown sock.

We walked another block or so without speaking. I realized he was becoming a good photographer. I was seldom sure about his subject choice but was impressed with his work ethic, attention to detail, and ability to see not only what was apparent to everyone's eye, but from his unique perspective. I was beginning to think I'd devote a section of the gallery to his images of used candy wrappers, smashed soft-drink cans, an occasional example of island roadkill, and now a Gold Toe sock. I'd seen worse in galleries.

The sun took its winter path over the island, illuminating the marsh side. We crossed the narrow part of Folly to the old Seabrook property, named after an early landowner who had dominated the real-estate holdings. Much of the area was now covered with McMansions, but still surviving among them were enclaves of timber, marshland, and remnants of a time gone by.

We took advantage of the late-afternoon light and captured several images that could as easily have been taken two hundred years ago. I enjoyed those scenes, and Charles didn't appear to mind the lack of photographable trash.

The sun and the temperature appeared to be racing to see which could go down the quickest. Neither outcome would be to our liking; we headed toward our respective domiciles. It was nearly dark, but both of us knew our way around after making this walk many times.

We strolled down the center of the street—our typical path, since sidewalks were few and far between.

"I bought a new old book at the Twice-Read Store last week," he said as he put the camera strap over his right shoulder with an air of finality. It was too dark for more photos. "It's a biography of Woodrow Wilson. I'm anxious to read it and, hopefully, learn some quotes from another United States president."

"That's just what I wanted to hear," I said in mock—well, maybe semi-mock—exasperation. "Why don't you …"

The sound of a large engine drowned out my insult.

What followed simply happened; there was no time to think.

I looked over my left shoulder and saw a dark pickup truck barreling toward us. Its headlights were off; only the very last of the sun's dying rays provided illumination. The massive projectile couldn't have been more than forty yards behind us, but I couldn't see the driver. The wide tires were pointed directly at Charles and me. There was no swerving, no screech of brakes, not even the warning of a horn. We were the target. I knew how deer felt standing in the middle of the road—headlights in the eyes or not.

I grabbed Charles's arm and yanked him to the right. He fell toward me, almost out of the road. His camera followed, still attached to the strap over his arm. I abandoned my tripod and rolled toward the grass berm a foot away. Charles dropped his cane and followed. The truck swerved toward us, still with no apparent intent to brake. The only thing between us and oblivion was a large, rusty, steel newspaper stand. Our guardian angel was a huge boat anchor holding the Charleston *Post and Courier* box; Charles and I would have been Folly's latest roadkill if the anchor hadn't been there. The driver yanked the steering wheel to the left to avoid the nautical barricade gloriously standing between the truck and the two of us.

The truck was gone as quickly as it came; it took longer for us to regain our regular breathing pattern. We had layered for winter, or our scuffs would have been much worse. My right knee hurt, and Charles complained of a pain in his left side; he had landed on his Nikon.

We were still sitting on the grass beside the lifesaving anchor. I was beginning to feel the cold ground through my slacks.

I called the Folly Beach Police Department, even though I figured it'd be an exercise in futility. My phone had fared well despite its abrupt contact with the pavement. I laughed as I punched the Send button. Ever the observant one, Charles asked what was so funny.

"Funny isn't the right word—although I'm not sure 'ironic,' or 'absurd,' or 'sad,' or 'scary' would be better," I said. "I'm laughing because I was wondering how many other residents of Folly Beach have the police department on their speed dial."

"I'd add 'pitiful' to the list," said Charles without hesitation. "You know, we've been on the ground together twice in the last few days. I don't have anything against you, but I'm not comfortable with this position."

I totally agreed.

I gave the dispatcher a brief explanation of what happened and was promised an immediate response. He didn't disappoint. I punched the Off button, and before Charles could retrieve his cane, which had wisely landed between the truck's tires, I heard the sirens of one of Folly's cruisers leaving city hall, only six blocks from our resting place. I glanced around and wasn't the least bit surprised to see no one looking out a window, driving nearby, or out walking a dog. Where were witnesses when you needed them? Winter at the beach.

*   *   *   *

Officers Robins and Spencer both exited the white Crown Victoria; the mesmerizing, flashing blue lights of the empty car reflected eerily off the nearby windows. Charles and I were both standing—more like leaning—against the anchor. I quickly told the officers what had happened. Charles and I combined all our knowledge and impressions of the event and told the officers the truck wasn't old or new, was maybe dark blue, black, brown, or green, with its headlights off; and we had no description of the driver.

"It didn't have any brakes, either ... the damn idiot didn't put a foot on the pedal," added Charles.

Officer Robins made some comment to the effect that with such a good description, they'd have the vehicle in a matter of seconds. From our limited contacts, I'd not noticed a sarcastic streak in him until now. The more diplomatic Spencer promised to stop all pickups on the island, but shared his suspicion that ours was well on its way to Charleston and points beyond. And, he added, there were a thousand places to hide a pickup truck, even on Folly. I knew that was accurate.

Robins speculated that our perpetrator was a drunk driver who hadn't seen us. Neither Charles nor I commented. We graciously accepted their offer of a ride home. Charles got out at my house. It was around seven—dinnertime—and we agreed a pizza would help soothe some of our wounds. Neither of us wanted to be alone.

CHAPTER 35

We were halfway through a large pepperoni and green olive pizza when Chief Newman knocked on the door. As strange as it seemed, I was relieved when he agreed to help us finish the doughy delight.

"You two okay?" he asked.

"Physically, just a few bruises," I said. "Emotionally, I don't think we're in good shape. It's not a very secure feeling, knowing someone tried to make us roadkill."

"Our cameras survived with minor bruises too," added Charles between bites. The chief didn't seem terribly concerned about the condition of our photo gear.

"Guys, there's no reason to think it was intentional," offered the chief. "This time of year, there's not much to do here. Drinking replaces surfing, sunning, and sailing for some. Too much drinking is a lot more potent than too much sunburn—it can affect more than the recipient."

"Brian, do you really believe it was simply a drunk driver?" I asked.

"Not really, Chris. I was opening with that company line to put you at ease. Did it work?"

He had a grin on his face, but I could tell it didn't run deep.

"Not yet," I answered. "Want to try harder?"

"It wouldn't do any good, would it?" he asked. Charles and I remained silent, staring at him. "Didn't think so. I got a call a few minutes ago from Detective Lawson. I called her as soon as I heard about your encounter. There was a report this afternoon of a stolen navy blue pickup—a 2003 Ford 150. It was taken from the parking lot at Patriots Point Naval and Maritime Museum in Mount Pleasant. The truck belonged to a couple from Connecticut touring the Low Country. They had left it unlocked—told the responding officer they thought the parking lot would be safe, since there were so many military ships there. Something about a sense of security. And people talk about the intelligence of southerners." Brian shook his head.

Charles chimed in as he reached for the last slice of pizza. "Don't suppose the person who borrowed the truck returned it to the Connecticut geniuses and turned himself in?"

A bit optimistic, I thought.

"No such luck. While I don't agree with the drunken-driver theory, I don't know of any compelling reason someone would target you two. That is, unless the rumors I've been hearing are true ... remember? Rumors that you're snooping around into something that's none of your business?"

"Chief—Brian," I tried, in my usual struggle with formality, "there's no doubt in my mind we were the target of that truck. Charles, agree?"

"No doubt," he mumbled, words competing with a mouthful of pizza.

I couldn't tell if Charles was feeling the accusatory stares of the chief as much as I was.

"What makes you so sure?" asked Brian.

"It was dusk," I said. "We were walking back from the west end of Ashley Avenue. We'd walked at least six blocks without seeing any vehicles parked on the road; believe me, we would've noticed. The truck had to be waiting on a side street. We heard the engine just before it was on us; it couldn't have come from far down the road. If it hadn't been for the seafarer's symbolic anchor, it would've swerved and not missed. We were supposed to be the bug on the windshield."

"Splat," said Charles as he clapped his hands together.

I gathered no United States president had ever been the near victim of a hit-and-run by a pickup.

Brian, leaning toward us with both elbows on the table, didn't pursue the logical alternative. He knew it, we knew it—no need to rehash it. The pizza was finished, and so were we. Brian offered Charles a ride home. I was surprised when he accepted; Charles was more shaken than he let on.

After doing the dishes from supper—by which I mean throwing out the pizza box, paper plates, and empty Diet Dr. Pepper cans in the waist-high Rubbermaid trash container by the back door—I settled in for a restless night of watching television. After an hour of watching the trials and tribulations of the gang from

Wisteria Lane on *Desperate Housewives*, I felt better about my minor complications. I still had that gnawing feeling that they weren't over yet.

Sometimes, one doesn't want to be right.

CHAPTER 36

The ringing of my cell phone rudely woke me at six fifteen. Phones are not known for bringing good news that time of day, so I was relieved to hear Bob's voice—sort of.

"You're a fuckin' disaster magnet," he began. "If you can manage to stay alive long enough, you'll be worse than Hugo."

"Morning, Bob. Thanks for your concern. I assume you're referring to our run-in with a truck."

"You're damn right. I had to hear it from Louise, who heard it on the police scanner. Shit, you didn't even give me the courtesy of a call."

Louise was the nearly eighty-year-old receptionist/office manager/gatekeeper at Island Realty, the firm Bob "worked" out of. She was some undeterminable relative of his. Rumors had it she had taken a liking to me when I visited the office during my visit to the island last year. Shortly after that, I had started calling her "Aunt Louise," although not to her face. Her scanner habit was a new one to me.

"Okay, okay," he said. "Now, with all that gooey sympathy shit out of the way, can I have the listing on your house when you turn up dead?"

"How could I resist such a nice request? I'll start reworking my will when I get you off the phone."

"That's what I like to hear. I love this early morning marketing. Oh, yeah, I almost forgot: are you okay?"

Bob was being almost sensitive; I wasn't going to spoil the mood by mentioning it.

"Fine, I guess. We weren't hurt but definitely were in someone's sights. On that topic, did you learn anything from your new best friend, Harry Lucas?"

"In fact I did. I learned that next to the television remote control, pawnshops are one of the greatest creations known to man ... at least according to Mr. Lucas, my professional acquaintance, not friend. I learned that pawnshops—in general, not his—have been around for three thousand years. I even learned that the nursery rhyme 'Pop Goes the Weasel' is referring to pawning. Apparently, a weasel is a shoemaker's tool, and 'pop' means to pawn. Go figure."

"Fascinating," I said, mixing sarcasm with a yawn.

"I'm telling you this now because I'll forget it by noon," Bob continued, ignoring my yawn-afflicted comment. "I even learned why the pawnshop has the three gold balls as its symbol ... don't remember why now. Your buddy Charles would've loved all that trivia shit."

"I should've been more specific," I interjected. "Did you learn anything related to the murder?"

He coughed a couple of times and continued. "Patience, my young friend. I'm leading up to it. I thought you'd like a history lesson about pawnshops first; I overestimated your curiosity. Disappointingly enough, Lucas didn't confess to the murder. Didn't even act like there was one, actually. I did learn he's in a heap of financial trouble. His divorce nearly wiped him out. From what I can tell, he's living on borrowed time and money. He does have a good amount of equity in the two shops he's selling. He can lower the price substantially to unload them. Two banks are ready to call their loans; maybe by spring."

"Anything about his relationship with Amelia?" I asked. I had moved into the kitchen and was trying to pour water into my underused Mr. Coffee.

"He, of course, expressed deepest sorrow in the death of Mike, despite his demeanor otherwise—said Amelia had suffered enough the last few months. And this is where it gets interesting: I casually mentioned you and that you had met Amelia after Julius's death. I told him I'd heard that he and Mrs. Hogan were dating. Guess what?"

"What?" I asked, just to irritate him.

"Don't interrupt," he said. "He knew all about your visit. He knew that you and some others he didn't know by name thought the death wasn't suicide. He seemed irritated that you were nosing in where you shouldn't be. That's a fairly common comment I hear about you, by the way."

"That's interesting, especially since we didn't say anything to Amelia about Bill's theory on the cause of death. Did he make any comments about Julius's death?"

"Yeah, said of course it was suicide, and that everybody knows that. I sort of didn't want to contradict him on that one. He did appear to sincerely care about Amelia—as sincerely as a pawn broker can. He did make one very fine business decision yesterday."

"Let me guess. You're now his Realtor."

"The longer you're around me, the smarter you get. Oh, yeah, one other thing: My new client doesn't have two damn boats. He has three. You know about the two large ones, his party boat and the oceangoing speedboat. He says he likes the peacefulness of fishing in the marshes and rivers in the area; both of those boats are too large for that. He keeps them at a marina in Mount Pleasant."

"And?" I said impatiently. I tried to hold back another yawn—not caused by the conversation, just the time it was occurring. Hurry up, Mr. Coffee!

"And he has a nice twenty-two-foot fishing boat he keeps at the Folly View Marina." Folly View was a small marina almost directly across the river from Charles's apartment—more of a working man's marina just past Mariner's Cay. "Interesting, huh?"

Interesting, to say the least. Bob mumbled something about having to go make his fortune and hung up before I could comment, say good-bye, or tell him I was sorry, but he had the wrong number.

✳   ✳   ✳   ✳

My memory's not what it used to be, but I don't remember having attended two funerals in a three-week period, ever. Not even when I had been surrounded by numerous relatives, friends, acquaintances, and even fellow workers, all of whom I would feel obligated to view in a casket, should the situation arise. Now here I was, in a new part of the world, knowing hardly anyone, and putting on what I had hoped I'd never have to wear again: a tie. I'd given most of my work clothes away before moving, but fortunately I had kept three ties, two sport coats (one for summer and one for winter), and a couple of dress shirts and pairs of slacks. I only saved one pair of black wingtips; they'd be appropriate at any dressy event. I prayed I wouldn't need the third tie.

Charles was waiting for me outside his Sandbar Lane apartment, pacing slowly and acting nervous and uncomfortable. His funeral attire was slightly more limited than mine; he had on the same thrift-store clothes he had worn to Palmer's interment. The chance of light snow was the top story on the news. For now, it was just cold.

"It's about time; you're only five minutes early. It's cold out here," Charles said. His hands were covering his mouth; he occasionally blew to warm them.

One thing I had learned over my few months on the island was that not only was there a shortage of chain hotels and restaurants (one and zero), there was a shortage of hellos, how-are-yous, byes, and other socially acceptable words that traditionally punctuated the conversations of normal humans. Then again, who had ever said the residents on this side of the Folly River were normal?

Charles climbed quickly into the car, then turned to carefully place his camera and cane on the backseat.

"Look, Chris," he said, "no mascots or college names on my coat."

I glanced over to him. "Good. I'm not a frequent funeral attendee—thank God—but I don't recall many university shirts at them. I think you'll be okay."

I also thanked God our conversations weren't recorded.

On the drive, I filled him in on what Bob had shared. I omitted the history of pawnshops; Charles didn't need more trivia to clutter his disjointed mind. He was familiar with the Folly View Marina and explained it wasn't as ritzy as its next-door neighbor, Mariner's Cay, a gated community where condos sold for baskets of bucks.

"There are two dozen or so deep-water slips at Folly View, and most are owned by locals," Charles said. "It basically serves as the parking place for small to midsized fishing boats, just like you thought."

The road to the Garner Baptist Cemetery contrasted drastically with the bucolic drive to Palmer's final resting place. The road was lined with industrial buildings and warehouses. The North Charleston area was not touted as highly as the historic sections of the beautiful city. Snow began to fall as we entered the cemetery property, located behind a small, traditional-looking church with its white paint peeling near the roof. The gravel and mud-covered circular drive was edged with decorative grasses, their plumes curving toward the turf, far beyond the time of year when they should have been trimmed. The mix of old tombstones and unattractive, concrete benches was surrounded by weeds that had not been cut for a couple of seasons. From what I knew of Mike, he would have been appalled by the condition of his new home.

Contrasting the ill-kept property was a line of high-end cars and luxury SUVs parked with the passenger-side wheels off the gravel. These must have belonged to Mike's friends and professional colleagues.

No funeral-home service had been offered—one of the few similarities to the Palmer funeral. Brief comments were to be made at the cemetery prior to burial.

I pulled up to the curb thirty minutes before the beginning of the service. Only the hardiest souls ventured out of their warm and cozy—and mostly expensive—vehicles until Amelia and her immediate family arrived. We were not among those hardy souls. Charles kept staring at the line of BMWs, Porches, Audis, Jaguars, and Saabs, shaking his head in disgust.

"Chris, look at that ugly Saab over there—lime yellow metallic, they call it," he said, failing to hide his displeasure. "With that new style and god-awful color, they've ruined a perfectly wonderful car. Mine has so much more class, so much more character. What's the car world coming to?"

I didn't want to mention that the ruined vehicle, as he put it, had made it here today—something I suspected Charles's "classic" model couldn't do. His had an enormous amount of class, style, and character for a piece of yard art.

Mike's family arrived in two vehicles, neither as new as the line of his colleagues' cars. The snow fell harder now, with some of it accumulating on the grassy areas and on top of the marble tombstones. Fortunately, the grave site was less than twenty yards from the drive. Amelia, dressed in all black, looked as if she had aged ten years since I had last seen her. A few of the snowflakes had accumulated on her black cloth hat. She was leaning heavily on Steven. Lance was not with the group. Sandy and her husband, Buddy, followed close behind, trying to walk in the shoe-worn path in the snow. A tall, distinguished looking, gray-haired gentleman walked behind the family. He looked older than Amelia, but not much. I assumed this was Harry Lucas. None of the church members from Julius's funeral were anywhere to be seen.

Mike's professional colleagues, occupants of the caravan of luxury vehicles, followed at a respectful distance. The look on their faces seemed more to be disgust than sadness—caused, I suspected, by a combination of having to take time from making money when the stock market was open, getting their fancy vehicles covered in slush, and having to stand in a cemetery that was too plain for their liking. I was possibly being unfair, but I doubted it. The only others present were Detective Lawson and her father, both in civilian clothes. I nodded to them; they reciprocated.

We gathered at the frayed funeral-home tent protecting the casket and open grave. Amelia sat on the front row of cheap, white folding chairs, her shoulders slumped and her eyes red. Sandy sat on her left, Steven on her right. Both leaned against their mother, providing comfort and warmth against the elements. The minister asked Amelia if she was ready to begin; she nodded.

My emotions ran the full spectrum. It was a surreal image: standing in the snow at a beach resort area, listening to the beautiful and haunting "Amazing

Grace" on a cheap, plastic boom box. It just didn't fit. I almost laughed until I started thinking of what my funeral would be like. Would there be more mourners? Would anyone be there at all? Unfortunately, many similar thoughts had begun sneaking into my head as I slid down the slope of late life.

Mindful of the snow, brisk winds, and frigid temperatures, the minister kept the service brief but respectful. For that, more than a handful of "thank Gods" were said.

Amelia went to each person as soon as the service ended to thank him or her for coming. She clearly didn't know most of the mourners, but remained gracious regardless of the weather. I admired her for that—another example of selflessness she had shown during my visit.

With a strained smile on her tearstained face, she introduced me to her "friend," Harry Lucas. His strong handshake was accompanied by the comment that yes, he knew who I was. He even said he'd heard much about me. Hmm.

"How's Bill?" she asked.

I told her what I knew, keeping it as brief as possible. Lucas looked everywhere except at us.

"I'd be honored if you'd visit soon to tell me more about his condition," she said before turning to speak to one of Mike's acquaintances standing nearby in his thousand-dollar topcoat and plaid Burberry scarf.

As soon as we got back in the car and turned on the heater, Charles said, "Did you feel as strange about it as I did?"

I didn't know what he meant—surprise, surprise—and had to ask.

"I kept standing there, thinking," he said, "the person who tried to send us to a resting place not dissimilar to Mike's here, was standing right beside you, in front of you, or behind you. I don't know about you, but that made me feel strange ... kind of creepy."

I told him I hadn't thought of that; also, I didn't tell him my thoughts about my funeral. Even if Charles had been ready to listen, I wasn't ready to share.

*   *   *   *

We pulled out of the cemetery and onto the paved road. It was just after noon, and the snow was easing some. I called Tammy to see if she was available to break bread with Charles and me. To my surprise, she said yes. She met us at a McDonald's just north of the city off I-26. Before sitting, she said she only had a half hour. She didn't have to tell us; it was evident in the way she rushed to the table, cell phone to her ear, her speech hurried. People failed to extend the courtesy of getting killed at convenient times; reporters covering the crime beat were at the mercy of the untimely events.

Instead of bread, we broke double cheeseburgers and fries—not quite health food, but it tasted good. We—or more accurately, Charles—told her of the brief, cold, and unusually sad funeral. Somewhere in the middle of the conversation, I slipped in the fact that Charles and I were lucky to be able to attend a funeral without the constraints of a coffin. She seemed more irritated that no one from the police had told her about our run-in with the pickup than upset that we had nearly been flattened into pancakes. All the same, I stressed that it was no big deal and most likely had been a drunken driver. After two kicks under the table, Charles got on the same page and downplayed the incident.

I could tell she was distracted. That wasn't hard to understand; she had to leave the restaurant and cover the death of a two-year-old girl who had allegedly fallen from the fifth-story window of a run-down apartment building. Tammy said the police were being closemouthed about the more logical explanation that someone had dropped or pushed the child.

"Why would a fifth-story window be open in this kind of weather?" she lamented. Suddenly, her investigative reporting switched tacks. "Any idea why Lance wasn't at the funeral?

She surprised me with the question; she must not have been as distracted as I thought.

"Guess he's the one who killed Palmer and Mike Hogan," Charles speculated. "If it was me, I'd be too ashamed to attend the funeral too."

Those words came from the same person who had taken photos at Palmer's funeral and said the murderer always attended the service. I wasn't ready to jump to so many conclusions, so I simply said, "No idea."

"If I get time, I'll check around and see if anyone knows anything about Lance or Steven," Tammy said. She looked at her watch—the second time in the last couple of minutes. I knew her half hour was up and said we needed to go. She agreed and gave each of us a peck on the cheek before heading out the door. I was learning not to ask if she would have any time soon.

CHAPTER 37

The snow was gone as quickly as it had arrived—another plus for the South. The morning was sunny, and the weather gurus projected temperatures in the low sixties by early afternoon. I, for one, was not the least bit sad to see the white stuff turn to mush, then to water, then to history.

The optimist in me grabbed the camera, heavy jacket, and even heavier tripod and headed to the beach, hoping to catch a shot or two of snow on the dunes. Before walking a block, I heard a voice from behind me and lower to the ground: "Hey, mister. Shooting pictures again?"

I was slightly startled until I recognized the voice. It belonged to a precocious ten-year-old I had met on my last visit to Folly.

"Hi, Sam," I said, while crossing my fingers and hoping I had the name right.

A big grin appeared, "Wow, you remember my name! I was afraid you might not recognize me."

"How could I forget? You were going to add red Christmas lights to your neighbor's blue, homemade Christmas tree, right?"

Sam's neighbor had an old tree stump in his front yard with gutter nails around it and blue beer bottles sticking from the nails—Folly art at its best.

"You should have seen it," said a very proud Sam. "Old Mr. Black didn't take the yucky old blue beer bottles off, but said my red lights hit the spot. Dad made me take them off New Year's Day."

"Sorry I missed it, Sam; next Christmas, I'll be here to see what you do then."

"I hope Mr. Black lets me do it again. Dad says he's a strange fellow. He laughs when he should cry, and he wears blue at Christmas—guess that's why his tree has blue bottles."

"I bet he'll let you put the lights on again," I said.

"I hear you're tryin' to find out who kilt that old furniture man," he said, with the drastic change of direction that children were so capable of.

"Where did you hear that?" I asked, without thinking about it.

"My friend Hector. He said some crazy, old photographer was thinking someone kilt the guy and was going to find out who. I figured he had to be talking about you."

I couldn't help but laugh, although a minimal amount of reflection revealed that it wasn't very funny.

Before I could say anything, Sam added, "I know how he got kilt; want to hear?"

Rendered almost speechless by a ten-year-old, I asked, "How?"

Sam stopped, looking around as if he wanted to keep his secret a secret. "A scuba diver grabbed the old furniture man by the leg and pulled him into the ocean, over his head. The diver could keep on breathing because he had that air thing on his back, but the furniture man couldn't. The diver guy just held him until he was dead, then let go and swimmed off."

I could tell Sam was as serious as a heart attack. "How do you know?" I asked.

"Seen it on a television show—one of them Mom don't want me watching. 'Cept on the show, the diver was in the dead guy's swimming pool. But I think drowning in the ocean would make somebody just as dead as in a pool."

No argument from me. "Where do you think Hector heard I was looking for a killer?"

"Don't know for sure," said Sam, "'cause he said everyone was talking about it and talking about an old photographer. Gotta go … maybe I'll see you again."

With that, Sam was off. I stood on the side of the street, pondering this latest exchange, then turned and headed home. For some reason, I had lost interest in finding snowflakes on the beach.

Charles called midmorning and asked if "we" were ready to visit Amelia. He reminded me that at the funeral, she had asked us to. I told him it was too soon after yesterday's funeral.

"Chris, don't you think she might need some friendly faces other than her family? Look who was at the funeral; she doesn't know those rich wannabes from his social circle. Heck, we're almost family."

I wasn't sure about us being family, but agreed he might be right about her needing friendly faces.

He met me in front of the house, his attire more subdued than usual, and we walked two blocks to the Hogan residence. The closer we got, the more I felt it might be a mistake. Maybe she needed some time alone, without two semi-strangers—regardless of Charles's elevated notion of our relationship—knocking on her door.

Buddy, Amelia's son-in-law, answered and appeared as surprised to see us as we were to see him. He was dressed in old jeans and a gray, logo-free sweatshirt. I could almost see Charles's disgust with this wardrobe equivalent of a blank bill-board just begging for a mascot. I introduced myself, and so did Charles. I told him I'd seen him at the funerals and a couple of times at the Dog. He said that "Mom"—whom I assumed to be his mother-in-law, Amelia, had told him who we were, and that he remembered seeing me at the restaurant. He also said he remembered the big fuss I'd made last spring. I didn't know if that was a compliment or an insult, but he said it with a smile and invited us in. I leaned toward compliment.

Amelia was sitting on the couch, staring into space. I could see Sandy through the large opening between the living area and the kitchen. She was putting a tray of cold cuts in the refrigerator.

When we got a couple of feet from her, Amelia shifted her gaze and broke into a big smile.

"Oh, Chris and Charles! Thanks so much for visiting," she said as she slowly stood and nervously smoothed out her two-toned, striped dress. She hugged each of us. Charles may have been right; we were becoming part of her family. "Won't you have something to drink? Sandy, do we have some coffee or tea for our guests?"

Sandy finally turned from her kitchen duties and looked our way. Her eyes were bloodshot, and she looked as if she had been crying.

"Hi, gentlemen," she said. "We have coffee and water, of course, but no tea."

Charles had perked up at being called a gentleman—a rare event—and said yes to coffee. He volunteered that I wanted some, then went to the kitchen to help Sandy. I was impressed.

Amelia asked me to join her on the couch; I sat on the opposite end and turned to face her. Buddy sat in one of the old, wooden kitchen chairs that had been moved to the living room to accommodate the unusually large number of people in the tiny house. I was generally a shy person, and this kind of socially awkward situation took its toll on me. I smiled at Amelia and Buddy, but had no idea what to say.

Charles saved the day. He delivered my coffee and some slices of coffee cake on a plastic picnic plate and proceeded to tell Amelia how lovely her house was, ask Buddy if he was ready for hunting season, and tell Sandy the coffee was some of the best he'd ever had. I was pleased to witness this "social director on a cruise ship" side of Charles.

Amelia seemed more comfortable listening, rather than speaking; I identified with that. Buddy kept picking at the worn arm of the chair.

I looked around the room and into as much of the kitchen as I could see from the couch. From my experience, after the death of a family member, neighbors, church members, and relatives brought food and flowers to the house—usually more than anyone could eat. I saw no evidence of that. That reinforced the comments from Amber, Charles, and Brian that hardly anyone knew the family. From what I was learning about Amelia, it was everyone's loss. A lone flower arrangement stood on the small table by the front door. I'd put my money on it coming from Harry Lucas; now, to find someone to bet.

Amelia said little about Mike. When she did, she referred to incidents from his childhood. I remembered her saying that she rarely had contact with him, despite the fact he lived a short distance away. She had seen him at Christmas, the first time since summer when he visited for a few hours. They had gone fishing in Steven's small runabout. All in all, it was almost as if she were talking about a stranger—so sad. Both Sandy and Buddy's comments reinforced the virtual estrangement; it didn't sound as if they had had much contact either. They didn't say anything bad; they just didn't say much of anything. Their facial expressions bordered on anger.

"Do the police know more about what might have happened?" asked Charles, never failing to go where angels feared to tread.

"We haven't heard anything from the police since they said it was a burglary gone bad," said Sandy. "Mom, you haven't heard anything, have you?"

"No," said Amelia, clearly uncomfortable with the topic. "They've been nice, but haven't said anything. It seems so unfair. Of the hundreds of condos around, why did someone pick Mike's? Why'd he have to be there? Why'd he have to get killed over stupid stuff? Why?"

These were good questions—but only questions, with no answers in sight.

"So, how's Bill?" asked Amelia suddenly, providing a welcomed change of topic.

I told her about my recent visit and that he'd be able to come home in a few days.

"I know he was such a good friend to Jay," she said. "I feel we're close." With a small giggle, she continued, "The three of us have one thing in common: few friends. We can't afford to lose any of them. Now that Jay's gone, I wouldn't want to lose Bill."

Knowing that she had only met Bill once, during which he had been borderline hostile, believing she had killed his friend, I couldn't see how she considered him a friend. Yes, he was a friend of Julius, so it was possible they were friends by association. I suspected she was really thinking more about her health situation—the friends she would soon be leaving. If a more helpless feeling could exist than the one that gripped my heart, I couldn't imagine it.

"When Bill gets back home, would you bring him over?" she asked. "Even better, maybe we could go out to a nice restaurant in the city. Jay really liked to eat; I bet Bill does too."

I assured her we'd be over as soon as possible.

"Mom, don't you think you need to rest?" asked Sandy.

Sandy stood and started walking to the door before her mom could answer—not so subtle. Being as bright as we were, Charles and I stood and offered our condolences. Amelia stood and hugged each of us. Tears filled her eyes, and she thanked us profusely for coming. That alone made the visit worthwhile. I hated to admit it, but Charles's idea to visit had been a good one.

Sandy didn't stop at the door; she followed us down the stairs and halfway down the walk.

Her eyes on the walk, she finally said, "Mom's getting worse by the day. Mike's death has taken months off her already shortened life. To be honest, I'll be surprised if she makes it to summer."

We both said we were sorry and asked if there was anything we could do.

"No. My damn brother's done it all. He hurt her deeply for years—ignoring her, acting like she was beneath him … beneath all of us, pretty much. And now this."

Not the most appropriate words for a eulogy. We left on that very low high note.

CHAPTER 38

"So, when're you going to stop dallying around and get this place open?" asked Charles. We'd walked back to the gallery from Amelia's.

I had known where he was going with the question. Rather than admit I was scared of opening and the possible rejection of my work, I promised to set up shop as soon as we got the flyers prepared and the final photos displayed ... barring unforeseen delays, of course.

"Good," he said. He looked around the half-bare walls and tossed his jacket on the straightback chair in the corner. "I was thinking I was going to have to sneak customers in here when you were away. How can I start earning big commissions if we're not open?"

This was the first time commissions had been mentioned, much less big ones!

"So, how'd you know Buddy was a hunter?" Changing the subject was in order. I led him to the office, so he wouldn't keep staring at the empty spaces on the gallery walls.

Charles raised his cane to his eye as if he were sighting a rifle. "Didn't," he said. "He's a young guy, works at a convenience store, looks kind of macho. I figured that was a better question than, 'Hey, dude, been to any good ballets lately?'"

"I wouldn't have expected you to judge a book by its cover—Mr. Presidential Biography and Shakespeare Reading Vagabond." I tried to hold back a laugh.

"Live and learn," he said. "And speaking of learning, what'd we learn today?"

"Let's see." I rubbed my chin and gazed at the ceiling. "Mike wasn't a finalist for any son- or brother-of-the-year award. Not many people have visited to offer condolences. Sandy's not a happy camper, and the coffee cake was way too good. How about you?"

"Ate too much too." He rubbed his stomach. "Besides that, Amelia appears desperate for friends. And you can add Steven to the long list of suspects with a boat."

Our rehashing of the visit was interrupted when Amber knocked loudly on the locked front door. She was still in uniform; her shift had just ended. The sunshine gave her clear, smooth skin an extra glow that wasn't evident in the harsh, white florescent illumination of the Dog. She looked lovely. Her son had an after-school meeting and wouldn't be home until after five. That had given her a rare two hours to herself; it was nice that she chose to spend them with us.

"So when's Landrum Gallery opening?" she asked as she looked at the walls with the same expression Charles had aimed at them. "Customers are beginning to ask what's going on over here. I've been telling them some northerner is going to open an adult bookstore and porn shop. Be ready to have a bunch of customers when you first open … and some protesters from the Baptist church."

"Did Charles put you up to asking about opening?" I asked, but didn't wait for an answer. "I guess I'd better get extra copies made of a couple of nude-statue photos."

"Good plan," she replied, followed by a slight giggle. "I'm doing my best to drum up customers for you. Got any of that beer in back you keep talking about, or is it an all-male club?"

"There goes the neighborhood," said Charles. "Now you're letting women in; next you'll have Bill over here; before you know it, Steven will get an invitation. What's next, a pony?"

"Funny you mentioned Steven," said Amber, ignoring Charles's discriminatory remark. "One of my less-than-regular customers told me yesterday that he heard that the new design shop in Charleston was already closed. My customer, Frederick, a late lunch eater—and gay, I might add—was talking about how hard it was to find a designer good enough for him in these parts. Said he'd finally found someone who understood his needs, as he put it, and now Frederick isn't sure he'll be able to locate him. Frederick has one of the McMansions out past the Washout … a real nice guy."

I was already in the back room, getting Amber's beer from the mini-fridge; I wasn't sure I had caught all her comments about Fredrick's quest for the perfect designer.

"Did he say who he was talking about or the name of the shop?" I yelled to the other room.

"No," she said, "but it'd be too big a coincidence if it were someone other than Ms. Hogan's son, wouldn't it?"

True, I thought as I handed her the cold Bud Light and encouraged the two of them to adjourn to the back room, where we all could sit.

Amber shared an amusing story about a couple of citizens we were acquainted with and the latest rumors about the newly elected city council members and how they were going to get Folly going in the right direction again.

"Councilman Metts was even talking about buying some of those cute little Segway scooters," she said. "He wants our police to patrol the city streets and beach—said they wouldn't need gas, and some of the other big cities were already using them."

"I wonder if Chief Newman knows about that brilliant plan," I said wryly. "I also wonder if the Census Bureau is aware that Folly Beach is a big city."

"Lord, let me have my camera ready the first time three-hundred-pound Officer Robins steps on a Segway," added Charles. He held his hands over his head, clasped together in a poor excuse of a prayer pose. "'All free governments are managed by the combined wisdom and folly of the people,' according to long-dead United States President James A. Garfield. I'll let you guess his answer to that one—wisdom or folly?"

That was the easiest question I'd faced that day.

"Gotta run—the rest of my family should be getting home anytime," said Amber. She kissed Charles on the cheek and hugged me before leaving—an interesting choice of departing affections.

✳   ✳   ✳   ✳

"I just heard an interesting rumor," I said, cell phone to my ear. "Thought you could check it out for me."

After Amber left, I had called Bob—her rumor about a design shop closing was way too close to everything going on to ignore.

"No, Bob, I'm not dead, and you can't sell my house yet. I'm here with Charles … yes, that damn worthless twerp … yes, the same one who's staring daggers at the phone. Okay." I turned to Charles. "Bob says yo."

After Bob got around to offending most every ethnic group and other minority—including, for some reason, the Daughters of the American Revolution—he agreed to ride past the Design Shop to see if it was open and to gather information. He got more excited when I suggested he could possibly snag a real-estate listing if it really was closed.

"That man should be glad I'm not rich," said Charles when I hung up. "If I were and wanted to buy a house, I sure would find another Realtor. Look at all that money he'd lose."

I assumed he realized Bob was making the same amount of money off him now as he would in Charles's hypothetical dream of wealth.

"It doesn't matter anyway," added Charles. "If Bob's your friend, he's a friend of mine. I guess being called a worthless twerp by someone like him isn't such a bad thing."

That was something to ponder as Charles headed home for the night. *What a day. How did I ever have time to work for a living?* I wouldn't ponder that one.

CHAPTER 39

Sunrise broke over the ocean for the kind of day the chamber of commerce coveted: sunny, with highs near seventy expected.

After the previous day, I wanted solitude. Breakfast at the Holiday Inn would be my second-best shot. I could have enjoyed the solitude of my kitchen, but would have had to fix breakfast. I was finally feeling comfortable in my house—boxes emptied, moving trash long gone, and the feel of "home" emerging. But the kitchen was still a stranger; a restaurant would trump that option every time.

Putting it mildly, midweek in early March wasn't going to break occupancy records at the island's only chain hotel. I had my choice of all but two tables. I walked past several silver-framed, black-and-white photos of Folly from times gone by and chose a spot overlooking the beautiful Atlantic and the Folly pier. The waitress, who I knew only by smile, welcomed me, made a benign comment about the weather, and took my order. The sun still drowsily rose in the east, backlighting the pier—a great photo op made more difficult with my camera at home. For a second, I wondered if the view would have been more majestic if Amber had been serving my breakfast.

The more I stared at the thousand-foot-long pier extending over the churning, ominous Atlantic, the more I became convinced of the accuracy of Charles's theory. There was no way the killer could have dragged someone that afraid of water out there without knocking him out with drugs or a blunt object, then carrying the dead weight a long distance. It would have been far too risky; the killer could have easily been seen.

My stuffed French toast arrived and interrupted the rehashing of the "dropped off a boat" theory. The arrival of Chief Newman interrupted my French toast—so much for my desire for solitude.

"I thought you might be here," said Brian as he stood by the table and looked down at me. "I went to the Dog, and Amber said she hadn't seen you. Then I dropped by your house—no answer there."

"Guess that's why you're such a good police chief, Brian—a mystery solver."

"Not really," he said. "Your car was at the house, so I knew you had to be at the Dog, here, or walking around with your camera. That was my next option."

Creatures of habit were much too easy to find, I mused. I needed to work on some variations, if for no other reason than to think of myself as not being so predictable. *That's what I should do*, I thought ... *but most likely, I won't.*

"Care to join me?" I nodded toward the empty chair. "I doubt you went to all that trouble just to wish me a good morning."

"Sure." He gracefully lowered his tall frame into the white wicker chair and looked around the near-vacant dining room. "Hey, P. J., could I get coffee and some dry toast?" he asked, then turned his attention back to me. "You're right about me trying to find you. Heard something last night I thought you'd be interested in. Yesterday afternoon, the sheriff's department pulled in Steven Hogan. He's being questioned about the death of his brother and the break-in at Julius Palmer's house."

"Wow, what happened?" Optimism and confusion collided in the pit of my stomach. "I just heard yesterday that his design shop closed."

"You get part of the credit about the break-in," said the chief at the same time P. J. brought his toast. "After you raised such a ruckus about Palmer being murdered, we took an extra look at his house. We first thought it was simply a burglary of convenience—funeral and all—but after going back, we found several of Steven's prints on items he wouldn't normally have touched. We knew he'd been in the house and worked with Palmer on decorating. But that didn't explain his fingerprints on a letter opener in one of the drawers and on an antique pillbox in the bedroom dresser."

I had underestimated the persistence and professionalism of Chief Newman and his department. Maybe he actually listened to what citizens thought.

"And get this," he said. "He waived his right to an attorney and admitted to the break-in. Detective Lawson called me after he let the cat out of the bag. Steven said he broke in a couple of hours before the funeral."

"Why?"

A huge weight lifted off my shoulders—at least partway, anyway.

"Said he'd heard rumors that Palmer had his mom in his will. When pushed, he said he actually heard that from Mike. He didn't really believe it and wanted to see for himself." The chief paused as if he wanted to tell me something else, but didn't.

"All that seems implausible," I said, waiting as long as I could before speaking. "If it were true, he would have found out soon enough. Besides, his mother inherits, not him."

"From other things he said, I think his new business was in trouble, and he was getting desperate. The sheriff's department found letters in his house from two banks threatening to call in their notes if they weren't paid in full in ninety days. He was going to ask his mother for a loan—or so he said."

"That's consistent with what I heard about the business. Was Lance involved?"

"Not according to Steven. He said Lance didn't have any idea what was happening. He said the two were 'bickering' the last few months; the money problems were driving a stake into their relationship."

"Lance wasn't at Mike's funeral," I said.

The chief nodded, then moved on. "But while he confessed to the break-in, he vehemently denied killing his brother. Unfortunately for him, according to phone records, the last call to Mike's house before his death was from Steven's cell phone. I think he was calling to make sure Mike was home. Steven's prints were all over the condo, and we can't verify his alibi for most of the day Mike was killed."

"Sounds circumstantial. Any evidence?"

"Nothing direct, but they've just begun the search," he said. "It won't mean anything in court, but it's interesting that Steven took shooting lessons in December. He brought a handgun to the shooting range, but there's no record of any being registered to him."

"Motive?"

"Money," he said as he pushed away his empty plate, leaned back in his chair, and stretched his lengthy frame. "He knew his mother had only a few months to live. He knew she was going to be more than three million dollars richer. With her gone, he was going to inherit a million bucks. Now, with Mike out of the picture, his bounty would increase fifty percent. In his current financial condition, that extra half million was worth killing for. Besides, from what we've learned, there was little love lost between the brothers." The chief nodded as if he had it figured out.

"So what incentive did he have for trying to run down Charles and me? Anything to tie him to Palmer's murder?"

"I wish you were half as tired of hearing this as I am of saying it," he said. He stopped nodding and fixed his cop's stare on me. "Mr. Palmer's death was suicide. Wishing it not to be won't make it so. Also, I still think the near accident the other night was caused by a drunk driver. We did find that stolen Ford pickup. It was in Charleston, parked on the street in front of the College of Charleston's administrative building. Whoever took it wiped the wheel and door handles clean. There's no reason to think it was the truck that almost got you two."

"Brian." I thought I might as well try again. "If you were in my shoes, you'd be convinced you were the target of the truck, not just an unrelated bystander who happened to be endangered when a drunk driver decided to navigate the streets. Please keep your mind open. Also, take a look at that pier." I nodded toward the massive wooden appendage sticking out into the Atlantic. "If you were deathly afraid of the water, can you, in good conscience, tell me you'd be able to walk to the end, climb over the rail, and step off into the Atlantic, regardless of how depressed you might have been?"

To his credit, Brian took a long—and somewhat contemplative—look over his shoulder at the majestic Folly pier.

"Chris, under that scenario, I don't think I could have done it. But none of us know how Palmer would've reacted. We really don't."

I looked at him, speaking only with my expression.

"I'd like to stay longer," Brian said, "but I've got to go solve some more crimes." He put a crisp five-dollar bill on the table for his coffee and toast. "By the way, when are you opening your gallery?"

"Did Charles put you up to that? Soon, I hope. And Brian—thanks for finding me."

He laughed, said "of course not" to the question about Charles, said bye to P. J., and left.

So much for a quiet breakfast.

I was tempted to walk on the beach that morning, but it was still too cool; maybe in the afternoon.

I was walking up the drive to my house when my cell phone rang. I was pleasantly surprised to hear Bill's bass voice.

"Chris, this is Bill," he said, unnecessarily. "They're saying I can leave this afternoon ... I hate to ask, being short notice and all, but would it be possible for you to pick me up?"

"That's great news," I said. "Tell me where and when, and I'll be there."

We decided on three o'clock inside the lobby of the hospital.

No sooner had I pushed the off button than it rang again. After a glance at the caller ID, I simply pushed Send and held the phone to my ear.

"You're not with that worthless twerp again, are you? I don't want to insult him over the damn phone."

"No, Bob, I'm not. Happy Wednesday."

"Why's everything so damn happy with you? It's just a damn Wednesday ... like all others. Do you want to debate that or find out why I called?"

"Why?" I asked, not wanting to debate anything with him—talk about a no-win situation.

"I drove by the Design Shop. The lights were off, the door was locked, and a small handwritten sign by the knob said 'Closed Until Further Notice.' There was also a more permanent note on the bottom corner of the door that gave a phone number to call in case of emergency. I had to put on my damn glasses to read it. I figured if I were ever in need of any damn design services, it would definitely be an emergency ... so I called." He paused dramatically.

"I suppose this is where I have to beg to find out what you learned?" I asked in mock exasperation that was starting to feel a lot like real exasperation.

"You're finally catching on," he said. "Well, I got the owner of the building, who lives up in Calabash, North Carolina—damn long-distance call. You owe me—again. I gave him my official Realtor shtick—saw building closed, thought you may need Realtor, yada, yada, yada. He finally told me the current tenant, a nice young couple of guys, were more than three months behind in rent. His lawyer had written them each month, and they're finally starting eviction proceedings. Don't look good for the quee ... alternative-lifestyle chaps. The owner— Mark's his name, if you're taking notes—told me that Steven even offered to give him his 'like-new' fishing boat he has docked at Folly View Marina. Said it was worth fifteen grand, but he would let him have it to cover the overdue rent. Mark, being the wise businessperson, said he wasn't in the damn boat business. Besides they're a dime a dozen here, and he wouldn't be able to unload it for anything near its value."

"Folly View Marina ... isn't that where you said Harry Lucas keeps his fishing boat?" I asked. "Lucas would know Steven, wouldn't he?"

"Same place. It's not that large, so I'd be surprised if he didn't."

I told Bob what I'd learned from Chief Newman. He said it was about time the police started doing something and guessed that the eviction was one of Steven's smaller problems. I shared the news about Bill, and he almost sounded pleased—pleased for Bob, that is. He ended the call on some insult about needing to sell some houses to pay for all the time I was wasting. I grinned and put the phone in my pocket.

To my great pleasure, the next three hours were interrupted by absolutely nothing.

*   *   *   *

Bill was waiting under the canopy outside the front door of the hospital. He looked a little heavier and stood more erect, almost regal—a good sign. He broke into a wide smile when he recognized my Lexus. He moved to the car more quickly than I'd ever seen him cover ground.

"Thanks for coming," he said in his deep, distinctive voice. James Earl Jones had nothing on my friend when it came to vocal cords. "I've had about all of this place I could stand."

He threw a large brown paper bag containing his possessions in the backseat. "They were fantastic and kind; the food and lodging was good; the therapy needed, I suspect; but I hated every minute. You don't know how much I'm looking forward to my own bed."

The trip back was unusually quiet. Bill looked out the window, his arms folded on his lap. He had said the food was good, but I knew he'd need a nice meal. I offered to take him to 11 Center Street Wine and Gourmet for supper; he quickly agreed.

Located in an old grocery store, 11 Center Street Wine and Gourmet was one of Folly's nicest restaurants. The tables were adjacent to attractive, functional wooden racks filled with wines from around the world. I was in Dockers and a nice long-sleeved casual shirt. I was underdressed compared to the dress slacks, blue oxford shirt, and navy blazer Bill had on when I picked him up at six. The Bill of old was on his way back.

We had our choice of tables and took a two-top in the front corner—it looked out on Center Street and also had a good view of the bar and other tables. I ordered a midpriced bottle of Napa chardonnay, and we chose to split an appetizer portion of conch fritters. He shared a couple of stories from his stay—all positive and slightly humorous. "Slightly humorous" was Bill's version of slapstick hilarity, so I was pleased. He was relaxed and didn't show any of the signs of hopelessness he had exhibited before his stay in Charleston.

Bill ordered the citrus scallop ceviche before he had finished the appetizer. He enunciated each word as if he were lecturing his impressionable students. I may have ordered it myself, if I'd known what it was. I played it safe with the sesame seed encrusted tuna.

He asked how I was progressing on the gallery and when it would be opening. I knew he wouldn't understand if I asked if Charles had put him up to that question. I said well, and soon—though I used several more words to convey the information. He wanted to spend more time talking about his students.

Bill interrupted the gallery update. "Chris, more than anything, I've missed the young minds that sit in front of me every day. Sure, they bring only about half their minds with them, but I've still missed them. I received three notes from them last week. They said the substitutes were okay, but they missed me. Bet it's because I'm easier on them."

"Are you going to class Monday?"

"Hope so," he replied. "I've got to call the dean tomorrow to see what he wants me to do. I hope they don't try to keep me out of the classroom. I don't know what I'd do if that happened."

"Whatever happens," I said, "you know you have friends here to help, in any way possible."

"The psychiatrist said I needed to establish a better 'support system'; those were his words for more friends, I think. I know he's right, but that'll be hard for an old hard-line loner. I've never felt close to anyone at the college, and you know how limited my scope of acquaintances is here."

It struck me that if he stopped using phrases like "scope of acquaintances," his scope might expand. But this wasn't the time to uncorrect his grammar.

"Bill, you have at least four friends you're not even aware of: Charles, Bob Howard, Amber, and someone I doubt you even know, Larry LaMond."

I almost added Amelia Hogan's name but didn't want to bring up the subject.

"And to play devil's advocate," he said, "how, may I ask, are these individuals—three I've only met once or twice—and Mr. LaMond, whom I don't even know, my friends?"

"Excellent question, Mr. D. Advocate," I said. "It's hard to explain, but these folks are my friends, and they ask about you each day, offering their help. My guess is, they like you because you—like each of them—are a little off center. Not bad, just off."

I didn't tell him each had also been convinced that Julius Palmer's death wasn't self-inflicted. My avoiding that subject only lasted so long.

He lowered his voice more than I thought possible and looked directly in my eyes. "My therapist said I needed to seek closure on the situation with my friend Julius. Until I'm one hundred percent certain, I will continue to struggle with my self-doubts and feelings of hopelessness. Chris, I don't want to spoil such a wonderful supper talking about it, but I'm still counting on you to help me find the truth."

My tuna fillet was fantastic, but probably would have tasted better without Bill's last comment.

All in all, we enjoyed a great supper, excellent conversation, and the comfortable knowledge that Bill was back among friends.

CHAPTER 40

I had failed miserably in avoiding people the day before, so I headed to the epi-center of erupting gossip and talk: the world-famous Lost Dog Café. I had beaten most of the regulars, so Amber gave me her high-wattage smile and pointed to my booth—the international symbol for "it's all yours." Coffee and gossip closely followed.

"I hear you brought Bill home," she said. "Folks say he's looking good and rested." She looked me in the eye, her head cocked a little to the left, waiting for confirmation.

I had stopped trying to ask who "folks" were.

"Hear more about our interior designer friends in Charleston?" I asked, leaving her unanswered question in that state.

"Not a word," she said. "To tell the truth, not much is ever said here about interior designers. Most of us know what they are but wouldn't have any more a clue what to do with one than a deaf zebra would with an mp3 player."

I had no response other than a smile—something I occasionally did, just not nearly as well and easily as Amber. I ordered breakfast.

Amber was only gone a minute before she was back at the table, friendly smile and all. "Are you in the market for a boat?" she asked as she slid into the booth across the table from me.

She must have been taking segue lessons from Bob or Charles.

"Can't say that I am. Why?"

"Didn't think so … thought I'd try anyway," she said as she pretended to clean the table with her white bar towel. "Cool Dude Sloan's going to give me a couple hundred bucks if I help him sell his thirty-five-foot 1988 Bayliner." She spread her arms as if she were showing me how long thirty-five feet was. "He says it's worth almost eighty thousand. I have no idea why he's got an eighty-thousand-dollar boat. Why do surfers need boats?"

I shrugged my answer.

"Anyway," she continued, "he doesn't know why he has it either, so he's trying to sell it."

From my limited knowledge of Sloan, I understood her confusion. "Even if I was interested in a boat," I said, "it wouldn't be an eighty-thousand-dollar one. I'll let you know if I hear of anyone."

"Thanks. I could use the money. He's only had a couple of nibbles. One's from Sean Aker. He said he needs a larger boat, but couldn't afford it until the lawyerin' business picked up come summer. Business ain't booming when no one's here, he said."

All of that boat talk had reminded me of something. I asked, "Where's this bargain-priced yacht? Who knows, I may want to take a look."

"I think over at the Folly View Marina," she said, her voice returning to normal. "He said it's named *Throw a Wave!* or something like that."

I wondered if Dude had any vested interest in the death of Mr. Palmer. Then again, including every boat owner on my suspect list would only let a dozen or so residents off the hook.

*   *   *   *

"Charles, Larry, it's my treat. Order anything you want; you've put up with my pizza too many times."

We were seated by one of the large windows at the River Café, looking out on the Folly River and the sun setting between the large oaks behind the restaurant and the marsh. Each entrée was about the price of the large pizza—our normal culinary fare. I owed Charles and Larry far more than a meal—both had donated hours to the almost-budding gallery.

Charles had decided earlier in the day that we—the "C, C, and L Detective Agency"—needed to meet and "figure out this murder stuff" once and for all. He had even offered his apartment for the meeting. I had never been in his apartment and for some reason was looking forward to it. The River Café was in the same old, rambling building as his apartment and was thus the logical location for supper.

Charles sat near the window and leaned his cane against the sill. He was fidgeting and looked uncomfortable in the nice restaurant. He studied the modest-length menu as if he were trying to find obscure quotes from dead presidents. Unable to find anything Chester Arthur had said, he finally settled on the local shrimp and grits. I smiled, thinking of my first meeting with Tammy, during which we had debated the pluses and minuses of grits. I hadn't found any pluses; she had said I couldn't be a southerner. To this day, I must still be a northern southerner.

Larry awkwardly asked me three times if I really meant it about picking up the check; after three reassurances, he chose the fried seafood platter.

Charles and I split the lowest-priced bottle of cabernet and spent several minutes laughing at Larry, who sipped a gin martini. The fragile, distinctively shaped glass was funnier than the drink itself.

"Larry, did you acquire a taste for the martini while living off the citizens of Georgia?" asked Charles at the same time Larry removed the olive skewered by the miniature, clear plastic sword from the glass and took a sip.

Larry shook his head no but didn't elaborate. I started to laugh, but when I saw discomfort in his eyes, I remained silent.

We didn't have to relive our normal argument about who got how many slices of pizza, so we had time to talk about our childhoods and memories of early visits to restaurants. Larry won the Most Interesting Conversation Award when he said he didn't remember eating in many restaurants, but had broken in to some of the finest dining establishments in his hometown. Charles and I couldn't compete with that; I knew Charles wanted to try, but didn't.

The muted, low-wattage light in the dining room wasn't conducive to serious murder talk—nor was it intended to be. Our plates were empty, the bottle of wine depleted, and Larry's second—humorous—martini drained, so we walked to Charles's place.

His home, less than a hundred steps from the door of the River Café, was everything I had expected, just smaller ... much smaller. The apartment wasn't really that small, but when you added floor-to-ceiling wooden bookshelves made of stacked concrete blocks and irregular pine boards on three walls in the living area, four walls in the bedroom, two walls in the kitchen, and one wall in the bathroom, the feel of a small cave permeated the place. These weren't just shelves; they were shelves full (not partially full, not mostly full, but full—full-plus if that was possible) of books. On second thought, "cave" was not the accurate term. The apartment looked more like an imploded library: hardback books, paperback books, dust-covered magazines, biographies, autobiographies, two sets of encyclopedias, at least four dictionaries, and two cookbooks all combined to decorate the walls.

The floor was carpeted—at least the part that could be seen from under more books stacked around the perimeter.

"Holy concrete block," said Larry. "Have you read all these?"

"All but the cookbooks," said Charles as he slowly looked around the room with new eyes. "The guy who sold me the dictionaries made me take them. I couldn't just throw them away, could I?"

"Charles, if you ever decide to put me in your will—Don't," I added.

"I'll remember that when I win the lottery," he responded. "And speaking of wills, who killed Palmer?"

By that time, we'd toured the apartment and found seats. (Correction: moved stacks of books from chairs, and then found seats.) I managed to squeeze into an old, worn, navy blue velour recliner by the door. A broken spring in the seat drew the immediate attention of the left side of my posterior. Larry uncovered a wicker rocking chair sitting in the corner beside a rack of college sweatshirts. I thought I'd seen all of Charles's sweatshirts; I was way wrong.

Before Charles sat in one of the chrome diner-style kitchen chairs he carried to the living room, he fidgeted with an old Magnavox console stereo—more like a record player—and several albums. Yes, albums—33 1/3 rpm, black, vinyl albums. He adjusted the volume so the Duprees' version of "You Belong to Me" could be heard without overpowering our conversation—if we ever got around to a conversation. I had forgotten how distracting the scratchy, grating sound of the vinyl could be.

"I'm playing that one for you, Chris," said Charles.

"I assume because you know it was written by some Louisville folks and not because you're trying to romance me," I said.

"I'm surprised you knew that ... but yes, because of the scribes."

"Thank God," said Larry. "I was beginning to feel like I was intruding on something."

"Okay, enough small talk." Charles could always be counted upon. "Who did it?"

"Pee Wee King and—" I said.

"No, no, no," Charles interrupted. "Who killed Palmer; not who wrote the song."

"To start things off," I said. "What evidence do we have that Palmer's death wasn't a suicide? Why do we want to ignore the best police minds and make it murder?"

"Proof? We have none," said Charles, slowly waving his arms in front of him as if the truth were floating there for all to see. "That's our big advantage over the police. We don't have to be constrained by such vague concepts as proof."

"Having some firsthand experience with the concept of proof," interrupted Larry, "I don't see how not having any helps us."

"Look at it this way," said Charles, my friend and lawyer-in-training. "The police didn't prove O. J. killed his wife and her unlucky amigo. But I know he did. Don't you? So, without proof, we're right; they're wrong. See? We've got the upper hand." He spread his arms out again, this time with his palms up, as if to ask how our advantage could be any clearer.

"Then let me rephrase my question: why do we think he didn't kill himself?" I asked and continued to move around to get comfortable in the chair.

"Easy," said Charles. "Bill said he didn't, and you believed Bill, and I believed you, and Larry believed me, and there's Bob—who knows what he believes—then Amber believed you and me, and Tammy believed you, as much as a snooping reporter can believe anyone. So, there it is—murder." I assumed he resisted the urge to add, "I rest my case!"

"I lost Charles about halfway through that jabbering," said Larry. "But I simply can't believe anyone who was as afraid of the water as everyone said Palmer was would walk to the end of the pier, out over the rough, dark, unforgiving Atlantic Ocean, and jump. That's all the proof I need."

"Also," said Charles, "we've been snooping around. Everyone knows that. The killer knows it and tried twice to shut us up."

"Twice?" said Larry with a questioning expression.

"Sure—tried to asphyxiate Chris and me, then tried a more direct route: run over our bodies with a big-ass pick-um-up truck."

"Charles, we don't know those things were intentional," I added, knowing as sure as I was sitting there that they were.

"See," he said. "Two more examples where proof means penguin poop."

After a few more minutes of the no-win debate, we had agreed to assume his death was not suicide or accidental. Motive was the next piece of the puzzle. Tammy's mantra that the motive for murder was either love or money was our guidepost.

Charles's bar was drastically more limited than the one at the River Café. He and Larry had a Bud Light; I opted for water in the absence of wine.

"With seven million dollars at stake, money would be my choice for motive," said Charles. "Besides, no one's even mentioned love when it came to Palmer."

"True," added Larry. "Amelia Hogan was his closest female acquaintance, and she said they were friends—nothing romantic. And Bill was his only other friend that I've heard mentioned ... don't think love hung around there."

"What about jealousy?" asked Charles as he headed to the kitchen to get two more beers. "Harry Lucas could've seen Julius as a competitor."

"I can see a little jealousy between the two," I said, "particularly from Lucas, but not enough to kill over. Money would be the stronger motivator for Lucas. Like you said, Charles, three and a half million would be a powerful reason for murder."

"So, if we eliminate love from the race, money wins," said Charles.

If only life were that simple, I thought.

"Who else would benefit if money was the motive?" asked Larry.

Excellent question. I named the most likely benefactors: Preserve the Past, Amelia Hogan and her three kids, and—if she were to marry him—Lucas.

From Charles's classic stereo, the Four Seasons were informing us that big girls didn't cry; Charles returned from the kitchen with the beer; Larry absently thumbed through a stack of dust-covered album jackets on the floor; and we continued to debate the merits of each suspect.

We eliminated Amelia—again. Julius had already promised he would take care of her and her family; she truly enjoyed his company and the time they had together; she sorely needed him to be near her for her precious few months left on earth.

Preserve the Past had a powerful three-and-a-half-million dollar incentive, but we couldn't see how any one person or small group of people would have directly benefited. Larry correctly pointed out that the leaders of the organization rotated annually, the membership consisted of some of the most prominent and well-respected members of the community, and no one person had access to the organization's assets. Were we missing something?

With the two primary beneficiaries eliminated, we quickly—okay, slowly—moved to the second layer or potential millionaires. Harry Lucas was our sentimental choice for gold digger. We wanted to figure out the puzzle more quickly but were enjoying the blasts from the past on Charles's record player and the beer from the present too much to rush. I had given in to peer pressure and was helping Budweiser's sales.

"So how can we blame Lucas for the nasty task?" asked Charles after putting on an old album by the Lettermen. "I don't like him."

"What's your problem with him?" asked Larry. "From everything you and Chris said, Amelia likes him. If she's such a good judge of character, maybe he isn't so bad."

"Appears to me that someone Amelia knows is a killer. So there goes your theory about her knowing character," said Charles, exercising his talent for finding logic where there was none. "Anyway, did you know they were first the Four Most?"

"Which four most? I thought we identified at least six suspects—that is, if you count Preserve the Past as one," I said, even more confused than Charles usually made me.

"Keep up with the flow," he said and pointed his cane at the antique sound machine. "The Lettermen called themselves Four Most before changing their name."

The sounds of "The Way You Look Tonight" provided a soft, comforting ambience while Charles stirred up confusion in the air. It was his house; we cut him some slack.

"Let's try again," persisted Larry. "Why don't you like Lucas?"

"How could anyone like a pawnshop owner? Seems to me, all they do is prey off the misfortunes of folks. A chance to pick up a mil or so would be bells to his ears."

"I agree," I said. "But for him to inherit, he'd have to marry Amelia—if she'd have him and she lived that long. Besides, he would have a fight on his hands with her kids over the money once she was gone."

"Don't forget," Larry added, "there's one less kid now. If Lucas could kill Mike and set Steven up for the killing, that would eliminate two of the three. His odds of beating Sandy would be increased drastically."

Larry had made a lot of sense, but my Pooh brain found that scenario way too complicated. Besides, Lucas needed money now—not after Amelia passed away.

"Okay," said Larry. "For the sake of argument, let's assume the lighthouse group and Lucas are out. How about the kids?"

"For one, I think I'd eliminate Mike," said Charles. "I don't think he'll be inheriting much."

"So why was he killed?" asked Larry.

"We don't know," I said. "But there are a couple of possibilities. First, he and someone else could have been in it together and had a fight over something. Another possibility—and a more far-fetched one, I'll admit—is that one of Mike's siblings killed Palmer, then killed Mike to increase the amount he or she would inherit when Amelia dies."

"Hell, Chris," interrupted Charles. "They all could have been in it together—Amelia, Sandy, Mike, and Steven. They could have killed poor Palmer to inherit a boatload of money—a big boat. A family that kills together, shares wills together."

"I don't suppose some dead president said that?" I asked, finally giving up on finding comfort in my chair.

"Don't reckon, but I don't know everything each of the forty-two presidents said."

I was beginning to yawn, but the conversation was doing a good job keeping me awake.

Larry wisely ignored the presidential utterances and asked who would have known of the will. "Someone must have known about the millions to even consider killing Palmer if money was the motive," he concluded.

"I don't know about Lucas, but each of the three children could have known," I said. "Remember, Steven did some design work at Palmer's house and could have seen a copy. Mike had been in Palmer's antique shop several times and had some of the pieces in his condo. And finally, Sandy works in Sean Aker's office. He prepared the will; Sandy could have even typed it."

"Which begs the question," said Larry. "Who tried to turn you two into road-kill? And how about the furnace? Guys, I'm not an expert, but it didn't look as if there was anything wrong with the pilot light."

"Long shot," said Charles, "but the chief could've been right that both were accidents." Had my friend finally conceded to logic?

"No way, not the truck," I countered. "Someone was waiting for us."

Charles, now standing and straightening a row of books, said, "If it was the truck the chief said was stolen in Mount Pleasant, that would lead toward Harry Lucas, wouldn't it?"

"True, but it could as easily have been one of the Hogan kids, wanting the police to think that." I continued, "Remember, guys, if he or she had succeeded, they would have found a truck with a rather messy front end and would have known for sure it was the stolen one—right from Lucas's backyard, almost." A coincidence?

"Now that we've narrowed down who tried to squash and asphyxiate us to every living soul on the planet except for the two of us, Julius Palmer, some soldiers stationed in Germany, and the cow that jumped over the moon," said Charles, "my question is why?"

"Why what?" asked Larry.

"All we've done is ask a few questions," Charles said. "The police have done that much, and nobody is trying to kill them. I can't see how we're a threat to anyone. Sure, Bill wants us to solve the crime, but so what? To be honest, the world wouldn't come off its axis if the two of us were dead. But it would raise the ire of the police—I hope. They'd start asking more questions and hopefully turning over a few more rocks to find who decreased the tax base of the island by two."

I didn't tell Charles that the two of us weren't contributing enough to the taxes of Folly Beach to keep city hall's lights on a week. He had a good point, though. What did we know? Who had we threatened?

We were talking in circles, getting no closer to solving anything and beginning to argue about who was better, the Beach Boys or the Four Seasons. We decided to call it a night. For the record, no matter what tone-deaf Charles and Larry had said, the Beach Boys won, hands down.

"A final thought," added Larry as we were taking the three long steps to the door. "Why don't we sit down as a group with Chief Newman and outline everything we know? Basically, give him a chance to reopen the case. Regardless of what he says, he does have some respect for our thoughts, and he's brighter than many give him credit for being."

"Let's think about it and talk tomorrow," I said.

CHAPTER 41

The ringing phone woke me from one of the best dreams I had had in months—I couldn't remember the details, just that it was great.

"Well, did you decide we should talk to the chief?"

"Charles ... what time is it?" I sat up in bed and wiped the sleep from my eyes.

"Six thirty—I gave you time to ponder it. Didn't want to call too early."

"Charles, you're all heart—and no patience. You called, so I assume you've made up your mind. We should call Brian, right?"

"Sleeping Beauty, someone could be up this very minute plotting how to get us; third time's the charm. Don't you think we'd better do something before he—he or she, as you like saying, politically correct and all—removes us from this fine earth? This island may not be heaven ... but I'm not ready to do comparative shopping. I don't know about you."

"Okay, let's see what Larry thinks."

"Been there, done that. He doesn't sleep the day away; he's a working person, remember? Those hardware people are up and at 'em early. He even thanked me for waking him at five fifteen—said who needed to sleep anyway. Good attitude, right?"

"Your human-alarm-clock trick worked on him too. Let me guess: he thinks talking to the chief is a good idea?"

"Yep. Smart man, that Larry; he gets right to the nuts and bolts," said Charles, chuckling at his own hilarity.

"Please don't tell me you woke the chief to tell him three raving maniacs wanted to talk to him before the sun peeks over the beach?"

"Course not. You're his good buddy," said Charles. "I thought you'd want to wake him."

"Tell you what, Charles. Meet me at the Dog at seven thirty. I'll spring for breakfast, and we can talk about what we want to tell Brian. If someone kills us before then, I'll apologize to you when we meet in the hereafter."

"Okay. If we get separated, I'll ask God to get you a message."

Friday filled early at the Dog, even during the off-season. By the time I arrived, the booths were full and most of the tables occupied. Charles had arrived and commandeered one of the prime locations. The smell of fresh coffee and bacon sizzling on the grill brought a smile to my face. Amber wouldn't bring my coffee to the table until I was there; she knew I liked it hot. She said Charles had tried to get her to have it ready, but she had refused.

"Amber, I appreciate that extra serving of consideration; our friend Charles misses a few of the subtleties."

"Chris," said Charles, who was wearing his University of Connecticut Huskies sweatshirt and footwear that could best be described as army surplus combat boots that had endured a nuclear disaster, "Do you know how stupid it sounds to hear you talking about subtleties when talking about a darn cup of coffee?"

Apparently he'd never been to Starbucks.

I slid in the booth. "So what's your plan?" I thought I'd ask first; he'd tell me anyway.

"Larry said he could take an early lunch and meet us. I thought we'd see if the chief was available; how about at the Almost Open Gallery? That'd give us privacy, and we wouldn't have to go to the police station. I don't think Larry'd feel comfortable there."

"Sounds like a plan to me; I'll call him in a little while." I was barely settled at the table, with the cook working diligently on my breakfast.

"Chris, you got that little silver phone in your pocket. Call him now, and get it over with."

I called the Folly Beach Department of Public Safety while once again pondering the depressing state of my speed dial. A few of the planets must have been aligned; Chief Newman was in. Even better, he agreed to meet at eleven—and didn't even ask why.

Breakfast tasted better knowing that had been arranged. We spent the time discussing what to say—and what not to mention, such as finding the body of Mike Hogan while we were trying to break into his condo.

*   *   *   *

Charles, as usual, arrived at the gallery fifteen minutes early. I realized it was a mistake, but since most of the sentence was already out of my mouth, I continued and asked him why he had chosen a Syracuse sweatshirt that day.

By the time he'd finished the history of the school colors, Larry had arrived. *Thank you, Larry!* I thought.

"So's there anything we aren't going to mention to the top local law-enforcement official?" asked Larry. He was rubbing his hands together to warm them. "I don't want to open any more cans of worms than necessary."

We all agreed the less we incriminated ourselves, the better.

Chief Newman knocked on the unlocked front door promptly at the designated time. With the obligatory courtesies exchanged, the former marine and no-nonsense chief of police asked why he was there. I offered him a soda or water. He declined. We moved to the back room, where Brian chose to sit in a well-worn side chair I had added for crowds like this.

I was elected spokesperson by glance, so I began outlining our suspicions and rationale. Our guest had turned the chair around and sat with his arms folded on the back, patiently listening as I talked about each of the Hogan children, Harry Lucas, and the Preserve the Past gang. He wasn't jumping up to leave or telling us we were a bunch of meddling troublemakers, so I continued the analysis of who had boats, who had the strongest motive, and how each of the Hogan children would have had access to the will. I told him I knew he would soon have figured all this out himself—we'd just spent more time thinking about it and wanted to share our thoughts. I didn't want him to think we were telling him how to do his job or suggest he didn't know what was going on.

I was surprised when he didn't interrupt. After I finished, he hesitated, looked at the table like he hadn't seen it before, and said he still wasn't convinced it was anything other than an unfortunate suicide. What we said made sense, he noted, so if—the big if—it was murder, our list would be his as well.

"Guys," he said, "I appreciate your efforts and applaud your devotion to Bill and his theory. I'm curious about something." He hesitated, then looked at each of us—for only seconds, but it felt longer. "The Charleston police said Kiawah Island Security learned about Mike Hogan's death from a phone call from an anonymous male. They even traced the call to a phone booth in Charleston—sort of between Kiawah and Folly Beach, for example."

"That's interesting," said Larry—his first words since he had told the chief he was fine and the weather looked nice at the beginning of our meeting.

"You guys wouldn't know anything about that, would you?" asked the chief with a look between a scowl and grin.

"Could've been anyone," said Charles in a lofty manner that wouldn't convince any court. I chose to remain silent, having remembered one of Charles's quotes that said something about you can't be misquoted if you don't say anything. I was thinking more in terms of "a lie isn't a lie if you don't verbalize it," but close enough.

"I guess that covers that topic," said the chief. "Chris, I see all these framed photos sitting back here; your showroom looks finished, so when are you opening?"

I was glad he had chosen to change direction, so I spent the next few minutes repeating the word "soon."

"He's afraid to open," said Charles conspiratorially. "He doesn't think anyone will buy anything, and he'll have to move back to Louisville—or go over to Charleston and become a Wal-Mart greeter."

Brian continued walking, erect and formal in his starched uniform, around the room, looking at the large framed photos leaning against the wall.

"As long as a career as a private eye isn't one of your options, I'll buy one when you open," said Brian. "A cheap one, that is—not one of those big-framed beauts."

"I'm thinking about having a preopening sale for some of my more loyal potential patrons," I said. "We'll be able to work out a better price."

"Sounds a lot like an attempted bribe to a local chief of police," said Brian, smile affixed—sincere, I hoped. "I'm a closet art collector, so I think I'd qualify for the 'loyal potential patrons' loophole.'"

With the attempted bribery charges dropped, we said our good-byes. Brian thanked us for our stumbling into "law enforcement" and said he always welcomed the help of vigilant citizens. He was a poor liar.

After Brian left, Larry looked at his watch and said, "We gave it our best shot. That's all we can do. Now I need to get back—the nuts and bolts are beckoning."

"Hold on," said Charles. "Those hardware thingies will wait. Nuts have been calling me all my life, sometimes you have to ignore them."

"Larry's right, you know," I added, looking directly at Charles. "We need to leave it to the police."

"Where have you two been?" asked Charles as he stood and began pacing around the small room. "The chief of the Folly Beach Police Department is begging us to help him solve the terrible murder of Mr. Palmer."

"What?" Larry and I said in unison.

"How do you figure that?" I continued.

"Didn't you hear him say he welcomed the help of vigilant citizens? Didn't you hear him say, by not saying, that he knew we were the ones who found Mike and reported it? Didn't you hear him not say he was upset about it?" He was pacing the entire width of the gallery, pointing his cane toward the ceiling with each "didn't."

"Yes," I replied, "no, and on the last one, don't know—couldn't understand the question. Now please explain, for those of us who missed some of the very clear directions the chief gave us, what you're talking about."

Larry nodded in agreement. He remained in the swiveling secretary chair, leaving the sale of nuts and bolts to others for a few more minutes. Now we had Charles outnumbered two to one—still not a fair fight for our side, but closer.

Charles gave us his supposedly clear-as-day explanation. We listened. We gave in. If Charles didn't leave his brain to science, the world would be a sadder place—more logical, but sadder.

The plan we devised wasn't as complex as the invasion of Normandy but seemed as daunting. It would involve the cooperation of Amber, Bob, Chief Newman, karma, luck, prayer, greed and fear in the killer or killers, and things we hadn't even thought of. And, in that mix, timing was critical.

No sweat!

CHAPTER 42

For sake of simplicity and our mental health, we had narrowed the most likely suspects to three; our primary suspect had plummeted off the list with the demise of Mike Hogan. Considering the population of the world, we knew our assumptions were a bit naive.

After some preliminary planning by C, C, and L, I spent most of Friday afternoon hanging the rest of the framed prints, taking another step toward opening Landrum Gallery and facing the reality of acceptance and rejection—or worse yet, apathy. Regardless of how optimistic I wanted to be, I had identified one or two ways to succeed and countless opportunities to fail.

My home-cooked supper consisted of a peanut butter and jelly sandwich, Doritos, two sweet pickles, and a Diet Pepsi. I clearly hadn't wasted time watching the food channel. My mind kept vacillating between the gallery and the semblance of a plan we devised—a plan to catch a killer. Bottom line: if I were in a casino, I wouldn't put any money on either winning. But with the gallery, all I had to lose was a pot load of money and gain a serious deflation of my ego. The stakes were drastically higher on the killer-catching journey—up to and including death. I was concerned about that last one—especially my own.

*   *   *   *

The weather gods had done everything possible to ensure a better mood—not only mine, but that of everyone on this laid-back barrier island. The forecasters in

Charleston had called for sunny skies with the temperature rising to the mid seventies—a treat for this time of year.

Unlike some of my South Carolina friends, I had waited for the earliest reasonable hour to call Bill and ask if he was up to visiting Amelia.

"Chris, that sounds like a great idea. I was thinking about her last night."

Still on my politeness kick, I then called Amelia to see if she was up to visitors. She said Sandy was there but would be leaving shortly; she also told me she welcomed a visit from Jay's friend. She didn't say it, but I counted myself in the number of people she would welcome as well. After all, she didn't tell me to send Bill by himself.

I called Bill back and said I'd meet him at his house, and the two of us could walk to Amelia's. This was out of my way, since Amelia lived quite near me, so I added that I'd be near his place anyway. The walking and talking would be good for both of us.

He opened his door before I reached the front porch. I was pleased to see him rather dapperly attired and with a broad smile—a far different appearance from not that many days ago.

"Thanks for calling," he said as he stepped onto the porch. "I've wanted to call Amelia since I returned but didn't know what to say. To be honest, I had been a little embarrassed to talk to her after all the struggles she's been facing. I know she'll ask how I am; considering what she's been through, I'm near perfect."

"She's been asking about you," I said as we began walking toward her humble abode. "It'll do her good to focus on something other than her problems."

I filled Bill in on the plan Charles, Larry, and I had hatched and what his role would be. He listened without comment, then rehearsed his lines before we reached Amelia's house. *Interesting*, I thought.

I was surprised when Steven answered my knock. The last I had heard, he was in jail. He didn't appear surprised; his mom had told him we were coming.

"We've never met," he began, "but unless I've badly mistaken, you must be Chris, and you Bill."

He looked at the appropriate person as he said it.

"Please come in," he continued. "Mom's expecting you."

I bit my tongue and didn't ask what he was doing out of the hoosegow. He led us the short distance to the family room. Amelia was already standing and approached us with a big smile and a hug for Bill. She gave a polite hug to me, but was clearly more interested in seeing Dr. Hansel. She looked much more together than she had at our last meeting; her flattering green dress was complemented by black pumps. Slovenly did not exist in her wardrobe.

"We could come back another time," I said. "We didn't know you had company."

"You most certainly will not; Sandy just left, and Steven surprised me with a visit. This is a good chance for you to spend some time with him. He doesn't get much time to visit with his new business in Charleston."

My tongue endured a second bite as I resisted the question "What business?" especially since Bob had found the bleak notes on the door of the Design Shop.

Bill wasn't as hungry for tongue. "My understanding was that the police were holding you for questioning in the murder of your brother," he said. "What happened?"

It was becoming obvious that Bill's therapist had talked with him about the importance of honesty—honesty with himself, honesty with others, honesty with people who might kill us all.

"Would either of you like something to drink?" Amelia nervously asked, acting oblivious to Bill's question.

We opted for iced tea—hot winter weather outside and all. Amelia played the gracious hostess and hurried to the kitchen.

"That's a fair question, Bill." Steven, who was seated across from us, looked Bill directly in the eyes when he responded, with no signs of defensiveness. "The police finally checked where I said I was at the time of my self-indulgent brother's death. Why they didn't do that before corralling me, I'll never know. They're convinced I wasn't able to be on the north side of Charleston and Kiawah at the same time. It was embarrassing, but thank God it's over."

"I'm glad to hear that," said Bill. "I know that must be a relief. Being in captivity, I'm beginning to learn, is a far more terrible experience than I could ever have imagined."

"I'm not off the hook," said Steven. His candor was refreshing; maybe he and Bill shared the same therapist. "The police also accused me of breaking into Mr. Palmer's house. Regretfully, it's true. I'll have to face criminal charges. They allowed me to post bail."

"Why?" I cleverly tried to sneak the question into the conversation. I hoped he would believe he was just thinking the question and reply. Occasionally, I impressed myself.

"After Mr. Palmer died, I began hearing rumors that he left a large amount of money to some lighthouse-preservation group and a woman on Folly Beach. I didn't want to be so crass as to ask Mom about it. I knew they'd been friends for years. Was it possible she was the one?"

Hmm … not crass enough to have asked his mother a question, but crass enough to break and enter.

Amelia had just returned with our tea. "That's enough about such an unpleasant topic," she said. "I'm sure Steven had his reasons and is willing to pay the consequences. Now, how are you, Bill?"

Bill gave an abbreviated version of his stay in Charleston and how he was doing so much better now—and ready to get back in front of his students.

Bill took his tea, added sugar, and continued. "Amelia, we both know that Julius wouldn't have killed himself. Chris and some of his friends believe they have some information that'll prove who was responsible for our dear friend's death. From what I've heard, I think they'll be able to prove who did it in the next few days. Isn't that wonderful?"

Bill had presented the comments exactly as he'd rehearsed—the problem was Steven hearing them directly. Great—the first part of the plan that had sounded so good yesterday was already going astray. We hadn't wanted any of the prime suspects to hear specifics this early—or directly from us.

"Is that true, Chris?" asked Amelia. "That would be so wonderful."

"Let's don't get the cart before the horse," I said. "We have suspicions, but we need proof. We have some leads and may possibly be able to prove the cause of death but may never be able to find out who did it."

I hoped I'd said enough so Steven wouldn't be too suspicious.

"I wish you the best of luck," Amelia said. "And speaking of good news, Harry Lucas and I've talked about getting married."

"That's wonderful," responded Bill.

"Thank you," she said. "I've resisted, my health being what it is, but he insists. Says while we might not have years together, the time we do is special." Her huge smile lit the room.

Special? That was an understatement. That announcement vaulted Mr. Lucas to the top of the list.

"Bill and I better be going," I said, standing up. "I don't want to interrupt the time you have with Steven."

"You two are welcome anytime. If you don't mind, I'd love to invite you to the wedding."

"I'd be honored," said Bill. "Any idea when?"

I remained silent, my best faux smile pasted under my nose.

"Not yet, but soon," she said. "It won't be anything fancy—just a short service at church. There won't be formal invitations but I'll be sure to call."

She hugged both of us. Gracious as usual, she said she was glad Bill was doing better, even instructing him to please let her know if she could help him in any way. And she was standing there with only a few months to live. If only I had so much courage.

Steven walked us to the door and said it meant a lot to his mother that we visited. He said she told him how much she enjoyed meeting and talking to Bill, but was sorry it was under such horrible circumstances.

One (mis)step in our plan down; more to go.

CHAPTER 43

"Damn late for lunch. You ought to be glad I waited on you."

These warm and fuzzy words from Bob resounded over the distinct slip notes of Floyd Cramer's piano classic "Last Date." I had just entered Bob's Charleston hangout, Al's Bar and Gourmet Grill.

"I figured you were already here when I heard country music," I said.

Bob was seated in his booth, his ample stomach touching the front of the table. Most likely, he had combed his hair in the last four days.

"Damn right—only kind of music," he said. "It's damn lucky that Al isn't racially challenged and stocks the jukebox with white men's blues music. He sticks in a few old jazz songs and some by the Supremes for his unenlightened brethren."

I was impressed by how politically correct my most non-politically correct friend was being. I wondered if it had anything to do with us sitting in a dark bar surrounded by twenty or so African Americans. Bob was rude, tactless, and boorish—not stupid.

"At least he doesn't have any of that rap crap on it," Bob continued.

Whoops, I'd given him too much credit.

Fortunately, Bob moved on. "So what's so important you made me eat late and sit in a dark room on such a lovely Saturday?" he asked between bites of what appeared to be Al's famous cheeseburger. "I could be out getting a glowing tan riding around in my Realtormobile."

Al came over and asked how I wanted my cheeseburger before I could answer Bob. Al had either remembered what I ordered the last time or knew the only decent food on his menu was the cheeseburger.

"Bob, I need a couple of favors."

"Then you're buying my lunch and two desserts—maybe more."

"Deal. Now, when're you meeting Harry Lucas again?"

"Early next week," he said. "He doesn't know it, but I have three potential buyers for his shops. Can't bring him anyone too damn quick; if he thought it was that easy, he wouldn't want to pay my hefty commission." Bob stuffed one of Al's gourmet French fries in his already full mouth and mumbled, "Why?" At least I think it was "why." It could have been cry, pie, or fly—surely he didn't tell me to die.

I explained what I needed. He called me a "total idiot hell-bent on self-destruction." I agreed with him for a change.

Al delivered my cholesterol-boosting meal, and Bob and I ate in silence for a few minutes.

"I remembered what Lucas told me about the three damn gold balls on pawn-shops," Bob said. "Something about some guy in an ancient European family of moneylenders fighting a giant by smacking him with three sacks of rocks. The sacks were pretty important and were made into the family crest. The sacks were butt ugly, so they changed them into balls and made them gold—which figures. Damn money-grubbing pawn brokers."

"Thanks for remembering; I feel my education is complete," I said, never looking up from my fries.

"Your way with words never ceases to amaze me. You said two favors; what's your last wish before you get yourself offed?"

"I need a place for Charles to stay for a couple of nights. Any ideas?"

"Since you know damn well that this tourist city has about a trillion fine—and not so fine—hotels and motels, I suppose you, or your worthless twerp of a friend, are too tight to spring for a room and want me to put him up. Close?"

"Bob, it's no wonder you have such a wonderful reputation for being generous and open-minded. I think Mr. Fowler'd be honored to take advantage of your kind offer."

"You're becoming as daft as your Folly friends—kind offer, humph. Okay, he's got a room as long as he needs it. Just don't tell me why; don't think I could handle it on top of your other damn stupid idea."

"Don't we all have the right to be wrong now and then?" sang Roger Miller from Al's color blind jukebox. *Please don't let this be one of those times*, I prayed.

✳   ✳   ✳   ✳

I felt strange as I punched the number on the phone. I'd had more than a hundred conversations with Amber, but this was the first time I'd ever called. I had kept her number, though; we did things for a reason, I suppose.

"Amber, Chris. No, nothing's wrong. I wanted to talk to you, and the Dog was closed by the time I got back from Charleston. Could we meet somewhere? I'd rather not talk at the restaurant. Okay, that's fine; see you in fifteen minutes."

I met Amber at Planet Follywood, a small restaurant that promoted itself as a "beach bar"—whatever that meant. It was within easy walking distance for each of us, just up Center Street from her apartment and two blocks from my house. It had some large windows, so it was brighter on the inside than Al's, but the atmosphere was similar—casual, very laid-back, and convenient.

Amber was seated when I got there. Other than looking tired after a full day of work, she looked great; she hadn't left her radiant smile in the Dog. In deference to the competing restaurant, she'd changed out of her logo-bearing polo shirt into a nice white blouse. I gave her a quick squeeze on the shoulder as I sat opposite her.

"Hope you don't mind," she said, "I ordered some jalapeño poppers, a beer for me, and red wine for you."

"Perfect,"

"Jason had play practice again after school, so I'm free until five. It's good he's getting into these after-school activities—not only for him, but for me. I'd forgotten how good free time can be."

We discussed Jason's expanding extracurricular schedule and the exceptionally nice weather before curiosity got the best of her.

"Okay, this isn't a social call," she said as she eyed me suspiciously, "not that I'd mind. So, what's up?"

"It's a little of both," I told her, wondering where that had come from.

I explained what Charles, Larry, and I had decided. I shared the complete, gory details of our plan and what needed to happen for it to work. She said it sounded complicated; I agreed. She said she didn't think it had a snowball's chance in hell of succeeding. I was more optimistic—but only slightly. She said she would do everything I asked. I couldn't have hoped for more.

With the scary stuff out of the way, our conversation turned lighter.

She asked about Tammy; I said she was fine. I didn't think it would be wise to share my frustrations about Tammy's work schedule and what appeared to be her inability to find time to spend with me—inability, or lack of desire.

A second drink and an order of nachos had provided us the energy to talk about some of her more … let's say … amorous customers and their top ten pickup lines; the latest gossip from the local city council members and their sense of inflated importance; and some of the thoughts the Canadian tourists had about the United States. Amber was disarmingly funny and a deceptively intelligent young lady. She was much more fun to be with in a darkened bar than Bob. That was not necessarily a big compliment, but it was intended to be.

*   *   *   *

I had had a busy day, especially for a retired person. I had filled the daylight hours with Amelia and Steven, Bob, and Amber. My stomach was trying to decide whether jalapeño poppers and nachos mixed as I sat at home staring out the window at the midwinter darkness. I remembered I still had the memory card from Charles's camera beside the computer. He had taken photos of everyone present at Mr. Palmer's funeral. I remembered him saying he was doing it because that was what police did; murderers attended the funeral of their victims, or something like that.

I downloaded the images into my computer and began reviewing his work. The photos were more interesting now that I'd met many of the mourners. I realized now that the entire Hogan family had been strangers to me that day. Most of the others I hadn't seen since, supporting my initial thought that they were antiques-shop owners or others from King Street businesses. I had no idea what I was looking for, but there wasn't anything good on television. I didn't have anything better to do.

Maybe it was just my slightly depressed mood or a little fatigue, but something didn't feel right as I studied the photos.

CHAPTER 44

I was awake at six—not the result of the alarm, not the phone ringing, or even someone rudely knocking on the door. Somewhere between my subconscious sleep and semiconscious waking, it struck me what had bothered me about the funeral images—and something my young friend Sam had said.

I waited patiently until six thirty to call Charles; after all, he would have shown me the same courtesy! We had a brief conversation, and he agreed to call Larry and wait for me to pick him up at ten. Hopefully, Larry would be available; this was his only day off.

Charles was waiting outside his less-than-palatial apartment, and we drove the short distance to pick up Larry at his small rented house on East Indian, within sight of Pewter Hardware. We took the five-minute ride across the Folly River and turned left just past Mariner's Cay, the gated, upscale development of condos, pools, tennis courts, and deep-water marina.

A hand-painted, wooden sign announcing "Folly View Marina, Private Property" was nailed to stanchions made of sawed-off telephone poles. Folly View stood in deep contrast to its neighbor—not that different from many inadequately zone-restricted, beach-area developments. Beyond the rusting chain "securing" the marina from the outside world was a tire-rutted parking lot covered with a mixture of crushed shells, gravel, and dirt. The lot could hold fifteen vehicles, maximum; the spaces were unmarked, so it was hard to judge the exact number. There was barely room between Folly Road and the chained entrance for two vehicles to pull off. The entrance to Mariner's Cay was watched over by a uniformed guard; the only living thing we saw at Folly View was a hearty cricket that had managed to survive the winter. We took one of the spaces and stepped over the nonthreatening security chain. No silent alarms were visible; the cricket watched.

The small parking lot was bordered on two sides by large decorative grasses proudly exhibiting their end-of-season wheat-brown plumes—an inexpensive way to ensure privacy for the property. Two cars were in the lot, but both were covered. From the dust on the canvas, they had been there quite a while. One was small and could have been a sports car, the other was an enormous 1960s auto. At the back left side of the parking area was a wooden bridge approximately twenty feet long bridging terra firma and the floating pier that provided access to no more than twenty slips for small and midsized boats. Half the slips were vacant.

We walked to the rear of the lot and looked toward the Folly River and the floating dock. From there we had a clear view of the River Café on the other side of the stream. The wooden bridge and floating dock were old but sturdily built; the boats ranged from the smallest johnboat to a couple that were easily seaworthy.

"I can get you a list of who owns the slips," said Larry. "Won't be able to get it until tomorrow, though." His hands were in his pockets, and he kept slowly turning his head from side to side, his eyes looking for any unusual movement.

"That'd be great," I said, not asking his source. I doubted it would take a list to tell the owner of the boat named *Fish Pawn*—a feeble attempt at pawnshop humor. Cool Dude's Bayliner, *Throw a Wave!*, rocked slowly in its slip, a handwritten "For Sail" sign taped to its front rail. The parentage of *Folly's Folly* and *Your Inheritance* would be more difficult. The smaller boats would rather be a number than a name.

We didn't find any murder weapons sitting on the dock or a note confessing to the murders of Julius or Mike, so we headed to the Dog for brunch.

"So what did we learn from that little journey?" asked Larry. He slid into a booth near the front of the restaurant.

Charles pushed in beside Larry. "Mariner's Cay and Folly View Marina don't pay the same amount of taxes," he brilliantly deduced, "but that's about it."

"Cool Dude Sloan can't spell 'sale,'" contributed Larry.

"We'll know more about what we learned after you get the property-owner list," I said. "We're pretty sure Harry Lucas has a boat there, and I'd almost bet a couple of the no-name boats belonged to Sandy Miller and Steven Hogan."

"And the other boats probably belong to members of Preserve the Past," said Charles. "So what?"

I skipped his question and said, "We now know the layout of the marina, how many boats are there, the level of security, and how the marina is easily accessed by most anyone without much risk of being seen. We know enough for now."

Charles and Larry ordered large meals, knowing I'd be picking up the tab. We shared pleasantries with Amber and Mayor Amato, one of the regulars.

"Let's talk about what we'll need before Wednesday," I said. "Charles, you'll have a cell phone by then, right?"

"Yep, if I can take it back next week. I hate those darn things—never wanted one; can't afford one."

"No problem," I said. "Just get one without a service agreement. I wouldn't want to ruin your way of life. Now, Larry, didn't you say you could get night-vision goggles?"

"They've been in storage for several years, but they should still work. I haven't used them in a long time—an arrangement I made with some law-enforcement folks in Georgia."

Just talking about it raised red splotches around his collar.

"Good, I'll pick up the small recorder. Anything else?" I asked.

"Yeah, how about a Bible, the Koran, a Talmud, and the Avesta?" asked Charles, counting the books off on his fingers.

"Think we'll need all those?" asked Larry, sporting a half smile.

"Sure wouldn't hurt—might as well cover all bases," answered Charles.

"Okay, Charles, what's an Avesta?" I asked.

"Chris, Chris, Chris. Your ignorance never ceases to amaze me. The Avesta—of course—is the holy book of Zoroastrianism."

I looked to Larry for support, but he was quickly becoming fascinated with his fork and didn't look up.

"And I'd know that why?" I asked.

"Remember those three wise men in the Bible—you've heard of the Bible, haven't you? Got one in every hotel room."

"Yes and yes," I said, hoping he would move along.

"Many biblical scholars believe those three cats who came to visit baby Jesus in the manger were members of the Zoroastrianism religion. But, yea or nay, there are tons of Iranians and Indians following the Zoroastrianism faith. Though you would have known that."

I confessed—a good thing in most religions, though I wasn't sure about Zoroastrianism—that I had never heard of them and asked Larry if he had.

He maintained his fascination with his fork, although his knife was now getting added attention. He looked up and said, "Sure, who hasn't? They can have a bunch of wives, right?"

Charles stared at both of us as if we were hopelessly religion-challenged; he may have been right.

"Okay, Charles," I said. "You're in charge of your cell phone and all the holy books you believe we'll need. Besides, you probably have all of them in that library you call home."

I wasn't the least surprised when they had two desserts each before I managed to get the check from Amber—the check, and an "I don't know what you three have been jabbering about over here, but good luck with it" speech, and a warm, strong hug.

Assignments were delved out, and we went our separate ways. I don't know what Charles and Larry did, but I spent Sunday evening making a couple of phone calls to other players in our grand plan. The rest of the time I spent worrying and wondering if I could have ever foreseen the odd twists of my retirement.

CHAPTER 45

A light drizzle filled the air; daylight had barely broken over the Folly pier. I was in no mood to see anyone, so I feasted on a healthy breakfast of Hostess Twinkies and orange juice; after all, breakfast was the most important meal of the day.

Just before noon, Bill appeared on my front step.

"Chris, I just left the home of the charming and sweet Amelia Hogan. Steven was there, helping her go through boxes she had stored for years. She said they needed to get rid of some stuff. I was afraid she'd be sad, but she acted pleased to be 'putting her house in order,' as she called it."

Steven's being there to hear Bill's story about what was to happen had been an added bonus. I'd been afraid Amelia might not have passed along the important points to her son. I invited Bill in; the cool, damp air made for an uncomfortable stand.

"Great, Bill. How'd it go?"

He broke into a large grin, stood erect, and said in his best bass voice, "I've never taken much pride in my creative storytelling skills, but I amazed myself."

"Good! Have some coffee and tell me about it," I said.

He poured of mug of steaming coffee, gave a nasty look at the empty Hostess Twinkies wrapper, and sat at the kitchen table.

"Amelia was pleased to see me. We were talking about what her life had been like without Julius as part of it. I told her, with Steven within earshot, that I heard that you and Charles were going to prove who killed Mr. Palmer. I told her Charles was out of town until Wednesday afternoon, and the two of you were meeting then to pick up the evidence."

"How'd she take it?" I asked and refilled his mug.

"She was surprised but said she was thrilled that someone knew he didn't kill himself. She wondered what kind of evidence you had. I told her I had no idea, but that you were going to be meeting around seven at some marina. She asked if the police were involved and what marina."

"What'd you tell her?"

"Just what you told me to," he said, as he scowled at my apparent distrust. "I didn't know what marina. I told her you were upset that the police didn't believe he was murdered. I said you called the police—blithering idiots that they are. I ad-libbed that part, but thought it sounded good. Regardless, she sounded excited and told me to wish you luck."

"Anything else?" I asked, pleased that the conversation had gone the way he described.

He took a sip and unzipped his jacket.

"No," he said. "I thought I'd better get out of there before I said something wrong."

"Good job. Want something for lunch?" I asked. I didn't know what I had to eat but would find something.

"No, thanks," he said. "It's a little early."

I suspect he was afraid my menu might not be to his liking—who could not like a Hershey bar for lunch?

"I have tuna salad at home," he continued. "Let me know if I can do anything else. It's great knowing something is being done to get the stigma of suicide off Julius's back."

Bill left with a spring in his step—something I hadn't seen for weeks. I wish I had his confidence.

*   *   *   *

"Bob, did I catch you at a bad time?" I asked once I was sure it was him on the phone and not his machine, which answered with a warm and inviting "What?"

"Almost always a bad time," Bob answered, "but I'm good enough to handle your interruptions."

"How's your houseguest?" I asked.

"Chris, you got to get this over quick. It's worse than having seven monkeys loose in the house. At least the monkeys wouldn't be quoting Chester Arthur, and damn few of them would be wearing a Drexel Dragons sweatshirt with a damn dragon spewing fire on it. In case you're wondering—and you better damn well be—Mario's the name of the damn dragon."

"Thanks for sharing," I said, trying to hold back laughter. "Believe it or not, I was not aware of Mario's allegiances."

"So, are we ready to catch a damn killer?"

"Depends on how good an actor you are," I said.

"Then lock him up!"

"Are you still on to meet with Lucas tomorrow?"

"Yep, nine thirty. I'm going to moan and bemoan how difficult it'll be to sell his properties, how much time I'll have to spend prospecting for potential buyers, how he's underpaying me for all the work, and more Realtor bullshit."

"And all the time, you have buyers waiting," I marveled. "What a wonderful business you're in."

"Don't have to tell him everything," he explained. "He's getting my umpteen years of experience and wisdom—priceless, you know. Besides, he's a damn pawn broker. I doubt honesty's part of his makeup."

I knew all pawn brokers weren't dishonest, but didn't waste my breath while Bob was on a roll. Besides, I wasn't ready to vouch for Lucas's ability to tell the truth.

"I hope you can take him for all he's worth on the real-estate stuff," I said. "Now, walk through our part of the meeting."

"Okay, first I'll tell him I know a couple of damn nutty people over on Folly who've been playing detective. These idiots decided that Julius Palmer didn't kill himself, and they're going to find the killer. I thought Lucas'd be interested, because he knows Amelia Hogan, who knew the deceased. How am I doing so far?"

"A little heavy on the nutty people and idiots part, but it'll work," I said.

"The stranger and more ridiculous I make you sound, the more I'll be able to laugh it off when I'm telling Lucas. Trust me; I can play with these guys."

"I'll need to know when to call," I said.

"I'll call you just before I meet him; wait fifteen minutes, then call. When I get your call, I'll write myself a note—just happen to do it where he can see read it. Don't worry, I've got it—Charles out of town, the note, the meeting, the big finish."

Being insecure when it came to risking my own neck, I had him go over the details again before feeling confident in Bob's part of the plan.

"Chris, I still think you're a damn fool for doing this, but good luck. Remember, I get to list your house if you get killed."

Two parts of the plan were in place; now I was off to lunch—and another piece of the puzzle.

Amber was sitting at one of the wooden tables in the rear of the near-empty Dog when I arrived. Much of the luncheon regulars had headed back to their job or respite.

"Afternoon, Chris. Are we ready for the showdown?" She nervously wiped the already clean table with the white bar towel.

"That depends. Are you ready to hear about your part?"

She placed my luncheon order and sat across from me. "Lay it on me."

I outlined her role and emphasized how important it was that she portrayed me as "nutty as a fruitcake" for trying to catch a murderer. "Tell him it's endearing, but stupid. The tricky part is for him to believe that Charles is out of town, and that you're supposed to tell me he left me a note in the office. You know I'm in Charleston until midafternoon, and you'll give me the message then. Charles told you the note tells me where and when to meet him.

"Amber," I continued, "are you sure he'll be in?"

"He's been here every Wednesday for as long as I can remember; don't see any reason why tomorrow will be different."

"Good. It should work," I said, with much less conviction than I would have hoped.

"Charles was all excited," she said. "Said he loved the story about having to go to Savannah to see his sick sister. Charles doesn't have a sister, you know. He said this was the best of both worlds. He didn't have to put up with a sister and buy her Christmas presents and stuff … yet, he could tell everyone how close they were. Such a sweet, loving family."

"Only Charles would be able to pull that off," I said.

"It's sad, in a way; he doesn't have any real family. This is his way of creating a nice, warm family. He's much more insecure than he wants people to believe."

Before I left, Amber grabbed my hand and told me to be careful—said she would have serious trouble coming to work if she didn't know I'd be there. I was touched and told her so. It could have been my imagination, but I saw a tear in her eye.

CHAPTER 46

I wanted to go home, get in bed, and pull the covers over my head. Knowing that may not be the most mature, adult, and mentally healthy thing to do, I went home and tried to walk through everything I knew about the deaths of Julius Palmer and Mike Hogan. Were the deaths related? Were we looking at the right suspects? Did our less-than-perfect plan make sense? What could we have done differently? And, the most important question: what in the hell was I doing?

I had a serious headache. Maybe the bedcovers-over-the-head thing wasn't such a bad idea.

*   *   *   *

I slept but didn't know when. I tossed and turned. The low roar of the aging furnace failed to lull me to sleep. I was relieved to see the clock turn six, so I could justify getting up. Coffee and a breakfast of two granola bars followed: health food for a busy—and hopefully productive—day. I would have preferred a warm and friendly meal at the Dog but didn't want to be around while Amber was completing her part of the great plan. Besides, I needed to go to the gallery to make sure everything was in place.

Amber called a little after eight and said, "Mission accomplished—the bug in the ear's been placed, and the bait taken ... maybe." She sounded more like her son with the spy talk, but I got the message ... maybe.

Bill and I had already put our own little bug in the ear of our assigned suspect, and now it was up to Bob to do his part.

On my six hundred and fifty-third pace between the living room and the kitchen (9:35 a.m. in clock time), the phone rang.

"Ready to enter Harry the Sleaze's office," said Bob. "Call me in fifteen." The line went dead.

Cryptic phrasing was part of the plan, I supposed. I knew what he'd meant and continued my pacing for fifteen more minutes, then took a deep breath and called Bob's cell phone.

"Yes, this is he. Oh, hi, Charles. Of course I remember ... thanks for calling back," Bob said to my silent end of the phone. "Can we get together next week about making an offer ... Savannah, okay ... I hope she's okay ... yeah, I'll be seeing Chris later today. We have a meeting about some house over there ... note about tonight under the keyboard ... yeah, at his gallery ... sure, I'll tell him ... sounds interesting. You really think there's a killer? Tonight, wow ... okay, yes, I said I would ... I'll call you Monday about getting together ... see you."

He hung up. When Bob was conversing with dead air, he made more sense—and definitely was more polite—than in any real conversation. Amazing.

All the seeds had been sown. Now it was showtime.

I spent the rest of the daylight hours staying out of sight. I drove to James Island and visited the Ravenous Reader Bookstore, catching up with my magazine scanning, then puttered around Office Depot. I achieved absolutely nothing. I returned to the gallery about an hour before dark, in time to hear Larry's knock on the back door. I'd been expecting him but was still startled by the sound.

"You were right," he said. "The lock's been jimmied."

"You sure?" I said.

"Yep. It wasn't too difficult, obviously." Larry was referring to his installation of a cheaper lock set the day before. "It didn't take a pro; I could've done it in my sleep. You didn't touch the keyboard, did you?"

"Just came in the front door and was waiting for you."

"Good," he said. He was in his element.

We went to the desk; I took a clean rag and lifted the keyboard. No surprise.

"The note's been moved," I said. "I left it facing the back. Someone put it back facing forward. I guess that narrows the suspects down a bit."

Larry had put on rubber gloves he had in his pocket; he carefully lifted the note and placed it in a clear, Ziploc freezer bag. He slowly read it: "Chris, I know who it was and can prove it. Meet me at seven thirty Wednesday night at the Folly Beach Marina. I should be back from Savannah by then."

"The prints on here may help," said Larry. "Especially if your idiotic plan backfires."

Larry gave me a handwritten list of the slip owners in the marina. We composed a fairly detailed note explaining everything we knew, then stapled it to the front of the freezer bag and placed them both in a large manila envelope. I wrote Brian Newman's name on the envelope with a black, fine-point Sharpie and left it on the desk. I prayed he would never see it—if he did, my genius plan had fallen flat on its face, and I had fallen somewhere else.

He wished us luck and gave me a brief, embarrassing hug.

"See ya later," he said.

I hoped he was right.

CHAPTER 47

I pulled my Lexus off Folly Road and up to the chain blocking the parking lot to the Folly View Marina; the analog clock on the dash read 7:29. I had been tempted to keep driving until the car ran out of gas, hopefully hundreds of miles from doom.

Two lights on a telephone pole provided minimal illumination on the front of the lot. A second pole at the walkway to the dock held two light fixtures that emitted nothing—hardly a confidence builder. The two covered vehicles hadn't moved. Additionally, there was a midseventies Chrysler parked just inside the chains and an old Dodge van near the back. It wasn't one of the popular minivans, but a bus-sized vehicle that decreased in popularity in inverse correlation to the rising price of gas. At least one, maybe two, of the slips were empty where boats had been the day before. I heard the roar of an occasional passing vehicle on Folly Road and distant, indecipherable voices from Mariner's Cay. Other than that, nothing. Even the cricket who had guarded the gate earlier remained silent.

I had never been happier to see someone than I was when Charles pulled up in his classic convertible. I silently apologized to his Saab for the nasty things I'd said about its ability—or inability—to run.

He slammed the door and walked around the front of his car to meet me.

"Hello, Mr. Photo Man," he said in a stage whisper. "Thanks for meeting me."

"How's your sister?" I asked, continuing our poorly rehearsed conversation.

"Much better. I'd hate for anything to happen to her; she's my favorite."

Such a happy imaginary family. I stayed far enough away from him so our raised voices wouldn't draw undue suspicion. "So what's so important we had to meet here?"

"Did you get the list of the owners?" he asked, in response to my question.

I handed him the list from Larry—source unknown. Charles took it with more fanfare than if I'd handed him the original Gettysburg Address.

I'd already circled slip number five. He looked at the list, hesitated, and gave me a quizzical look. I ignored him.

We slowly walked toward the back of the lot and headed down the wooden bridge separating the land from the floating dock. I don't think either of us wanted to get there first. The temperature must have been in the fifties; I was shivering—partially caused by a brisk wind coming from the ocean, partially by what we were doing. I almost fell off the narrow plank. I told Charles it was my clumsiness but knew it was really fear. The sound of Charles's cane hitting the wooden planks reverberated in my ears. If Charles weren't blocking my way, I would have been in the car in ten seconds, including the time it would take to unlock the door.

I knew at least one person—maybe more—had read the note; the odds were good we weren't alone. I kept thinking how stupid our actions were with each step along the deserted, nearly dark pier. The numbers were hand painted in yellow on the wooden deck at the end of each slip. We had to pass three before we reached number five. Its occupant looked like the hundreds of older fishing boats dotting the coast and intercoastal waterways. Its paint was peeling, its surfaces were addled with rust, and an old, brown, paint-stained tarpaulin covered the pilot housing. We stood about three feet down the pier, next to the bow of the old boat. Charles was uncannily quiet. His cane had stopped tapping.

I was startled—but not the least bit surprised—at the sight of a shiny, chrome handgun pointed at us from the edge of the tarp. Attached to the gun was the right hand of a very angry Buddy Miller.

"Keep your hands where I can see them, keep walking, and climb aboard," he said. "Why the fuck couldn't you two mind your own business? Never mind … shit. Get in here, now." His command sounded like a growl.

I didn't know what was on Charles's mind, but I knew we needed to obey or try to find a way to attack. Buddy was only six feet away. Could he shoot both of us before Charles or I could subdue him?

I couldn't see any upside to getting shot. And our odds of escape decreased drastically when I heard the not-so-pleasing voice of Amelia's angelic daughter behind us.

"You heard the man!" barked Sandy, not nearly as sweet as during our previous conversations. "You get in the boat now, or your miserable, snooping, trouble-making lives end right here." She was dressed in black, her wool pea hat pulled down over her ears. I could only guess that she had been in one of the boats we had passed.

The double-barrel shotgun she pointed at us sealed the deal. It wasn't nearly as shiny as Buddy's handgun, but its barrels looked slightly larger than the barrels of the cannons protecting the battery. I could tell Charles wanted to say something. Wisdom won out, and he kept his mouth closed.

Climbing onto a rocking boat, in the dark, with two guns pointed at us was not a simple task. I nearly fell against the side of the swaying boat; Charles's cane hit me in the thigh. Sandy didn't help make the task any easier with her barrage of questions.

"How'd you know it was us? Why did you even get involved? Why, why ... shit, never mind."

She and Buddy were beginning to sound alike.

"You don't mess with our friends," responded Charles with more bravado than a reasonable person should have under the circumstances.

Charles and I finally made it on board; Buddy kept his pistol pointed between the two of us, easily able to change its direction and silence the target of his ire. Sandy was already on the pier, loosening the old, rotting ropes securing the boat.

I interpreted before they shot Charles on attitude alone.

"Why kill Mike?" I asked to neither of them in particular.

"Don't get me started," growled Sandy from behind us. I didn't know what was going to happen, but clearly the Millers were running the show. "I'm the only one who ever cared about Mom. I visited almost every day, did whatever she wanted, always was there for her. Yet, who the hell do you think she was constantly talking about? Mike this, Mike that, Steven this, Steven that." Her mocking tone said it all. "She was always worried about them, wondering if they were okay, looking forward to their fuckin' visits—the visits so damn rare I could count them on one hand."

"That had to drive you crazy," I said to keep the conversation going. I hoped it would be hard to shoot and talk at the same time.

"I'd put up with it for years and guess I could have continued to until I learned about Mom's cancer. I knew about Palmer's will; shit, I typed the damn thing. Then the doctor told her how little time she had ..."

"Calm down, Sandy," interrupted Buddy. "No need to say more."

"Shut up, Buddy," she said, not taking her eyes off me. "You know where my beloved brothers were then? Nowhere around … fuckin' nowhere around." She held the rope in her left hand, resting the barrel of the shotgun on her bent elbow. Both hands were visibly shaking, but her grip on the shotgun was still in control.

"So how'd you con Palmer into going out in the water?" asked Charles.

My need for talk rather than being shot was rubbing off.

"Come on, Sandy," said an irritated Buddy. "Get in the damn boat, and let's get this over with."

"Give me a minute," she said, sloughing off his irritation. "There's no hurry. These two aren't going anywhere,"

Not only was she in charge, but she liked to hear herself talk—a good sign.

"Palmer was a creature of habit," she continued. "Every day, he closed his shop, stopped at the bank, deposited the receipts, and then stopped at the Piggly Wiggly. He told Mom he had to have his fresh vegetables. All I had to do was be at the store, fill my cart, wait for him to head to the checkout line, act surprised to see him, talk a little about Mom, and wait for him to offer to take my groceries to the car. He was such a gentleman—his bad luck. No good deed goes unpunished."

"Then?" I nudged. I figured she wanted to unveil her masterful plot, even to a soon-to-be departed audience. Buddy was the one I was worried about; he didn't want to hear the story again.

"That was the touchy part," she said, "but it worked. I was afraid someone might see us in the parking lot, but it was nearly deserted. Know how vulnerable someone is when putting a sack of groceries in the backseat?" she asked with a giggle.

I failed to see the humor but waited.

"I just gave him a tap—okay, a hard tap—on the head and pushed him in after the bag of food."

"Enough," said the impatient and increasingly irritated Buddy. He pushed the barrel of his gun in Charles's ribs. "Sit!"

I thought I could guess the rest and didn't want to risk Buddy's volatile side by pressing for more information. I stopped asking questions and prayed Charles would follow. He did as he landed hard on the steel crossbeam, his cane flying to the rear.

"Why the hell didn't you two just drop dead in your damn gallery when I shut off the pilot light?" Sandy asked. "Why didn't you let Buddy run you down in the middle of the damn street? Why—"

I had never thought I'd love the next words I heard.

"Police! Get your hands up!" bellowed the recognizable voice of a former military police officer and my favorite police chief in the world—maybe in the universe.

At the same time, the immediate area was bathed in the cold, white light from handheld spotlights coming from three sides. Four smaller flashlights were rapidly bobbing toward slip number five. The lights were blinding and disorienting. Brian and three of his officers had come running from the old van parked in the lot; the sounds and spotlight from a police boat approached from the north.

Like the obedient citizens we were, Charles and I reached for the winter stars. And thank our lucky stars, so did the Miller family. The shotgun clanged to the bottom of the small, rusting boat.

"Did you get it all?" the chief asked me, never taking his eyes off Buddy and Sandy. Officers Spencer and Robins grabbed the gun Buddy still had in his hand and picked up the shotgun. They yanked Buddy off the rocking boat, escorted Sandy slightly more gingerly, and pushed both to the wooden deck.

"I think so," I said and stepped off the boat to the slightly more stable dock. "The recorder worked fine before we headed out here."

I took the cell phone–sized audio recorder from my jacket pocket, rewound the tape, and hit the Play button. After the words "testing, testing …" Buddy's unfeeling, sharp voice said, "Keep your hands …" I smiled and handed the recorder to the chief.

"I saw everything," said Brian. "Larry's night goggles were great. Remind me not to ask him where they came from."

"What night goggles?" I said.

"If the city's budget wasn't so tight," Brian continued, "we'd have our own high-tech tools. Did they tell you how they got Palmer into the boat?"

"Not everything, but if you have the sheriff's forensics experts check the boat, I'd put money on finding blood or at least prints somewhere in there that belonged to Palmer."

Brian had seen everything and now had a recording of the chain of events, including complete—or nearly complete—confessions. There was little else to be said. The Millers were not-so-politely escorted to one of the two Crown Victoria cruisers parked along Folly Road just outside the chained entry. I thanked Brian for listening at least one more time; he expressed irritation with citizens snooping where they shouldn't, then mumbled thanks under his breath. I told him I had things to do, and I was dismissed; I had no problem with that.

Charles admitted for once he couldn't think of a single appropriate presidential quote. "I need to walk home and get my head back on straight," he said.

Doesn't that imply it was on straight before? I thought. Regardless, I completely understood and watched him walk toward the Folly River bridge and home, the white "NYPD" on the back of his black sweatshirt decreasing in size as he walked.

It wasn't even nine, and yet it seemed like midnight. On the drive home, I shook almost uncontrollably, both from nerves and the cool, damp air. I walked in the house on shaky legs. I had two calls to make: one I needed to, and one I wanted to.

I poured a large water glass full of cabernet, sat for a few minutes staring out the window at absolutely nothing, and then called Tammy. I caught her on her drive home from the scene of Charleston's most recent murder. She had once told me there were fewer than thirty murders a year in the majestic city, but it felt like one a day, as busy as she was.

She was thrilled to hear the outcome of my evening's activities. But getting to "thrilled" took some time.

"That's about the most stupid thing I've ever heard," she said in response to my good news. She was almost yelling. "What an idiot," she added in case I'd missed the "stupid" part.

I didn't disagree, which took some steam out of her ranting. After a few minutes, she went from a boil, to a simmer, to a cooling off, and the "thrilled" part finally surfaced. To be honest though, I couldn't tell if she was thrilled about my safety or because she didn't have to cover a double murder after a hard day of reporting on other mayhem.

She finally convinced me she was glad I was alive and said we needed to get together soon. Neither of us defined "soon."

We said our good-byes, and I began, once again, to stare out the window. The glass of wine was now mysteriously empty; I couldn't have that!

Then I made the call I'd hoped all day I'd be able to make. Bill was home; he said he was grading papers. He sounded in good spirits; I planned to elevate them more.

I gave him an abbreviated synopsis of the night's events. He only interrupted a couple of times with "Thank God." His voice cracked as he spoke; I couldn't tell if he was in tears or his allergies were kicking in.

"Does Amelia know?" he asked, after composing himself (also known as wiping a runny nose).

"I don't know, but I doubt it," I said. "From what Sandy said tonight, I doubt she'd be the person her loving daughter would use her one call from jail on."

Bill said he should get over to her house; someone needed to be there when she found out. He'd tell her and take her to the jail, if that was what she wanted.

"Want me to go with you?" I asked.

"No," he said. "You've done more than enough—much more than enough. It'd help me more than anything to do this by myself."

I didn't say it, but I agreed.

I asked him to let me know if there was anything I could do. He said he would, thanked me, and then thanked me again.

I felt drained as I stood on top of the world. Another glass of wine was on my agenda.

CHAPTER 48

The next forty-eight hours were a whirlwind. I had thought retirement would bring sleep, with no need to pay attention to clocks. I would wake up when I wanted and go to bed whenever. Wrong!

Thursday morning was thrust upon me prematurely when my phone did its alarm-clock imitation, ringing at five sharp—as sharp as anything can be at five.

"Damned if you didn't do it again," said the pleasant, cheerful, and unmelodious voice of the best Realtor in the second biggest of the island's three small realty firms. "Shit, Chris, get it through your thick skull. I don't want to have to sell that shack you live in again; when in the hell are you going to stop trying to get yourself killed?"

My increasing maturity and deeper understanding of my real-estate agent stopped me from asking how he had learned about last night. I simply wished him a pleasant morning. He hesitated, perhaps disappointed I didn't ask how he knew. That gave me some satisfaction.

"So when are you going to have that grand-opening reception of your overpriced photo gallery?" he asked, completing one of his characteristic transitions. "I've got to get some free food and booze out of you before you stumble on another disaster and get killed nosing in."

"Sunday evening. You and the lovely, patient, and angelic Betty are most cordially invited—seven o'clock." I hung up, managing another ray of satisfaction before sunrise over the beautiful Atlantic.

My pleasure quickly waned when I began thinking what needed to be done to prepare for a grand opening in three days. The rest of the morning was devoted to taking notes and making lists—food, drinks, personal invitations, and paper goods. I also cleaned, finished pricing the photos, and finalized the flyer Charles had promised to deliver to the occupied homes.

I had done everything possible—busywork, in the eyes of most—to get my mind off the previous night. Had I really risked my life to prove that someone hadn't killed himself? Someone I'd never met? Couldn't there have been a better, and safer, way to do it?

Creeping into my thought pattern was a feeling that maybe I made a difference in the lives of others; I had finally made a mark, however small, on the world. What a great feeling—even better than hanging up on Bob.

I was more comfortable about the grand opening when Saturday rolled around. Charles, good to his word, had delivered approximately three hundred flyers. I had accused him of throwing most in the trash once he was out of sight.

"Hell's bells, Chris. Why would I have done that? I couldn't get rich if no one came."

Bill not only had been the one to tell Amelia about what happened, but had visited her three more times. While he had to deliver bittersweet news, he said he was able to comfort her. I could tell it was all the medicine he needed.

Tragically, medicine was not an option with Amelia. No one could imagine what was going on in her head. Her daughter and son-in-law had been charged with murder—not only the murder of Julius, but of her son. Her consolation was that her true friend Julius Palmer hadn't taken his own life.

Bill said Steven visited each day and even talked about moving back to Folly.

"Lance has come with Steven most visits," said Bill. "The two seem to be such a nice, uh … they seem like nice acquaintances." "Couple" was a word Bill struggled with.

Bob called each day—to see if I was still alive, I suspected. He had even offered to bring anything I needed. I didn't want to tax his kindness. All he needed to bring was Betty. He said he could "damn well handle that," if she'd let him.

CHAPTER 49

I was amazed at the turnout. The weather cooperated to create a nice night for a walk through the streets of Folly Beach. Not only had Bob and Betty honored me with their presence, but they also brought Louise from his office. I was surprised when Amelia walked in wearing a beautiful burgundy dress, much less somber than I'd ever seen her. It had been less than a week since one of the worst days of her life. She was escorted by Bill, looking like the distinguished professor in his dark corduroy slacks and camel-colored blazer.

I was more amazed when Charles arrived—not that he was there, but that he was wearing a white, long-sleeved sweatshirt without a single animal, mascot, or school name—or, for that matter, any ornamentation at all. And I thought I'd seen everything.

No sooner had Charles pirouetted to show his sportswear (nearly hitting two patrons with his cane) than Brian Newman entered, escorting his lovely daughter, Karen Lawson. Both were casually attired. *No work for either of them tonight,—please!*, I thought.

Country crooner Tom T. Hall shared his wisdom about old dogs, children, and watermelon wine in the background. I had filled the jukebox with country songs in honor of Bob—okay, not really a jukebox, but an mp3 player—and because I liked the music as well. I'd never sat in Miami but could almost taste the whiskey and smell cleaning agent in the bar as I listened to the music. I watched Bob standing on the on the other side of the room, eyes closed, mouthing the lyrics. He'd kill me if he knew I'd noticed.

By seven thirty, Larry had arrived, followed by Cool Dude Sloan and a couple I'd met when my previous house burned last year. They were followed by two elderly couples I didn't recognize.

"Don't get all excited," said Charles. "Those wobblies are here for the food."

"And you know that how?" I asked as I watched them shuffle to the food table.

"Oh, no reason," he said, "other than I've seen them at every free event on the island for the last five years."

Did he realize that only a fellow moocher would notice such things?

I was pleased that most people—other than the free-food moochers—were actually looking at the framed works and flipping through the bins of the matted, unframed photos.

I stood in the center of the gallery, talking with Amelia and Bill about some of the Charleston photos of the historic district. She laughed at something Bill said about two of his students. It was one of the better moments of a great evening.

"Before you hear it from someone else," said Amelia, "I wanted to tell you that I won't be seeing Harry anymore."

I didn't know if I should say I was sorry or happy, so I stuck with the old standby: "Oh."

She was standing close to me with her head turned toward Dr. Hansel. "Bill told me some of the things you learned about Harry," she said. "I just don't need someone like that in my life. I wanted to thank you, Bill, and your friend Bob for uncovering the true Harry."

I hated that she wouldn't have someone close to her during the next difficult months. Bill allayed those concerns.

"I told her I'd be there for her, for anything she needed," said Bill, beaming with a sense of belonging.

Amelia hugged him and whispered a thank-you.

I was interrupted by Larry, who had just arrived and wanted to say hi. I thanked him for helping me stay alive and finding the killers.

"Thanks for giving me a chance to use my talents for a good cause," he said. His physical stature grew far above his normal jockey-sized body; his eyes seemed a little less sad.

Tammy Wynette was standing by her man; Charles was trying to herd the two food-mooching couples away from his favorite finger foods; Sean Aker—a late and surprising arrival—was talking to Amelia, hopefully not about her daughter; and Amber had just guardedly walked through the door. She looked lovely in a simple, light blue dress—the first time I'd seen her in a dress. I felt butterflies in my stomach as I went to meet her.

"Tell you the truth, Chris, I've never been to anything like this," she said. "I almost didn't come."

"You better be glad you did," I said and gave her a hesitant hug. "If you weren't here in the next few minutes, I was going to go to your place and drag you out."

"Thanks, I feel better."

"You better—besides, look around. Your friends are here."

"Where's Tammy?" she said as she slowly looked around the gallery.

"She had to work."

She demurely diverted her gaze to the floor and said, "That's too bad."

I didn't hear any regret in her voice. Did I want there to be?

I pointed her toward the food, and she said she'd see me later, then walked away.

Interesting … it wasn't exactly angels singing from on high, but Roger Miller was in the background observing that with love, there were two ways to fall. Coincidence, good timing, fate, or just a great line from a great song at the wrong—or was it right—time?

*   *   *   *

"Don't tell Dad I told you," said Karen Lawson, who had snuck up behind me when I was talking to Amber. "He told me he really appreciated your help with the Palmer case. He grumbles, but admires your persistence and courage to follow your convictions."

A little taken aback, I was beginning to say thanks for sharing when Chief Newman—Brian—walked over.

He shook my hand. "What're you two whispering about?" he asked.

"I was telling your daughter how much I appreciated your listening to my concerns and helping catch Mr. Palmer's killer."

"Sure you were," he said. "Chris, what made you think it was Buddy in the first place?"

"I didn't, for sure—that is, not until he pointed the gun at me. I suspected it when I looked back at the photos Charles took at Palmer's funeral. Sandy and Buddy were walking behind Amelia and Steven. Tears were falling all around the two of them … and they were dry-eyed and even appeared to be smiling. Nothing about that made sense, but it got me thinking." I realized my glass of cabernet trembled every time I even thought of what had happened—or what might have happened. "That's why we had to get the story about the note to both Sandy and Harry Lucas. I didn't really know who it was then. And remember, Steven wasn't off the hook. I didn't eliminate him until Larry said the lock to this building had been jimmied. Steven didn't know about the note."

"Not bad," said Karen.

"Oh, yeah," I added, "I never could figure out how the driver of the pickup knew Charles and I would be out walking until I realized Charles had practically announced it in the Dog that morning. And Buddy had been there when I left. Charles said he just missed me, so I figured Mr. Miller was still there and over-heard Charles's proclamation that we were going out to take photos around the island. Buddy knew it before I did."

"Hmm," said Brian, with a look on his face that could have meant he didn't believe a word I said or that I was the luckiest person in the world.

"I also wondered how they knew we were looking so hard for a killer—why we were being targeted," I continued. "Then I remembered what a new young acquaintance, Sam, said about his friend telling him everyone was talking about us. I forget how small a community this is."

"Maybe I should offer you a job," Brian said. "Your track record on catching bad guys is better than that of anyone I have."

In the unlikely event he was serious, I quickly declined. "As one of the newest citizens on your island, I'll leave the policing to you and your force." The three of us ran out of words at about the same time and moved our separate ways.

Bob was clearly getting irritated that he wasn't getting sufficient attention, so he pulled Betty over to the spot vacated by Brian and said, "Well, shit, Mr. Artist. My lovely wife wants me to buy these two overpriced—way overpriced—photos. I told her I could take pictures of the same thing, and she wouldn't have to waste my hard-earned money … but no, she has to have these."

"Dear," said Betty with a halfhearted scowl on her face. "You could take pic-tures pointed in the direction of these lovely scenes, but your charming, chubby finger would be in front of the lens, or you would forget to put film in the cam-era, or something similarly stupid would happen. Why don't you pay your friend, so we can have some good art in our house?"

My first big sale, and to Bob—would wonders never cease?

Charles, the self-proclaimed gallery manager, quickly grabbed Bob's credit card and ushered the Howard family to the never-used register.

There was only so much to say and look at in a small room filled with photos, especially when the food trays were nearly depleted. The two mooching couples left, and I could tell Cool Dude was running short of social energy. Bob was getting in a halfhearted argument with Charles over why county music was the only true music of America. I heard Charles profess his ignorance of the musical genre and quote the long dead United States President Ulysses S. Grant. He—Grant, not Charles—said something like, "I only know two tunes; one of them is 'Yankee Doodle,' and the other isn't."

Bob kindly didn't challenge the genesis of the quote—actually, I knew he wasn't being kind. He just didn't give a damn, as he would say. I wondered what Grant's other tune had been—but not enough to ask.

Charles broke himself away from the captivating conversation with Bob and loudly spoke above the decreasing din.

"Folks," he shouted, his right arm waving his ever-present cane in the air, his left holding a can of Bud Light over his head, "if you can break away from your jabbering a minute, please gather around."

Since most folks were bored with the conversations, they obeyed his request.

"Ladies and gentlemen," he continued. "I propose a toast to Chris Landrum, the newest resident of our beloved and eccentric Folly Beach. May he have a long and prosperous life among the finest people on earth—and may you buy a bunch of these photos to keep this gallery open and provide me with huge commissions."

I appreciated the sincerity of Charles's toast—most of it. I really appreciated that he was able to get it out without being interrupted by police sirens.

Maybe there was hope yet: hope for a peaceful, pleasant, and long life among my friends.

Maybe.

Breinigsville, PA USA
31 August 2010
244633BV00004B/7/P